STOLEN MOMENTS

Sionna took a deep breath, rejoicing in the calm of the night even as she felt the first taps of raindrops. She could hear the cars speeding by just over their heads on the Wilson bridge. There were hundreds of twinkling lights that lit up the houses and the waterfront as far as the eye could see, and in the darkness, they were like little playful dancers.

The water sparkled from lights and the half moonlight. Sionna was turning to tell David how wonderful it was when she realized he had come to stand right behind her. She caught her breath and stared into his eyes. He stared down at her, and before he could stop himself their lips caught in a tender, searching kiss.

As Sionna returned his kiss, David grew bolder and wrapped his arms about her. He pulled her to him as his kiss explored the sweetness of her mouth. Sionna tingled all over. Her body was a buzz of excitement as he pressed her even closer to him. The raindrops came faster and harder, matching their growing passion for one another.

Sionna gasped for air even as she was melting inside with pleasure, falling like a feather into his charms. She didn't want to fight it, to resist her feelings. She only wanted him to go on kissing her, filling her with his passion.

"Do you want me to stop?" David asked, feeling his desire grow and wanting to find control before passion took possession of him.

"No," Sionna whispered, staring boldly into his eyes.

STOLEN MOMENTS

Dianne Mayhew

BET Publications, LLC
www.bet.com
www.arabesquebooks.com

ARABESQUE BOOKS are published by

BET Publications, LLC
c/o BET BOOKS
One BET Plaza
1900 W Place NE
Washington, D.C. 20018-1211

First Printing: September, 2000

10 9 8 7 6 5 4 3 2 1
Printed in the United States of America

One

It was raining hard again. It seemed it was always raining and with it came the sadness she could not shake. The feeling was still there. Midnight was the worst, with the constant tapping of the rain reminding her of her sorrow. It had been more than a year since he left her and still he stayed on her mind like a rich molasses. She only wanted to stop thinking about him, to let him be and to move on. It was late, she was tired and she just couldn't take it anymore.

Sionna heaved a sigh, then got up and turned off every light in the house, as if switching out the lights would turn off the memories of him. She switched off the television set, then curled up under her heavy white quilt blanket. She laid her head on her feather down pillow and squeezed her eyes shut, hoping to shut out the pain for just a moment. What she needed, she decided, was to get some rest and shake off her melancholy. It was time she let go of the past, and she was determined to get over it.

Yet as she lay there embraced by the darkness, her determination slipped away. And, as so often, just around midnight when the night became a smothering blanket of emptiness, she would feel the weight of her sadness like a suffocating hand. And she wanted only to cry a thousand tears, to drown in the drenching rain that stamped upon her window and relieve herself once and for all from her sadness.

He was gone. She had to face that fact. Her handsome, loving husband was no longer with her. And she, Sionna Michaels, was doing something she thought she would never do over anyone. She was grieving endlessly and was finding that she was having the most difficult time letting go. But she was so lonely, so tired of fighting her pain. She missed Joey tremendously. The short period they had known together had been the most beautiful time of her life. Yet she wanted to feel joy again, with a touch of passion and a tinge of love. Since Joey left, it was as if all her dreams had floated out the window into the oblivious darkness of days gone by.

It happened the night she had come home late from work and found that Joey wasn't home yet. Normally he would be sitting in his suede blue chair, smoking one of his awful cigarettes that she complained would be the death of him. But that night the house was silent. Their house was fairly huge, so she was used to not seeing Joey immediately or hearing a response from him when she arrived home. But his car was not parked outside, either.

She set her purse on the coffee table and switched on the soft blue light in the foyer that Joey had insisted on purchasing during their honeymoon. He loved blue. Blue furniture, blue lights, blue nights . . . he had proven to be very blue in the end.

She recalled going into the living room and sitting on the sofa before checking the answering machine. As the messages rolled on, she switched on the television set and was about to turn up the volume when a message no one ever wants to hear blared over the speakers. It was Southern Unity Hospital. There had been an accident. They needed her to call right away or to come to the hospital.

It had been all she could do not to faint. Instantly she knew Joey had been hurt. Instantly she knew it was more than just a minor problem. Instinctively she knew to cry.

With shaking hands, she had called the hospital, told

them who she was and was given the bad news. Joey Michaels had been in a fatal car accident. No, no one else was hurt. It appeared to be a deliberate collision into the ditch just off the parkway. They would appreciate it if she could come to the hospital. They would advise that she take a taxi if she could. Of course she would.

And that's all she could remember. Everything after that was a blur. A thankful blur. She remembered calling her mother. She vaguely recalled her mother making the funeral arrangements. The funeral itself was all but a blank. She only knew that David Young, the man Joey had said so much about, was not there. Then the police gave the worst news of all to her. They had determined that Joey's accident had indeed been suicide. Worse yet, she had no doubts that it was accurate. The way Joey had been acting those last days was clearly not the way a man in his right frame of mind would act. She accepted their determination, as painful as it was.

Then it was over. The funeral passed, the police went away, the days passed and finally her mother went home. She was alone. She took a few weeks' leave of absence from her job and sulked around the house, day in and day out, refusing visitors, including her twin sisters. And she would have kept up that way if it were not for her mother's insisting that she had to go on. Joey would have wanted it that way.

She finally picked up the phone and called her job at the paper. They were happy to have her return to work. Months went by and she dove into her work with an enthusiasm a fresh college grad couldn't match. But still, when she got home at night, she found herself thinking about the last few weeks with Joey, and the pain would pour over her as if she hadn't gone all day without it.

She relived the night she was told of Joey's suicide over and over, so often she couldn't remember when it began and had no clue when it would end. She only knew that the dreams she had envisioned for her life with Joey were ripped from her in one merciless moment. She closed her eyes and fought back thoughts of blame. Blame she knew was unreasonable, unfair. Yet each time she thought of Joey's growing depression those few short weeks before he committed suicide, the image of David Young invaded her thoughts.

He was the man she blamed for her misery, a man she had never actually met. He had swept into Joey's life like a fierce lightning bolt and completely destroyed them. For that, she could never forgive him nor stop thinking of him.

When she and Joey married, Joey's career was beginning to soar. He had just landed a major contract for the architectural firm where he was employed, and he was sure he would soon be promoted. It was only three weeks after he bid for the contract that his firm, On-Site Associates, merged with the much larger New York-based architectural firm of Buerhler Architects, a company where Joey's one-time college friend, David Young, was employed as head of the design and construction division.

At first, Sionna was under the impression that Joey's relationship with David, as well as the new contract he had gotten, was going to do wonders for his career. Then the merger took place and Joey's world was turned upside down. The new president brought in his own people and terminated several managers from the On-Site management team, and before Joey could blink and get a full grasp of the situation, he was being offered a severance package that would have easily pacified an ordinary man. But Joey was no ordinary man, Sionna soon discovered.

She rolled her eyes, trying not to dwell too deeply on how hard Joey took his termination from the company. At the time, she didn't think it was that major. He had been given the choice to resign and accept the six months' pay with benefits that extended for a year or to take a demotion to an assistant design technician under the new director of construction services, David Young. Sionna had asked why

Joey hadn't approached David to see what David could do. At that, Joey had stormed that David was the reason he was being booted from the company. He had accused David of stealing his ideas and shooting them upstairs as his own. David Young was not the friend that Joey had thought him to be, and Sionna was perturbed.

Joey chose to leave Buerhler rather than be humiliated into working in what he deemed a role for a novice college graduate, under a guy who had proven to be his perpetual foe. Joey kept repeating to Sionna that he had been played by Buerhler, by David and by the entire design team. They had used him and set him up. Sionna could not understand how a man whom Joey had looked forward to seeing had suddenly turned into a backstabber. But Joey insisted that David was behind his getting fired and if it was the last thing he did, Joey was going to make David pay.

With a wretched frown, Sionna guessed that by committing suicide, Joey thought he was getting the ultimate revenge against David and Buerhler. She wondered if he even once thought of the pain and distress it would cause her.

Worse yet, if Joey expected sympathy, he didn't get it. Although the memory of that day was vague, she was sure that only a few Buerhler staff members showed up at his funeral, but she was confident that there was no sign of his so-called friend, David Young. Based on Joey's accusations, she didn't expect David to show up. And she didn't want him to.

Joey was so bitter about his termination by the company and his broken friendship with David that he had no time to think about Sionna. Rejected and frustrated with a loneliness that started even before his death, Sionna resorted to working more at the paper. During the time away from home, she naturally saw less and less of Joey. As suddenly as they had met and fallen in love, she found herself married to a completely different man, a stranger.

It was as if all the spirit was stolen from him at the loss

of his job. She found herself married to a man she barely new. It dawned on her during those last few weeks together that the time they had spent together had been no more than a few precious stolen moments, then reality kicked in. And what she had left was a brooding man, a solemn man, a defeated man.

The unexpected groaning of the house invaded Sionna's thoughts. She looked solemnly around her, thinking how the house was still settling into its foundation. The rain had ceased and suddenly she could hear every sound in the silence. During silent moments like these she could hear the creaking and groaning of the house as it nestled itself into a permanent position. This night it was as if the house was groaning in unison with her. Slowly she sat in Joey's blue suede chair. She laid her head against the arm of the chair, her loose hair spilling forward as she crossed her legs and attempted not to cry.

Two

Sitting alone in Joey's old chair left Sionna feeling cold. Sighing, she sat up and thought it was just too lonely a night. Using all her energy and forcing the thought of David Young from her mind, she found the strength to rise, and with tearstained cheeks she grabbed the phone. She was calling her mother. She needed her mother to console her and then she would be all right. She knew her mother would help her realize that everything was going to be all right and that she could shake off her blues.

"Mom," Sionna gushed the moment her mother's familiar voice cleared the line.

"Sionna, sweet, I was just thinking of you," her mother Rose whispered on the other end of the line.

"Were you?" Sionna asked, relieved that she was not disturbing her mother, although she could hear the sleep in her mother's voice.

"Of course. You're my baby and you've been through a lot. How is everything? Are you all right?" Rose asked, her voice gaining strength as she spoke.

Sionna couldn't help but sigh. Was everything all right? She couldn't say. She only knew that she had to stop holding onto her growing hatred of David. She had to get him off her mind before she exploded with the deep-seated passion of hatred she was feeding every minute.

"Sionna?" Rose called, her voice growing agitated at her daughter's prolonged silence.

"I'm here, Mom. I guess everything is all right," Sionna added, trying to clear her head. She started toward the window and stared into the street, watching in sad reminiscence as car after car drove by.

"Sionna!" Rose's sharp cry startled Sionna. It was as if Rose could hear her daughter's sad thoughts and wanted to her shock her out of her misery.

Sionna winced, turned from the window and with a shaken laugh asked, "What was that for?"

"Sionna, sweet, you called me. Now you stop worrying me. You're starting to scare me, child. What's going on? Are you sure you're okay? Because you just tell me and I'll come down there. You know that, don't you?" Rose said firmly.

"Yes, Mom. I know. And right behind you would be the twins. Honestly, I can't deal with the stress of company right now. I have a lot going on right now. I just called you because I wanted . . . I guess I just wanted to hear your voice, Mom." Sionna's voice broke and she suddenly wished she hadn't called her mother. She was simply having an awful day. Besides, not only was she causing her mother worry, but she couldn't talk without wanting to cry.

"I suppose I'll just have to live with that then, Sionna," Rose sighed, not wanting to upset her daughter more. A moment of silence fell between them before Rose, conscious of her daughter's sadness, asked, "When are you going back to work? You've been on leave for several weeks now."

"I know, I know," Sionna sighed. She didn't want to discuss work. She had asked for an extended leave of absence to give her time to clear her head. After Joey's death she had taken a short leave of absence, but it had not been long enough. After putting in months of hard work, she realized that she needed to get a grip on things. She had to seriously check her emotions, so she had requested another leave of absence, which her boss had reluctantly agreed to. And as much as she didn't want to disappoint him because he had been so considerate throughout her entire ordeal, it was what she needed. At first she had planned to go home to Georgia, to get away for a while. But she found she could not leave. It was as if she was trapped inside the house and couldn't tear herself away. Even after a year she couldn't shake the connection she had with Joey and her home.

"Sionna, you can't take off work for weeks at a time every time you have a bout of depression. Besides, how will you be able to pay your bills?" Rose insisted.

"Joey," she choked on his name. "He had a decent savings and Buerhler gave him an outrageous severance package. Even without his money, Mom, I would be fine. Believe it or not, I haven't touched his account. So don't worry about me. I won't disappoint you," Sionna added. Sitting on the sofa and curling up, she tucked her feet under the pillow and switched on the television set.

"I'm not worrying about you disappointing me, but what about your job, Sionna? I would think your job would be a great distraction for you. Don't they need you?" Rose asked, although the agitation in her voice clearly identified her concern for Sionna.

Sionna released a laugh and shrugged. "Mom, please, it's just a local paper. Trust me, Mom. I know what I'm doing and I know how often and how long I can take off before Mr. Eikton thinks of firing me."

Rose didn't respond. And Sionna used that moment to get off the phone. Softly, Sionna said, "I'm going to try and get some rest, Mom. You go back to sleep and I'll call you tomorrow. Okay?"

"I guess. Good night, baby," Rose responded a little stiffly before hanging up the phone.

The moment her mother was off the phone, Sionna glanced at the clock. It was just a little past eleven P.M. and the local news report was just starting. If the nightly rituals she had formed since Joey's death continued she would have a long, restless night ahead of her.

Feeling a little distracted at that thought, she stared at the television set in a daze before shaking her head. She swung her feet off the sofa and switched off the television set. She switched on the lights and began moving the furniture around, trying to become distracted from the anguish she was feeling. When she was done, she realized that although she had completely rearranged her family room, the blue suede chair had not been touched.

"I need to stop this," she mumbled.

She was frustrated with herself, frustrated with her life. She wanted to get past the grief, to move on. But she kept falling over the same pattern of blame that wouldn't relieve her from thoughts of David Young. He once again popped into her thoughts at the sight of Joey's favorite blue chair. She could almost see Joey sitting there, laughing as he read the comics in the Sunday paper, frowning as he pored over blueprints, or just smoking a cigarette that left blue haze over his head. That chair was his central location more often than not, and Sionna decided it was time to get rid of it, if she did nothing else.

She continued to clean up and reclean up until she felt exhausted enough to fall asleep. With feet that were beginning to drag from the late hour, she went to her bedroom and lay facedown, straddled across her bed. As she lay there her mind raced in a ton of directions and again she found herself dwelling on David Young.

Had he any idea of the damage he had done? Did he care? He couldn't possibly care, she thought bitterly. If he did he would have at the very least sent a card or flowers, or given her a sympathetic call. Something. But he had done nothing.

She knew his type, she decided in disgust. Although she had never met him, she was sure how he would look. He was most likely an arrogant, self-consumed, thoughtless man who had the ability to have everyone hanging on to his every word. Joey had said David was fun and likeable, at least that was how he had described David before the merger. By the time he had lost his job, David was described as a conniver, a liar, and a cheat.

Sionna was sure that his deceitful personality was the only thing that got him by. He wouldn't be good-looking; men like him never were. No, he was a base liar, a conniving backstabber and a braggart who probably threw money around to show off his position. A position he had stolen right from under the nose of her husband. She envisioned him living the life, enjoying his new role as managing director, and it embittered her more. He didn't deserve that position. He didn't deserve to be laughing and feeling joy while she lay in a lonely bed pining for a man that was forever lost to her.

With a sudden burst of renewed energy, she jumped from the bed and went into the closet. With careful precision she began going through Joey's old work papers. She wasn't sure at that moment what she was going to do, she only was certain that she had to do something.

One thought had dwelled on her mind for too long: to meet David Young and ask him why. She was now determined to do that. She was going to meet him and make sure he was fully aware of how he had devastated her life. And once he knew the damage he had done, she would watch him crumble with despair and regret and beg her to forgive him. Which, of course, she would reject. She envisioned herself walking away from him as he sobbed and pleaded with her to take away the pain. But she wouldn't look back. No, she would let him feel the full effect of what he had done to her family.

She nearly laughed aloud, realizing how foolish the idea of his pleading for sympathy was. He was not that kind of man. She was sure of that. Yet she knew she had to come face to face with him to be at peace.

Confident that coming face to face with David Young was the only way to turn her life around, she brought Joey's box of papers to the bed and began carefully reading through the material. She especially read the new employee information he was given only a few days before he was told he was being terminated. In the employee profile for new management, she found a short biography of one David Young, but there was no picture. It didn't matter, she was sure her instincts were right. She was confident she would know him in one glance. Feeling more empowered now that she had read about the Buerhler organization, she set the box on the floor beside the nightstand and lay back on the bed, this time her hands snugly tucked under her head.

A glimmer of a smile curved her lips as she came to the conclusion that all she needed was to meet David and tell him just what kind of a lowlife bastard he was. Only then would everything be all right.

Even as the wind whispered softly outside her window, warning her not to pursue such a reckless obsession, Sionna closed her eyes in stubborn determination. And as the crickets sang songs of warning deep into her consciousness, Sionna remained confident that she had made the right choice. What could be so wrong about at last telling David just how she felt? What was wrong with asking him why he had broken Joey down until he ran himself into the grave, literally? After all, Joey claimed that at one time they were best friends. Well she was Joey's widow and she had a right to confront him. He had an obligation to explain himself. It was time they met.

Three

Her black high heels rang loudly over the gray marbled floor of the lobby. She opened her purse and took a quick glance at her face to be sure that her makeup and hair were in order before she pushed the button for the elevator. Had she been paying attention she would have known by the admiring glances sent her way that she looked breathtaking. She had dressed carefully that morning, choosing a chic black suit and black high heels that accentuated her long, shapely legs. Her hair was pinned back in bouncing curls and her makeup was immaculate, perfectly showing off her exquisite features.

She considered her face in the mirror, scrutinizing her finely plucked eyebrows, her carefully lined wide eyes and her softly colored full mouth, confident that the chocolate-brown lipstick she chose was a perfect accent to her caramel complexion and the subtle poise she wanted to present. Patting her hair in place, then patting the corners of her mouth to ensure she did not have an overflow of lipstick, she got on the elevator. Once inside, she pressed the button numbered sixteen, then took a step back and waited patiently for the elevator to reach her destination. She was alone on the elevator but it wouldn't have mattered. She was so focused, so specific in her decision to confront David Young face to face that nothing could have distracted her.

The elevator stopped and she took a cautious step into the tumult of the offices. Telephones were ringing, women in classic corporate suits were racing back and forth from their desks to the fax machines, copier machines, following their supervisors with pen and pad in hand as their supervisors dictated memos. The office was a busy hub and no one seemed to notice as Sionna Michaels paused in the middle of the corridor and looked for a door with David's name on it.

With determined eyes, Sionna glanced around the office, peering at each door. When she didn't see an office with David Young's name, she became disappointed. A woman was walking past her. Sionna halted her in midstride and asked in a calm, low voice that belied her anxiety, "Could you tell me where to find Mr. David Young?"

"Down the hall, two doors on the left," was the woman's brusque reply.

A moment later the woman continued on her way and Sionna headed down the corridor. She was composed, confident and firmly secure in her decision. She would have no regrets on the morrow and certainly none later in the evening. After all, she had dreamt of this moment for much too long to allow anything to go wrong. Her black high heels were expensive. Her hair was done up immaculately. Her suit was a Chanel original. She was perfect and she knew it. Now was the time to bring David Young to his knees. Now was the beginning of her sweet revenge. Taking precise steps, she reached the door with large black letters spelling his name, David Young. At last, she thought.

It was then that she paused. That she hesitated. That she thought perhaps, just perhaps, coming here was a mistake. And it was then that the door flung open.

He was a tall man, at least six-three. He wore a well-tailored blue suit with an almost lost blue-striped black tie. His stance was confident and bold yet nonthreatening behind his casual smile. And it was a beautiful, pearly white smile, offset by dark, penetrating eyes that seemed to reach right into her soul. It was all Sionna could do not to gasp behind the surprise opening of the door and his equally surprising good looks.

He was a little taller, a lot younger and much more handsome than he had the right to be. Just looking at him filled Sionna with resentment, and suddenly her apprehensions were gone, replaced with her months of built-up frustration and loathing for the man she blamed for the death of her husband.

David Young paused, surprised by the sight of the beautiful young woman at his door. For a moment he openly stared at her, then, realizing who she was, he smiled and leaned back against his door before saying in a deep, throaty voice, "Wow. I had no idea you would be here so quickly."

His voice was fascinating, strong and throaty, and Sionna was captured by it. She frowned, becoming aware by his statement that he thought he knew her.

"Why would you?" she asked carefully, watching him with a suspicious gaze, although she was confused.

"I just got off the phone with the agency. They're fast," he added with a pleased smile.

Sionna's eyes narrowed, realizing that he thought she was sent by some agency. But to do what? Curious, yet feeling empowered by her hidden identity, she relaxed her shoulders and said flippantly, "We try to provide prompt, efficient service, Mr. Young."

She was testing the water, hoping his response would tell her what role she was playing. Her eyes were a little wider than she would have liked as she waited with bated breath to see if he was in fact her infamous David Young.

David grinned, nodded his head slowly and, stepping aside, waved her inside his office. As she passed him, he said, "I tell you what, there is no way that I am going to allow our first day together to start off with misters and misses. Just call me David. Everyone else around here does."

"Okay, David," Sionna murmured, her eyes narrowed in

hostility as she entered his office. She had no idea what prompt service she was providing, but she couldn't wait to tell him who she really was. She had no doubt that it would wipe that happy-go-lucky grin right from his face.

David didn't catch her sudden stiffening as she fully entered his office. He didn't notice her hands gripping her purse much too tightly. He didn't hear her teeth grinding in aggravation as he offered her a seat in front of his desk. In fact, Sionna was sure the only thing he would ever notice was himself. This was Joey's friend? They were nothing alike, she decided firmly. Certain that her time as a fraud would be short—because she had every intention of telling him her true identity fairly soon—she refused the seat he offered.

David hesitated, confused by her refusal to have a seat. Releasing a slight cough, he accepted her decision and sat on the edge of his desk, not comfortable with the idea of sitting down while she stood. They stared at each other for a few moments before David cleared his throat. He was baffled by her behavior but thought perhaps she was just uncomfortable or nervous. Deciding it was his job to make her at ease, he said, "Please, uh," he paused, glanced at the yellow legal pad on his desk for the name he had scribbled, then continued, "Karen, please have a seat. I gotta admit, I'm a little uncomfortable having you stand there," he added with an imploring smile.

Knowing she would look completely foolish not to take the seat, Sionna forced her stiff legs to bend, and she carefully sat down. She couldn't believe what she was doing even as she was doing it. Pretending to be this Karen person, whoever she was. Sionna knew it was wrong but he had made the initial mistake. How far was she going to allow the error to go? She wasn't sure but for now she was content to see which way the wind blew. She only hoped this Karen was no architect. That role she could not play.

"I'm sure you're very experienced so I'll just start by

letting you ask the questions," David said, settling more comfortably in his seat. Sionna frowned, not sure what he meant for a moment. Then her instincts as a reporter kicked in and she smiled.

"I prefer that you tell me a little about your expectations and then I can ask questions from there," she said. David, as she expected, nodded in agreement. He was content to take the lead, having no idea that he was helping her to conceal her identity.

He began tapping his desk with his pen as he stared up at the ceiling as if it helped him to formulate his words.

"I guess my main expectations include being able to count on you to keep me on track. I receive proposals every day, most of which we can't use, of course. And now that Buerhler is in full swing and no longer bid for our contracts, I have to pay close scrutiny to those freelance designs to be sure we're receiving the best designers for the new construction site at the museums. . . . Is something wrong, Karen?" David asked hesitantly, noticing Sionna's sudden frown.

Sionna blinked, not realizing that her expression had changed so drastically.

"Karen?" David asked, watching Sionna in worry.

"I'm . . . I must apologize. I was taken aback somewhat. I thought Buerhler did all of its bidding. In fact, I was under the impression you had acquired a firm for that purpose and that you were a designer as well. Are you saying that you don't bid on sites?" Sionna asked, watching David with dumbfounded dark brown eyes.

David chuckled and dropped his pen, then relaxed and leaned back in his seat.

"Nah, we merged with On-Site, but that was mainly to acquire their contracts with some of the bigger builders that we otherwise couldn't touch, specifically museum renovation. What I do for Buerhler is manage the builders. I can design but haven't had to in years. To be frank with you,

Karen, I don't miss that aspect at all. I see so many great designers, I get just as much pleasure in choosing the designer as I used to when I designed in college," David admitted.

"Oh," was all Sionna could say. She was feeling sick, weak. How could she have been so foolish? This man hadn't replaced Joey. Joey's role had been completely eliminated. But Joey had been so sure. He had been so adamant about it. David was not even a designer or bidder. It made no sense. Why had Joey lied? Or maybe Joey never really knew what was going on and latched on to the first conclusion he could.

"But anyway, I need someone who can handle my busy schedule here, as you probably noticed on your way up. Answer the phones, keep track of my appointments."

"I'm sorry, Mr. Young, but I can't . . . there's been a mistake. I have to leave," Sionna said hastily, coming to her feet. With the reality that Joey may have been misinformed about David's role in his losing his position, Sionna lost her nerve and wanted only to get out of David's office before he realized she was a fraud. She stood so hastily that she dropped her purse, and before she could get her wits together, David had come to his feet and grabbed the purse for her.

"I don't understand. What mistake?" David asked with a frown, holding the purse as he watched her. Sionna was trembling, certain he would call security the moment he knew who she really was. She just wanted to get away, to escape, and to forget the entire fiasco.

"You wouldn't understand. My purse please," she whispered so softly that David had to bend forward to hear her. He frowned, sure he had done something wrong, and he was uncomfortable with allowing her to leave before clearing the air. Before he could ask more questions, a tap on the door distracted them both.

Sionna, her head reeling from the foolish mistake she

had made, stared at the door, sure it was security. David went to the door, a frown creasing his usually pleasant face as he opened it.

A woman he had never seen before was standing there, a briefcase in one hand and a manila folder in the other. She looked very professional.

"Can I help you?" David asked impatiently, glancing at Sionna as she approached the door, her eyes wide and nervous.

The woman at the door smiled, placed the folder under her arm with the briefcase and purse, then offered David her hand.

"Karen Kimper. I'm your new assistant."

"Karen Kimper?" David asked, dumbfounded as he glanced between the two women.

"Yes, Mr. Pfeifer from human resources said you would be expecting. . . ." Before she could finish her sentence, Sionna swept past her and raced down the hall. David was too stupefied to move. At Sionna's hasty exit, Karen stumbled and dropped the briefcase and folder. David stared at the folder at his feet, then quickly reached for it. He opened it up and with a steadily increasing frown, he stared down the hall.

"Karen Kimper for sure this time," he asked harshly. Karen blinked in confusion and nodded.

"Yes," she answered with a confused shrug.

David's eyes narrowed. Gathering his bearings, he ordered brusquely, "Have a seat in my office. I'll be right back."

He too raced down the hall, glancing from left to right in search of the wayward woman who had lied about her identity. Seeing her nowhere in sight, he hurried onto the elevator. He had to find her, to find out what she wanted and what was going on. It seemed like the elevator stopped on every floor before reaching the lobby, as he brimmed with frustrated impatience. Once in the lobby, he received a strange look from two older white women walking by before he realized he still had the mysterious woman's purse in his hands.

Keeping a firm grasp on the purse, he raced for the exit and practically skidded out onto the sidewalk just in time to see the woman he had believed to be Karen Kimper flee inside a yellow taxi. Disappointed, he narrowed his eyes in bewilderment, watching the cab until it disappeared from view. Sighing heavily, he glanced at his watch. It was barely nine-thirty and he knew instantly it was going to be a long, tormenting day. He had to find her, he thought with an irritable frown. Balling his fist in consternation, he realized again that he was holding her purse as it crumpled within his grasp. Then his frown slowly dissolved as he smiled down at the purse as if it were his best friend. His agitation faded as he walked calmly back into the building while carefully opening and examining the contents of the mysterious woman's purse.

"Yes," he declared a little louder than he had intended when he discovered a wallet amid the cosmetics. "Now let's see just who you are," he said as he got on the elevator.

Four

"Hello," Sionna answered the phone, her eyes half open as she leaned over the bed, the phone nuzzled between her shoulder and ear.

"Sionna Michaels?" a male voice asked.

"Yes. Who is this?" Sionna responded, instantly alerted. She sat up in the bed, her sleepiness gone as she reached for the clock to check the time.

"David Young," was the short reply.

It was just past nine in the morning. Fingers suddenly weak with nervous energy at the announcement that David was on the line, Sionna dropped the clock and nearly dropped the phone. Her heart began to pound in anxiety.

He finally called. She had known he would once she realized she had foolishly left her purse behind. It had been a nightmare she couldn't seem to get over. The cab driver had called her a liar and threatened to call the police before she fortunately found twenty dollars in her blazer pocket. She had thankfully kept her house keys in her hand from habit. But the worst thing was knowing that David was in possession of her purse and that he knew exactly who she was. She could barely tolerate thinking about it. She thought for sure by the time she got home he would have called, but he didn't. In fact, he didn't call at all that day or night and Sionna had the most difficult time sleeping, and this time it wasn't because of Joey. Taking a deep breath and trying to control her wretched nerves, she found her voice.

"I expected you to call sooner," Sionna said, forcing dryness to her voice. She didn't want him to know just how much of a bundle of nerves she actually was. Again she kicked herself over and over at leaving her purse behind. It was stupid. Without her purse he would have never known who she was and the whole bizarre incident could have been forgotten. Now, anything was possible. She swore under her breath.

"I thought I would let you sweat after that little trick you played on me yesterday," David replied easily, the teasing in his voice lost behind his words for Sionna.

"Trick? I didn't mean it to be. However, I'm still sweating," Sionna said, her honesty causing David to feel contrite at teasing her. And she was certainly in no mood to play games. He knew who she was. He knew Joey. The game was over and it appeared that she had been played enough.

"Hey, I was just joking about making you sweat. But, on a serious tip, if you would kindly tell me what that was about yesterday, I would appreciate it," David said.

"I can only apologize, Mr. Young," Sionna whispered desperately, unable to put into words how she had come to his office with the intent of humiliating him, only to be humiliated herself. It had never occurred to her that Joey's situation on the job was anything other than what he claimed. For the first time, she doubted Joey and felt anger that he could have so baldly lied to her. "Besides," Sionna added, needing an excuse, "you made the actual error when you called me Karen. I just . . . I just allowed it," she finished lamely.

"Uh-huh," was his reply, although Sionna could imagine his confused frown. "That tells me a whole lot. I tell you what," he added after a moment's pause. "I'm willing to wait until we have dinner tonight for a better explanation. There's a nice cozy Italian diner I was thinking of. Is Italian food all right with you?" Even as he made the offer, David questioned himself. He didn't know anything about this woman, and for the life of him, he couldn't understand why he wouldn't let it go. But he had to see her again, and her refusal to explain her behavior was an easy excuse to see her again.

Sionna sat very still. She wasn't sure what kind of a game David was playing, but she was no fool. She hadn't committed a crime. She had only wanted to confront him, demand an apology or acknowledgment of the role he played in her husband's suicide. How could she have known that Joey had so drastically twisted everything? She didn't have to dine with this David Young. She didn't owe him anything more than an apology. After all, he knew who she was and that should have been an explanation in itself.

"I can't have dinner," she said firmly. "But again, I apologize for yesterday. If you would kindly return my purse, it won't happen again."

David laughed. In fact, his laugh was so hearty that Sionna frowned up her face wondering just what was so funny about her apology.

"My address can be found in my wallet that I do need, so please, if you can return it I would appreciate it. Now if you'll excuse me, I'm late for work," Sionna said stiffly, lying about her job to get off the line. She didn't want him to press her any further and she didn't appreciate his laughing at her.

"You know," David started thoughtfully, his voice devoid of amusement, "I've done a little homework, Sionna Michaels. You were married to my old college friend Joey Michaels, which sort of explains why you came to see me. Still I ask myself, why would Joey's widow come to see me? The same woman who hadn't even bothered to invite me to his funeral. And since I'm no detective and still can't figure it all out, I'm kindly asking you to clear it up for me.

So, again, is Italian food all right with you?" David insisted, his words clearly a threat.

Sionna's eyes narrowed with anger and her nervous apprehension faded with irritation. Was he trying to use strong-arm tactics with her? He wasn't fooling her one bit with his nonchalant tone. She knew a barely veiled threat when she heard one. Cautiously, she considered her options, and though annoyed but very aware of the mistake she had made, she answered softly, "Italian is always a good idea."

"Then it's settled. I'll meet you at six-thirty at the Little Italian Shop in the Pavilion. Do you know where that is?" David asked.

"Of course," was Sionna's reply.

"Six-thirty," David repeated before hanging up the phone, barely able to contain his pleasure at her agreeing to meet him.

Sionna held the phone in her hand a moment longer before carefully placing it on the hook. So now she had obligated herself to again come face to face with David. Only this time, he had the upper hand and they both knew it. What kind of recklessness had gotten her into this mess? Sighing heavily, she lay back against her pillow, closed her eyes and waited restlessly for time to tick by, wishing she did have to go work. It would be a welcome distraction from the sticky situation she had gotten herself into.

With his elbows resting on his desk, David clasped his hands together, thoughtfully rested his chin on his hands, and stared at the telephone with satisfaction. He didn't know what was wrong with him, but he was determined not to let Sionna Michaels simply walk out of his life without at least understanding why she had pretended to be Karen Kimper. Of course she hadn't caused him any harm, if only a slight distraction for the past twenty-four hours. She was amazing, that woman. He couldn't be sure if he was more intrigued by her brazen entrance into his life or her mysterious exit. He only knew that he wanted to talk to her again, to meet her again.

It had taken all his patience not to call her yesterday. He knew she would have expected that, and after giving it some thought, he decided it would be smarter to make her wait for his call. He was sure his patience had unnerved her and now the ball was in his court.

"David?" Karen called, opening his door after a quick tap on it. Lost in thoughts of Sionna, David gave Karen a blank look before realizing he had her waiting at the door.

"Yes, come in, Karen," David said hastily, quickly setting thoughts of Sionna Michaels aside.

"These just came for you. Also, Charles and Stan are meeting in the conference room and wanted to know if you could join them for a moment," Karen said as she handed him several packages. David took the packages, grabbed his jacket off the back of the door and followed Karen from the office.

"Give Charles a call and let him know I'm on my way. Oh, and Karen," David called before Karen could sit down.

"Yes?"

"Be sure that wherever I am you find me if I haven't already left by 5:45. Okay?"

"Not a problem," Karen said easily.

"Oh, David!" Karen called before David could disappear down the hall.

He paused and glanced back at her, "Yeah?"

"Jaunice Sumner called. She said she'd be in town tonight and that you should page her after six."

David frowned at her message. Jaunice was in town. She didn't give up, not Jaunice. He had to appreciate her determination to win, but he was starting to lose his patience with her. Although he had to admit that even though Jaunice was a beautiful woman, she was the wrong woman for him. She had said it herself. And during their weeks apart, he came to realize that she was right. A relationship between them would never work.

It was amazing to him how for nearly two years he had convinced himself that Jaunice was the only woman for him, that she would make the perfect wife. But then she complained that she needed space. Fine, he could understand that. And he thought for sure when he moved from New York to Virginia that Jaunice would feel less crowded. Then they saw less and less of each other, and still she cried that she needed space, that he was smothering her. He couldn't understand it at first, then he found it was beginning not to matter. Of course he tried to work it out. He had put in two good years with her. But if she didn't want him, who was he to force the issue? So when she officially broke up with him two months ago, he graciously backed down and agreed that they could still be friends.

With a rueful smile, he recalled how once he would have been excited to get a call from Jaunice. But today she was cramping him. There was a time when he would have done anything to get Jaunice to change her mind about how she viewed their relationship, but now he just wanted her to finish what she started and let their relationship evolve into a mutual friendship. Now she was in town and expected him to jump at her command, but he had a date that he had no intention of canceling. And he certainly was not going to cut short his date with Sionna, if it could actually be called a date, he thought ruefully. After all, he had practically forced the woman to see him. No, he would not cut short his meeting with Sionna.

Jaunice would simply have to wait.

Five

The conference room was a clutter of blueprints, proposals and used paper cups strewn about the table and chairs. Stan was smoking a cigar while bending over one of the blueprints. Charles was on the telephone, talking fast and loud.

David entered the room, took one glance around the untidy room and grinned. Those white boys always amazed him. They broke all the rules, from smoking in the building, although Stan was always careful to do so only in the conference room, to wearing jeans with their white heavily starched shirts and ties. They where characters.

Stan was too cool, always intact, in command. But David knew that deep down inside, Stan was nervous and anxious more often than not. His job was always being threatened by someone younger, more creative and more charismatic. Of course, Stan would never admit it even though everyone knew he was in the office from sunup to sundown, including weekends. His blatant disregard for the smoking law and his lack of professionalism was a facade to cover his insecurities. His tall, awkward body and dusty blond hair that was always out of place was a perfect facade to hide his weakness.

And Charles, well, Charles was just the opposite. He was short and bulky and had dark hair with premature gray strands through it. He didn't have discretion or charm. He knew his job and did it well. But at five o'clock he was gone.

Saturday and Sunday, no one need call, he wasn't home. And answer his pager? Never.

"Hey, David. Check this out. You ever seen anything like this?" Charles whistled the moment David came in.

David walked over to him and studied the blueprint of the new Smithsonian building they were working on. "What am I looking for, these hidden entrances in the basement? Or are they exits?" David asked, scanning his magnifier over the blueprint.

Charles pushed his glasses back on his face and stared at David. "Hold on, Kevin," Charles said hastily. He put the phone down, and with an edge of irritation that David didn't immediately know what to look for in the blueprints, he said, "No. There's something else strange about these designs. Look closer."

"I'm looking. Let's see. It's a government project. I've seen designs like that before. I don't get it," David answered easily as he settled one foot in the chair, bent over and searched the blueprints in more detail.

"Exactly!" Charles snapped. "We've seen designs not only like these before, but exact replicas. I recognize them from my school days. Stan, he recognized them from some of his research for government projects, and now you. So what's happening here? Why are we all familiar with blueprints that for all intents and purposes are supposed be fresh ideas brought in from On-Site?" Charles finished, eyeballing Stan and David as if he suspected they knew more than they were letting on.

"I don't know. You tell me. I'm just a little curious," Stan grumbled, crossing his arms over his chest.

"Who knows. It's the Smithsonian. We didn't actually use any of the On-Site designs, did we? And besides, they're probably just a standard design," David said.

"No, but Stan and I found this stack in the files for the Smithsonian, and I got to tell you, I'm curious about what's happening here," Charles responded.

David shrugged, not finding the blueprints interesting. "I don't have a clue and I don't get the big deal over them either."

"I would think after eleven years in the industry you would have a better clue about what's happening here," Charles insisted.

Stan looked at David with a smirk after Charles's comment, then shook his head with a bright smile. "Tell him, David, he's been in the industry nearly twenty years—"

"Seventeen," Charles snapped.

"That's still longer than David. So why don't you have a clue?" Stan asked.

" 'Cause I never . . . hey I don't have to deal with this. I was just curious," Charles said loudly.

"Tell me something," David said slowly, sitting in the chair and looking at Charles and Stan. They both fell silent, then Charles started to frown.

"What? What?" he rushed David.

David was careful. Although Stan and Charles had called him into the conference room to discuss the blueprints' uncanny resemblance to other prints they had seen before, David was too curious about Joey to focus on the question of the blueprints. When he first found out that Joey had left the company, David had vaguely wondered why. But it wasn't until he met Joey's widow that David seriously questioned what happened to Joey, his one-time friend. Not certain of where the conversation would lead or just how deeply affected he could be by the mystery behind Sionna, he didn't want to tell Charles and Stan that Joey and he were old college friends. After all, he hadn't seen Joey in years, and when he heard they were working for two companies that were going to be merged, Joey was terminated before they could reunite. And the next thing he knew, Joey was dead and buried before David could pay his respects. Thus he was cautious of how he approached his questioning.

"There was a guy who used to work here. Joey L. Michaels. He used to be one of the bidders for On-Site before we came in. Know anything about him?" David tried to keep his tone normal. He didn't want to give the impression there was anything strange about Joey.

Charles shrugged, saying, "Never heard of him."

"I did. He won the bid for the new development. This one in fact, Charles," Stan answered carelessly as he pointed at the blueprint for the new museum. David stared at it as if it were the answer to all his questions.

"Get out! I heard that was a pretty big deal about a year ago. So what happened to him? Another builder stole him from us?" Charles asked, looking impressed.

"Not quite. He died some weeks after he was terminated," David said.

"Terminated? Why?" Charles whispered as if he were being told a very important secret.

"He wasn't a critical employee after the merger. You know we don't bid . . ." Stan answered callously.

"So we terminated him," David said dubiously, realizing that he had never inquired into the fate of Joey. It had never occurred to him to ask more questions, even though he and Joey had a brief friendship during his last year of college. He felt bad, realizing for the first time that he had been so wrapped up in his relationship and pursuit of Jaunice that he had barely given a second thought about Joey.

"How did he die?" Charles asked, unable to contain his curiosity.

"I hear it was sudden. I'm going to know real soon though," David answered smoothly, not wanting to divulge too much information before he himself knew what had troubled Joey to the point of suicide.

He didn't want to share too much with them. He didn't want them to know about Sionna Michaels's visit. He only knew he was filled with curiosity. Even more so than before.

So Michaels was a strong bidder. David recalled that Joey was not a great designer, so it made sense that Joey had gone into bidding for firms instead of designing. He had won the museum contract and then was fired, which was something David did not understand. He sighed. Dinner with Sionna was going to be very interesting indeed. He knew one thing for sure: Sionna had come to him for something and it had to do with Joey. That much was clear. Just what she wanted, what her intent was, he was clueless. But he was determined that before the night was over, he would find out.

Six

Sionna chided herself all the way downtown to the restaurant. She should have worn a simple pair of jeans and a plain blouse, she kept thinking. In hindsight, as she got out of the cab, she realized that her sleek blue dress and blue high heels could easily be mistaken for an attempt to make an impression on David. It was a grave mistake. And yet, why it mattered what he thought of her appearance she couldn't fathom, or at least she didn't want to admit to the slight attraction that she instantly felt for him. She only knew from the moment she saw him and looked into his dark eyes that she was all wrong about him. Everything she thought she knew about her husband, everything she thought to be true, was suddenly a fog of misconception and even perhaps lies.

As she stepped out of the cab, she glanced up and down the sidewalk, wondering if she would see David approaching her. But in the bustle of faces she saw no one that could be him. Pausing for another moment, she took a long deep breath and chilled her nerves. It was just dinner, she thought sternly. It was simply a chance to clear the air, to apologize for her *I Spy* behavior. A chance to get beyond the past and move on with her life. Feeling a little more confident with her reasoning, she found the Little Italian Shop and, taking a deep breath, entered its doors.

The Little Italian Shop was by no means little. In fact, Sionna was impressed with its size. Yet somehow she could appreciate its name. There had to be several dozen tables throughout the restaurant, each covered with snow-white tablecloths that at closer glance had soft rose petal designs etched on them. The tables all had carefully decorated handkerchiefs and one fresh red rose set in the center of what appeared to be an ancient pale vase. The vases were beautifully handcrafted and Sionna wondered if the owners didn't fear theft.

As large as the place was, it had an air of coziness that created an atmosphere of seclusion at each table. Sionna wasn't sure what was more cozy about the place, the softly lit blue and pink candles that decorated each table, or the low, dimly lit ceilings, or the friendly waiters and waitresses that greeted the diners with bright smiles. It was a lovely place indeed. And if she weren't careful, Sionna knew she could get lost in the ambience of the restaurant and forget why she had agreed to meet David.

David felt Sionna's presence even before he saw her. Something about her alerted every nerve in his body. She had walked into the restaurant and paused just inside the doors near the hostess check-in desk. She was a sight, he thought, captivated by her unpretentious beauty.

Her hair was free of the pinned-up curls she had worn the first time he saw her. She wore a blue dress with sleeveless straps that curved around her body in a soft silhouette. The blue was becoming, he thought, appreciating how pretty she was standing across the room from him. A half smile curved his full mouth as he watched her, and he didn't bother to look away when she caught sight of him checking her out. In fact, his smile broadened when she returned his blatant scrutiny.

Their eyes locked, and as if the room stood still, Sionna slowly approached David. She thought with a narrowed gaze that it was interesting how he had managed to find the most secluded spot in the restaurant. She had news for him. Whatever he thought was going to happen wasn't going to, of that she was determined. She may have behaved like a ninny the other day, but that was then. She held back an amused smile, having no intention of encouraging any expectations he may have outside of giving her back her purse. No matter how fine he was.

"Can it be that you're even prettier than I remember?" David wooed, coming to his feet as Sionna reached him. As if they were old friends, he took her hands and held them for a moment in greeting.

Sionna's senses were startled by his touch, but somehow she managed to hide her reaction. She paused at his comment, focusing on their hands to give herself a moment to regain her composure. *Get it together girl,* she thought, *you don't even know this man to be reacting like this.* Taking a deep breath, she calmly released her hands and responded in a voice that was more steady than her racing heart, "Could it be that you've mistaken yourself for Casanova?"

David laughed, not the least bit offended by her statement. "Not at all. I just find myself acting the fool whenever you're around," he responded as he helped her to her seat, then sat back down.

"Do you? And this being our second and last meeting," Sionna said sarcastically, careful not to use the word date.

"Really?" David asked, leaning back in his seat. Her statement affected him more than he would have expected, and he couldn't keep from admitting, "I was kind of hoping for a different outcome."

"I don't think so, Mr. Young," Sionna said softly, using his surname as a shield against getting too familiar with him. His dark gaze was intense and was arousing emotions in her that she thought were lost with Joey's death. She was a little shaken by how taken she was with David, and she was beginning to feel like a skittish kitten.

"Why not?" David asked with a crooked smile, disappointed by her abrupt rejection but not ready to give up just yet.

Sionna shrugged slightly, then murmured, "I just need my purse."

David furrowed his eyebrows, puckered his mouth as if he wanted to say something and ran his thumb across his chin in a thoughtful gesture. Then he reached his arm to the side of the table and came back up with her purse. He set the purse on the table, keeping his hand lightly on it as he considered Sionna again.

Sionna glanced at her purse and his hand that was resting on it before allowing her gaze to fall back on David. Her look didn't waver even when he leaned forward, his keen gaze taking in every inch of her face as he said, "I have to ask you, Sionna Michaels, why did you come bursting into my life if you had no intention on staying awhile?"

His words were said with a hint of light banter, but Sionna tensed, sensitive to his underlying sincerity. Every instinct in her screamed *take your purse and run*, but she couldn't just get up and leave. Instead she responded in a voice full of regret, "You would never understand." She was very aware of how she had behaved and how they had met. No amount of attraction could change how she had come into his life in such a bizarre way. She would never forget how foolish she had felt when he accidentally cleared himself of guilt.

David considered her with a half smile, his eyes gleaming in curiosity before he suggested, "Try me."

Sionna sat back in her seat and laid her small black purse in her lap. How could she explain to this man looking so baffled across from her that she had actually blamed him for the death of her husband? A quiet glance at him and she knew she couldn't expose her deepest emotions to him. After all, he was a stranger, even more a stranger now than before she had met him, more so than when she had been sure he had callously taken her husband's job. Sighing and trying to build a believable story, she finally spoke.

"It was just part of my job. I'm a reporter," she began blandly.

David nodded as if to say he was aware of her position. She realized then that her press identification card must have been in the purse she had left in his office. She grew more confident.

"I was going to milk you for information about your firm's designs and the museum project. That's why I was there," she ended swiftly. In an odd way, what she said was true. Joey had worked on the museum project before he was fired from the company and she had intended to find out why the company had replaced Joey with David. After all, the museum contract created a lot of revenue for the company and more industry recognition. It wasn't a complete lie. Not totally, she insisted, as if to massage her conscience.

David didn't respond. He sat back and considered her with a perceptive smile, his eyes clearly expressing his doubt with her story. But Sionna refused to fidget beneath his unwavering scrutiny, although she was becoming more uncomfortable by the moment.

"Interesting," David finally said, tapping his fingers on the table.

"Yes. The public is always interested in knowing where their taxes are going," Sionna said, trying to sound natural.

"I'm sure," he said coolly. "I guess I was wrong then."

"About?" Sionna asked.

"About you. About your husband. I thought maybe, just maybe, grief-stricken and all, you had come to the firm to find some sort of closure. I thought the fact that Joey and I were friends in college may have inspired you to want to meet me. But that would have been too romantic," he added, searching her face for a response.

Sionna felt weak with worry. Could he have guessed her

intent so easily? Was she that obvious? Or had David's off-handed comments about how he got with the firm mean nothing? After all, he had thought she was his new assistant, not the wife of the man he had driven to commit suicide a year before. With a frown, she realized she was back to blaming him. But somehow, sitting across from him in the soft lights of the restaurant, she couldn't see him as having had anything to do with Joey's situation. And meeting him made it even more difficult to swallow Joey's description of David's role in the loss of Joey's job.

She felt her cheeks flush with embarrassment. David had known Joey, even if it was just for a short while during their college days. It made sense that he connected her visit with his relationship to Joey, she reasoned.

"Are you all right?" David asked, noting her slight frown, hoping he hadn't pushed her too far with his questions.

She focused on him, relaxing her face as she responded. "Yes. It's just that the mentioning of my husband is always a little upsetting, even now."

David looked instantly contrite and gently reached across the table and patted her hand sympathetically. "I'm sorry. I should have been more considerate."

"No need to apologize, David. It wasn't as if it was your fault," Sionna added, considering him with a discerning gaze.

David was uncertain how to respond to her comment so he simply remained silent. Initially he had asked Sionna to dinner because of the sheer fascination she had ignited in him. He was curious who this beautiful woman was, but now he was compelled to get the truth from her. To find out just what her true intentions were the day she walked into his office. Her lame excuse about doing a story didn't sit well with him either. And her obvious brooding and Joey Michaels's death were no coincidence. Just how in love was she with Joey, and was she holding onto the memory of him? Was there room for her to love again? he wondered.

"So, are you hungry?" he asked, swiftly changing the subject.

"If I weren't, the aroma alone would have made me," Sionna answered with a laugh, delicately sniffing the pleasant aroma that was left behind as one of the waiters passed their table carrying a steaming bowl of mussel soup and pasta.

"I thought you would like this place," David said proudly, ignoring the fact that it was his ex-girlfriend who first brought him to the Little Italian Shop.

After they ordered, neither of them spoke, finding themselves at a loss for words as they both considered how to broach the subject of her visit to his office. Sionna hoped that perhaps he wouldn't question her further, that he would take pity on her, offer her purse to her and call everything a truce. Of course, she could see by his deliberating gaze that there was no chance of that happening. Finally, David leaned back in his seat and decided to put Sionna's story that she was a reporter investigating his company to the test. He asked, "So what do you want to know?"

Caught off guard by his question, Sionna blinked and asked, "Excuse me?" with a puzzled look at him.

"What did you want to know about Buerhler the other day, you know, when you left your purse with me?" David repeated in a mocking tone as he reminded her of her hasty exit.

"Oh," Sionna breathed. "I guess for one thing why the museum is taking so long to be built and why it's being built so far from the traditional museum location and basically why all the secrecy on the renovation project," she rambled, trying to think of as many logical questions as she could while appearing nonchalant. But it didn't work.

David chuckled, his dark eyes full of amusement as he asked in a low, husky voice, "Tell me something, is it that I just make you nervous or are you just not used to digging for information?" He paused, then added before she could answer, "Or is it that you're not the most seasoned reporter? You tell me."

"I've been a reporter for seven years," Sionna said indignantly, not amused by his offhanded questions.

"Yeah? And how many of those years were spent on investigative reports?" David asked dubiously.

With a narrowed gaze, Sionna glared at him, then coolly responded, "Almost two years."

"Almost, ha!" David said. Thoroughly amused, he added, "So how many stories have you done in these almost two years?"

"Look, David," Sionna snapped, aggravated. "I happen to be a very good reporter. I spent my first five years after college working in all areas of the newsroom, newspaper and even some radio, thank you. I know the business, David, just as I am sure you know all about being a construction worker," Sionna added, purposely using the incorrect term for his profession. Her time with Joey had taught her that architects and designers didn't like being called construction workers. The look on his face gave her satisfaction, and it was her turn to look smug.

"Architecture," David corrected, feeling slighted by her interpretation of his job. "Although I spend the majority of my time on the actual development and technical aspects of reviewing designs, I am familiar with the drawing up of designs as well," he felt compelled to explain.

"Really," Sionna stated with sarcasm dripping from her voice.

"Yeah, really," David mumbled. "You realize of course that Joey and I studied at the same university. We even hung out for a while. Our degree is pretty much the same, although he went into design investments and I went into management. I don't get how, being married to Joey, you don't understand what I do," David insisted, glaring at her in annoyance.

Did he charge into her office, lying and pretending to

be someone else? Was he wrong to try to figure it out? Was he wrong to want to know more about this intriguing woman? And maybe she wasn't so intriguing after all, he thought, sulking a bit from her sarcasm. Maybe she was just some lovesick lonely woman with a reckless nature. The thought of her being reckless brought Jaunice to mind, and he knew instantly that she was nothing like Jaunice. From the moment he had made it clear to Jaunice that he agreed with her decision to end their relationship, she changed. Suddenly they had a future, she decided. Suddenly she couldn't get enough of talking to him. Suddenly she wanted to see him and the thought annoyed him more. He glanced at his watch, certain that Jaunice was wondering why he hadn't called yet. She would just have to get over it.

"David," Sionna murmured gently, taking his scowl to be toward her. Having no clue what was really bothering him, Sionna reached across the table and took his hand. He frowned, wondering what this new approach was about.

"I'm sorry, David. I must seem like some kind of nut to you. And I apologize. I better go," she added, releasing his hand and coming to her feet.

"But you haven't eaten yet," David said hastily, feeling an unexplainable panic at the idea that she was leaving so soon.

Sionna smiled, shrugged her shoulders and said regretfully, "I really have to go. Thanks for my purse," she added, then hastily left the table.

David stared after her, confounded. She was a mystery to him, an incredibly beautiful woman who seemed sincere yet impossible to understand. He had met her and sat with her as planned, and still he really did not know who she was. He watched as she disappeared from the restaurant, and with an unreasonable fear he couldn't decipher, he hated the idea that it could be the last time they would meet. With a firm decision that chiseled his jaws, he determined that it wouldn't be their last meeting. She may still be grief-stricken over Joey or just looking for a story. Either way he was the right man to help her and he was going to see to it that he saw her again.

Seven

"David!" Jaunice laughed in delight at the sight of him. She draped her arms about him, still wearing her coat. It appeared she had just arrived, and before David could respond, she greeted him with a firm kiss meant for his mouth but which landed on his cheek.

David didn't return her enthusiastic greeting. In fact, he turned his head before their mouths could meet, irritated that Jaunice had not only intruded on the privacy of his home but had come over unannounced. Before she left for New York several months earlier, he had asked her to give him back his key. She had promised to mail it, but she never did. Now she had the audacity to stand in his doorway and greet him as if she were the perfect happy homemaker. He scowled, wondering what would have happened if Sionna had been with him. What was Jaunice thinking? They were no longer a couple.

"What are you doing here, Jaunice?" David demanded, pulling himself free of Jaunice's excited hold and at the same time avoiding her second attempt to kiss him.

"I was hoping to surprise you, especially seeing how I missed your page," Jaunice said, ignoring how he had twice shunned her kiss. And she certainly wasn't going to dwell on his lack of response to her message to page her, conveniently deciding that it had to have been a fluke rather than deliberate on his part. David wasn't like that. No matter what she thought of him, he was a gentleman.

"I didn't page you, Jaunice. I was . . . busy," David said, careful not to mention his date with Sionna. The last thing he wanted to do was get into an argument with Jaunice, and besides, it was none of her business what he was doing. After all, he had not seen her in months, and her showing up looking adorable didn't change one thing.

Although he had been able to avoid her kisses, his eyes wandered carelessly over her carefully prepared hair to her dainty, strapped stiletto high heels. She wasn't a tall woman, around five foot four, so her stiletto heels didn't dramatically increase her height, although they did give the illusion that her shapely legs were longer beneath her flared floral miniskirt. She was wearing a matching floral semitransparent blouse that hung softly over her petite form. Her white leather jacket was oversized, and if it weren't for the way it hung off her shoulders, she would have been lost in the jacket. She was attractive, David admitted, but she had also made it clear when she left him three months earlier that she did not want to be his woman. And so be it, he thought firmly, his gaze hiding his appreciation of the work she had put into her appearance.

"Oh," Jaunice murmured, stepping away from him as if he were a stranger. She was not at all pleased with his reaction. She gave him a sidelong glance with a hint of a pout, her red lipstick making her full mouth even more sensuous. Her eyes were darkened by mascara and earth-toned eye shadow. She looked sultry, with her straight black hair lying flat against her smooth brown face. And up until David arrived, she had felt sexy. Didn't he know that she had called him because she genuinely missed him and his many compliments? But, she thought with a slight frown, his response was not a compliment and she was a woman who thrived on compliments.

David felt chagrin beneath her crestfallen gaze. He didn't want to hurt Jaunice; there was no bitterness between them. But what they had was over. She had seen to it when she broke up with him a few months earlier. What did she expect, that he would wait for her to change her mind again? Sighing heavily, he turned from her and locked the front door, then dropped his keys onto the counter in the foyer before giving her his attention again.

Jaunice was perturbed. When she broke up with David, she had no idea how much it would hurt once he no longer wanted her. The first few weeks after they broke up David kept calling her. Jaunice could tell he wasn't taking their breakup well. Then David stopped calling altogether but he would still talk to her and ask when they were going to discuss getting back together whenever she called him. In time, even that changed and he was neither calling her nor returning her calls.

She then had second thoughts about breaking up with David. It didn't matter that weeks had turned into months. She felt strongly that his love for her was not confined by boundaries of time. Yet it was his silence that prompted her to impulsively come to Virginia. She needed to see him, to reassure herself that she was not making a mistake. David wasn't helping her to come to a decision, either. He was closed-mouthed and unemotional. She didn't know how to take his reaction. All she knew was that for the first time she wondered if he had fallen in love with someone else. The thought was devastating.

Feeling a need to console her, which was unreasonable because he was a free man by Jaunice's own doing, David walked up to Jaunice and opened his arms in a gesture to welcome her and to call a truce between them. Jaunice visibly relaxed and easily slid into his arms. Relieved that her fears were unfounded, Jaunice gazed up at him with an adoration he thought she had lost. David knew in that moment that holding her was a mistake. He could tell she would read all the wrong things into it.

"Missed me, David?" she asked in a low, silken voice.

"Jaunice," David murmured regretfully, wishing he had remained firm and not given in to her tragic pout.

"Well, I missed you," Jaunice said. "I realize every day I'm not with you that I should have moved down here months ago when you asked me to." She nuzzled her cheek against his as she intentionally reminded him how he had asked her to move in with him.

"Like you said, Jaunice, there are dozens of capitals that need building architects, but there are only a few fashion capitals, and New York is where you're staying," David said dryly, going downstairs into his basement without bothering to offer her to follow.

Jaunice scowled at his statement, recalling exactly how she had flippantly dismissed the idea that they should live together. He was callous to bring it up, she thought in growing annoyance. "I know that, David, thank you," Jaunice snapped, following him down the stairs. He was standing at his bar preparing a drink for himself. He looked up at her approach, realizing that she still had her jacket on. He didn't suggest that she take it off, hoping that she planned to leave soon so he wouldn't have to ask her to go. That would be awkward for both of them.

"Would you like a drink?" he asked in such a formal voice that Jaunice itched to slap his smug face.

Did he think he had her begging for him now? Well, he was wrong and they would soon see just who wanted whom. Besides, he had to be playing a game, she concluded. There was no way a man could change his feelings so drastically in such a short period of time. She was certain that he thought pretending to be uninterested in her was his way of trying to win her back. With narrowed eyes, her confidence was boosted. She was onto him now, so he might as well stop trying to play Mr. Nonchalant. He still loved her, she thought proudly, her conceit blinding her.

"As a matter of fact, David, I would," Jaunice answered sitting on the high stool. She pulled off her jacket and set it on the high stool beside her; then, with both elbows on the bar, she leaned forward and gave David one of her most seductive smiles.

"I'm out of wine. How about a soda?" David asked, looking over his assortment of drinks, refusing to acknowledge the game she was playing.

"No, I'll have what you're having," Jaunice said, considering his drink with a raised eyebrow. She sat up straight.

"Scotch?" David asked, hesitating at her request.

"That's what I said, baby," Jaunice sung.

"All right, but I hope you're not driving," David said, the concern he was showing lost behind the fact that he apparently expected her to leave.

Jaunice frowned at his comment. Leaning forward, she hissed in a questioning voice, "Driving?"

"Yeah. You know how you are when you drink, Jaunice. You can't handle your liquor very well and I have an early day tomorrow, so you know, we'll have a drink then I have to ask you to understand I need my rest," David answered carefully. He was trying as politely as he could to let her know he wanted her to leave.

Jaunice was floored, saying in an incredulous voice, "What?"

"Jaunice—" David began, putting both hands on the bar as he stared at her in open agitation.

"Oh, now wait, David. Are you really trying to tell me you don't want me to stay tonight. You're really telling me that you are not interested in sharing a passionate night of making love with me?" Jaunice asked, attempting to be seductive, although her tone gave away her growing impatience.

David took a step back and scratched his head, uncomfortable. The last thing he needed was a misunderstanding between them, and making love would create a huge misunderstanding. Staring into Jaunice's seductive gaze, he frowned. She was making it very difficult to let go in an amicable way.

"Are you expecting us to be lovers without any form of commitment? Is that what you're telling me you want, Jaunice?" he asked matter-of-factly, hoping the blandness of his words would dissuade her from her plans.

"I miss you, David. After all, it's been almost three months since we made love. Why do you think I called?" she answered, not at all bashful.

"To talk," he answered with an edge of impatience.

"Lighten up, David. It's okay if we aren't committed," Jaunice said airily. Lifting herself from the stool, she wrapped her arms about his neck and attempted to kiss him again. David gruffly removed her arms from him and took a step back.

"That's enough, Jaunice. It's not okay. Not with me anyway," David added firmly.

"Are you saying you don't want to have a passionate night of making up?" Jaunice asked, staring up at him with wide, disbelieving eyes.

David stared at her, irritated, torn between wanting to send her away and wanting to give her what she wanted. He sighed, knowing making love to Jaunice would be a serious mistake. "I like to think we're going to have a quiet night of friendship. You don't have to leave, Jaunice, all right. I think we're beyond that. But," he added with emphasis, "we are not going to sleep together either."

"Sure, as if you could keep your hands off me," Jaunice scoffed, completely disregarding any sincerity she heard in his voice. She crossed her legs, watching his eyes with satisfaction as they followed her movement. As far as she was concerned, he still found her desirable even if he wanted to pretend differently.

David didn't respond as he downed his drink. She was still beautiful to him. He had to admit that. But she was also manipulative. He couldn't trust her and he had no doubt that every move she was making was well-planned. Their eyes caught and David felt like a fool. Why was he turning her away, he thought, momentarily weakened as he stared into her rich brown eyes with a sense of confusion. Then Jaunice said with a big smile, "So, have you eaten? It's early yet and I'm starved. How about we ride downtown and visit our Little Italian Shop?"

Her suggestion was like a douse of cold water. At the mention of the Italian shop, David snapped back into reality. He had taken Sionna to the place that Jaunice had claimed as their private spot. Worse yet, he realized, Jaunice had discovered the Italian restaurant. Although they were no longer committed to each other, he felt it would be completely uncool to let Jaunice know that he had taken another woman, an intriguing and exciting woman, to their favorite spot.

David answered carefully, keeping his gaze on his drink as he said, "I'm kind of tired, and like I said, I have to get up early so I plan to go to bed real soon."

Jaunice didn't notice his discomfort. She didn't hear the hesitancy in his voice, and with a content shrug, she gave him a knowing glance.

"I do believe I like the idea of going to bed better. I like that idea a lot," she laughed, deliberately playing on his words.

David frowned. He hadn't meant going to bed with her, and he knew she knew it. He was tempted to insist that she leave right then and there, but a part of him that had known her and loved her couldn't be as indifferent as he wanted to be about the situation.

On the one hand, Jaunice had put him on the back burner. She had ignored his calls for nearly two weeks after she first broke up with him, then for weeks after that she barely contacted him. When she finally wanted to talk he had discovered that his heart had cooled toward her. It seemed only then that she wanted to talk to him, to see him and talk things over. He had avoided the subject, no longer sure how he felt. Now he was certain, especially after meeting Sionna, that he did not want to renew what Jaunice had ended between them.

Of course, her timing couldn't be worse. He needed to clear the air, to tell her about Sionna. But if on the other hand Jaunice was here to let him know that she actually didn't want to continue a relationship with him, because he knew her well enough to know that making love to Jaunice did not mean a commitment from her, then he wouldn't feel it was necessary to ever mention Sionna. He held back a sigh of exasperation. If she were here to tell him that she wanted to get back together, then he was in trouble, because then he would be compelled to tell her he had met someone else, if only to get her to end any expectations of their having a future together.

Jaunice was utterly baffled by David's behavior. During the past week, she had begun to have second thoughts about breaking up with him and had begun to wonder if she had made a dreadful mistake. After all, it wasn't every day that a man like David came along. He was handsome, well-built and in good health with a great job. He was considerate and loving and, most important, he loved her completely. Yet up until a few weeks ago, she wasn't sure of how she felt about David. Did she love him or did she love the fact that he loved her? Those were questions she had to answer. Breaking up with him didn't make the matter any clearer and going out with other men didn't help either. In fact, it wasn't until she called the week before and got a dry response from David that she realized she still wanted him. The worst thing that could happen was for him to stop wanting her, and by all indications from his demeanor, her worst fears had come true.

"Jaunice, there's something we need to talk about," David began, his sense of right not allowing him to keep silent about his feelings for her. He couldn't make love to her, not knowing that all that was left between them was a fleeting physical attraction, and even that was barely there. He needed to let Jaunice know he was deeply sorry to hurt her, but it was definitely over.

"Yes, David," Jaunice whispered huskily, completely clueless about his intent. She was certain that he was going to confess his undying love for her again.

"I met someone else," David blurted, keeping his eyes on the bar counter as he spoke.

Had he been looking up he would have seen Jaunice's expression change from a dumbfounded gape to a contemptuous scowl. He heard her gasp and there was no way to ignore her frustrated yell as she jumped from the stool and stamped a high-heeled foot into the carpet in a fit of anger.

"You met somebody? You met somebody? How could you?" Jaunice stormed, putting her hands on her hips and glaring at him in total contempt.

"You broke up with me, remember? What was I supposed to do, sit around and twiddle my thumbs and hope you would change your mind?" David stormed back. He had not expected such a vehement reaction from her, although he realized instantly that he should have expected no less from Jaunice.

"Yes! If you loved me you would have waited before you slept around!" Jaunice yelled.

"Hold your voice down, Jaunice," David demanded. He walked around the bar and sat on the stool. With a thoughtful gaze at her, he admitted, "I haven't slept with anyone, Jaunice. I simply met someone and I thought you should know."

"Oh, gee thanks. You're so kind," Jaunice snapped in bitter sarcasm.

"Jaunice," David began softly, certain her sardonic words were a cover for the hurt she was feeling.

"No, David. Don't try to explain. You have that right,"

Jaunice muttered. But seconds later she sat back down beside him, and with narrowed eyes she demanded, "Who is she?"

"She is nobody that you would know. I barely know her myself," David added in raw honesty. He conveniently omitted that he had had dinner with her just a few hours earlier, certain that if he admitted to having taken Sionna to the restaurant, Jaunice, in the state of mind she was in, could not handle it.

"Oh, please . . ." Jaunice scoffed.

"I just thought you should know, Jaunice. I don't think it's a good idea to start something we are not prepared to finish. You were uncertain before about us and now so am I. Besides I haven't seen you in weeks."

"What does that have to do with anything? I could have been your wife, traveling, and you could still have met another woman. So please, don't run me that line about my not being around. You've probably been messing around all the time," Jaunice added nastily.

"No, I haven't. And I think you know me better than that," David responded. He stood up and sighed. "Look, I'm tired, and you've had a long day. I know how you hate to fly, so why don't we just go to bed and talk in the morning. You can ride in with me to work and we can talk when neither of us is tired. Are you all right with that, Jaunice?" David asked, feeling as if Jaunice was staring right through him, her gaze was so unwavering.

Jaunice continued to glare at him, her mind reeling behind the impact of his words. Who did he think he was, treating her as if she were the desperate one? She was no angel, but she certainly didn't like what she was hearing. Did he sleep with that woman or was he lying? Somehow she couldn't believe he was as innocent as he was portraying himself to be. Furious and determined to get to the bottom of what was going on, Jaunice had to force herself to calm down before she could speak.

"Jaunice?" David asked, frowning now at Jaunice's continued silence.

Blinking at the sound of her name, Jaunice scooted from the stool, turned in a slight circle and shrugged her delicate shoulders. She said smoothly, "You're right. I'm tired and we both need to think. You hear me, David? Think. Think about what all this means for our future. I'm leaving tomorrow afternoon, so you don't have much time to make up your mind," Jaunice added sternly. Before he could respond, she walked to the stairs and, turning to consider him over her shoulder, she asked, "So where am I sleeping tonight since it won't be with you?"

David held back an amused laugh. She was going to hold that card to the end, he realized. Walking to the stairs with her, he moved in front of her and guided her up the stairs. She followed him, her narrowed gaze shooting daggers into his back. And when she realized that he was heading for the guest bedroom down the hall from his room, she seethed inside. He stepped into the room, switched on the light and stepped aside to allow her to enter.

Jaunice sauntered into the room, hands on her hips as she swept her gaze over every item in the room, from the floral heavy draperies to the full-sized bed. The room was nice and she recalled when he had first changed the colors at her suggestion. She never thought she would be sleeping in the room, however, and she was gravely disappointed.

"You know where everything is," David said, clearing his throat.

She swung around to give him a disgusted look before saying between clenched teeth, "Yes, I do."

David hesitated, then, bobbing his head in discomfort and feeling foolish for standing at the door, he said, "Well, okay. I'll see you in the morning."

Jaunice didn't respond. She calmly walked up to the door and without blinking slammed it shut in his face, causing David to blink in surprise. Staring at the closed door, David again hesitated. With a heavy sigh, he left her and went back to the basement. He needed another drink, he thought, drained by his resolve not to fall for whatever game Jaunice was playing. He would just be happy when she was gone. Then he could get on with his life and get to know Sionna Michaels better.

Eight

Sionna sat cross-legged on her bed. Her encounter with David had been exhausting yet exhilarating on several levels. Not only was she able to finally put a face to the man she blamed for her husband's suicide, but she was able to bring a sense of closure to the depths of frustration he had represented. She had not expected to become even more attracted to him, however, and because of that she determined she had isolated herself for too long. He would not have been as attractive if she hadn't blinded herself from looking at all men since Joey's death. No, she wasn't going to foolishly become interested in David, especially considering that she still didn't know what he had done to cause Joey to hate him so much, and looking at how much she still didn't know about him, she was beginning to believe she would never truly know what happened between the two men.

Sighing, she looked up and gave an inquisitive frown, as if the blank ceiling could answer her questions. Looking around her room, she determined that she needed to get inspired, to come alive again. It was time. Time to release the pain she had held onto ever since Joey's death. Time to begin living her life like a normal young woman. She felt ashamed, though. Ashamed that she couldn't stop thinking about David, her husband's so-called enemy. He was far different from what she had expected, far more kind and interesting than she had imagined. A hint of a smile touched her lips, and Sionna sighed. She had no business smiling when he came to mind, she scolded herself. Her problem was that she had too much time on her hands and it was beginning to show. She needed to get back to work, to let go of Joey and David. Besides, David was the one man she should steer clear of if she ever wanted to get past her grief over Joey, because he would forever remind her of Joey and she could not bear that.

Feeling a sense of urgency that overwhelmed her, Sionna impulsively grabbed her phone and dialed the newspaper.

"Mr. Eikton," Sionna said brightly.

"This is not Sionna," Mr. Eikton guffawed, although by his tone Sionna knew he was well aware of whom he was speaking to.

Sionna grinned, pleased to hear his gruff but very welcome voice. "That's right, Mr. Eikton, it's Sionna."

"Tell me you're ready to come back to work again," he added, referring to her previous leave of absence when Joey died a year before.

Sionna sighed before obliging him with a humble, "Yes, I would love to come back to work, this time without a break, other than vacation and sick leave and . . ."

"Okay. Okay. I get it. No problem. And have I got a story for you," Mr. Eikton said with a burst of energy that gave away his excitement over her returning. He always carried on as if they had some incredible news story to break when all they ever covered was local fluff and community activities.

"Great."

"Good response because I need a draft tonight and I want to run it this weekend."

"Tonight? This weekend?" Sionna groaned. "But it's two o'clock. I'm not prepared—"

"Are you a reporter or a fumbling wannabe? Because if you're a reporter, you are always ready," Mr. Eikton said.

Sionna squeezed her eyes shut, sat back in her seat and

after a brief, thoughtful pause, she answered, "I guess I'm a reporter."

"All right. Then we have no time to waste. Some local computer programmers are suing their company for giving them the boot. I got one of their phone numbers. Call the guy, get the story, write it up and have a draft ready for me by nine A.M. tomorrow. Got a pen?" he asked and paused expectantly.

Momentarily regretting her impulsive decision to go back to work three weeks earlier than planned, Sionna grabbed a pen off the nightstand, then picked the phone back up and said, "Got it."

"If I told you once, I've told you a million times, the pen and pad is your best friend. Keep a pen in your hair if you have to, but keep one on you. And a pad, you should carry it like it was glued to your hand. Are you hearing me, Sionna?" Mr. Eikton demanded.

"Absolutely," Sionna answered quickly.

Mr. Eikton was the lecture king. He should have been a professor instead of running a local newspaper. He knew a lot and had the respect of his industry colleagues. Sionna had learned a lot from him and she always kept his lectures in mind. So when he began rambling off the name of the contact and his phone number, she scribbled intensely, trying to focus, as he had repeatedly told her to do. When he hung up the phone, she immediately dialed the contact's phone number, as he would have lectured her to do. But there was no answer after several rings, and she finally hung up.

She had done it. She had picked up where she left off and was ready to live again. She was disappointed that she didn't get an answer from the contact, nor did she get his voice mail. But she was certainly not going to let that stop her. Getting off the bed, she left her room and went downstairs. She turned on the television set and switched the channel to the local all-news station before grabbing a Pepsi from the refrigerator.

She went back to her family room and sat on the sofa in front of the television set. Trying to have patience, she couldn't help glancing at the clock every few moments. She would give the guy a few hours to get home from wherever he was since he had just gotten fired, then she would call again. An hour had barely passed before Sionna, a bundle of nervous energy, grabbed the phone again and dialed his number.

"Hello?" a sleepy male voice answered on the second ring.

"Mr. Hillman? Mr. Greg Hillman?" Sionna asked, excited that she had gotten through.

"Who's asking?" the male voice demanded with a hint of anger.

"My name is Sionna Michaels, Mr. Hillman," Sionna answered, sure that the man was Greg Hillman. "I'm with the *City Desk*. I wanted to talk to you about your lawsuit."

"From whose point of view, theirs or mine?" Greg demanded in a huff.

"From the most objective point of view, Mr. Hillman," Sionna answered cautiously. This man was angry and she didn't want to upset him any further. She would have to use kid gloves if she were going to get a story out of him. Or at least any information that was ethically worth reporting.

"I don't want to talk about it," he said gruffly.

"Wait, wait a moment, Mr. Hillman," Sionna gasped, desperate to keep him on the line, sensing that he was going to hang up on her. "I promise you, I won't be a threat to your case. I believe in fact that given the right information, I can help it. We have a circulation of thirty thousand readers just within the metropolitan area. And what you need in any case is civil support. My paper can get you that." Sionna's pitch was good, she thought, but by his silence she wondered if it was good enough.

"Yeah, well why are you the only paper calling me? I bet everyone else is calling Buerhler," Greg finally grumbled.

Buerhler! That was Joey's company. That was David's company. His words froze Sionna and she sat absolutely still. Was she destined to never escape that nightmare?

"Buerhler? As in the architectural firm?" she murmured, barely able to speak.

"Yeah! They merged with On-Site about a year and a half ago and now I'm out. I'm suing those bastards. I worked for On-Site seven long years without ever receiving a complaint. Then—suddenly, here comes Buerhler complaining about this and that and I'm at fault, then suddenly they no longer require my services. They give me this big severance pay as if they're sorry, but they ain't sorry. Not yet!" Greg blurted in growing frustration as he spoke.

Sionna listened in shock to Greg Hillman's complaints, recalling that her husband's words were the very same, his complaint about how they dogged him out of his job the very same as Joey's, except for one thing: Greg didn't accuse David of stealing his job. She was very curious to learn what Greg knew about David Young and what he thought of David Young. With a mixture of natural curiosity linked with her role as a reporter and her interest in David, Sionna was anxious to calm Greg down and get as much information as she could from him.

"Mr. Hillman, are you available to meet with me tonight?" Sionna asked impulsively. She held her breath, anxiously awaiting Greg's reply. "Or breakfast tomorrow," she added, worried by his silence.

Greg hesitated before responding in a mumble, "Yeah, I suppose I can do breakfast tomorrow. Where do you want to meet?"

"How about the House of Pancakes, about eight A.M.?" Sionna suggested, excited that he had agreed to meet with her.

"It'll have to be earlier. I have a nine o'clock interview."

"Okay, you set the time," Sionna agreed hastily.

"What about six A.M.?"

"Yes. Just ask for Sionna Michaels when you get there," Sionna added. A moment later she hung up the phone and stared with wide-eyed fascination at the television set. Anyone watching her would have thought an amazing movie was being shown. But Sionna was actually still in shock. Why Mr. Eikton had not warned of the association the story had to her husband's death, she had no idea. What she was certain of was that she was even more curious about Buerhler and David now, and Greg Hillman was the answer to her questions.

Nine

David awoke just past daybreak. In fact, he had barely slept at all. Just knowing that Jaunice was in the house was enough to keep him alert. He didn't trust her, not because he thought he was so irresistible, but because he knew she had an agenda and wouldn't stop until she succeeded. So every little sound disturbed him, and it was with heavy eyes that he finally realized he wasn't going to be able to fall back to sleep. Irritable at the lack of sleep he had gotten and knowing he would have to get up soon for work, he grabbed a pillow and covered his head, holding it over his face as if it could force him to get some rest. But it didn't work. With a scowl at the clock, he groaned. It was barely past five A.M. Realizing it was no use to try and get any more sleep, David reached for the remote control and turned on the television set.

Jaunice's eyes popped open and her first thought was of David. She sat up and stretched, although her face was set in a frown as she stared down at the empty space beside her. It was all she could do last night not to make a fool of herself and go to David in the middle of the night. It was about three A.M. when she finally realized that not only was he not going to come to her but he was very likely fast asleep. Awakening in the depth of disappointment, she wasn't sure if she wanted to yell in frustration or laugh in amazement. If he thought that by having them sleep in separate rooms he could convince her he didn't love her anymore, he was mistaken. It had only aggravated her more and instilled more resolve in her to win him back.

For David, time ticked by like the annoying dripping of a water faucet. He couldn't shut it off, he couldn't speed it up, he couldn't make it work for him. He only knew he wanted Jaunice out of his house as soon as possible. Yawning, he stretched and sat up in the bed. It was a little past six now and he could not lie through another revolving news report. Getting up, he went to his closet and pulled out a suit and a pair of shoes. He went into his bathroom and grabbed the shoeshine and a cloth. Then, picking up his shoes, he proceeded to shine them, needing to find something to do to speed time up. As he sat shining his shoes and peering at the television set, he heard the door down the hall open. He paused and stared at his door, watching for any signs of movement. None came. Relieved, he carefully placed his shined shoes on the floor and went back into the bathroom, dropping the cloth in the bucket and replacing the shoeshine in the cabinet. Then he started the shower and with a heavy yawn, prepared to shower. Jaunice was up and he might as well prepare himself to see her. He reminded himself as he stepped into the shower that he needed to get his key from her.

The house was illuminated with a twinkling of light from the dawn sky. David's house was built in cottage style although it had all of the modern conveniences. There were three steps leading to the floor where his room and two guest rooms were. There was also a main bathroom on the floor, a full bath in the guest room that Jaunice was in and a full bathroom in his room. The main floor boasted a huge foyer and family room, which David rarely visited. The main floor also had his library that he had built to be as big as the family room. He needed the space to view the many designs that crossed his desk. Just outside his library was the kitchen and breakfast area where he always ate. His dining room was small and cozy and, as with his family

room, he rarely used it. The house was well-lit with an un-
usual number of ceiling windows and skylights planted
throughout the house. David's main objective when he had
the house built was to be able to see the sky at all times.
Even in his bedroom he had a huge skylight fixture that
served as his natural alarm clock.

The house was warm and cozy, but it was built without
the thought of privacy. In losing that privacy, he heard
Jaunice clearly as she got up and left the floor. A few minutes
later the smell of bacon assaulted his senses. Realizing he
was hungry, David hurried and dressed. He started for the
kitchen, pausing to check the front door for his morning
paper. Glancing through the headlines, he entered the
kitchen with his head down and said, "Breakfast smells wonderful."

"Why thank you, David." Jaunice greeted him with a
bright smile, pausing over the plate she was filling with eggs,
bacon and pancakes.

David looked up, surprised by her pleasant tone. He
wasn't prepared for what he saw and he nearly dropped the
paper.

"Jaunice," he muttered, stunned.

Standing with a hand mitten and plate and sheer scarf
wrapped about her waist in the form of an apron, Jaunice
was completely nude. David didn't know what to say. He
could only look at her in shock, his gaze going from her
stiletto high heels that she rarely was seen without to her
bare legs to her flat abdomen to her pert, petite breasts.
Jaunice held a mischievous, triumphant gleam in her eyes,
enjoying David's shock and uncontrollable gaze.

"Are you hungry?" she asked just as naturally as if she
were fully dressed.

David caught her eyes, narrowed his gaze and dropped
the paper on the table with a loud bang. He pulled on his
jacket and fixed his collar before saying in a voice that
clearly expressed his aggravation with her, "I have to get to

work. We can talk later, when your clothes are on. I'll call you. Later." Then, like a madman, he hastened from the kitchen, grabbed his keys off the foyer counter and left the house, never looking back.

Jaunice grinned, not at all hurt by David's abrupt retreat. His reaction was a triumph. He desired her, of that she had no doubt. She could see the bulge in his eyes and knew he felt the same all over. When he stormed from the kitchen, she set the plate on the breakfast table and raced for the front door, watching through the window as he sped his car out of the driveway. She giggled, shaking her head in amusement that he would rather run away and fight what was a natural reaction than to admit he still wanted her. She would have him soon, she thought confidently as she walked slowly back to the kitchen and cleaned up. When she was done, she dressed in her best navy blue pantsuit. If David thought her performance this morning was her last effort, he was wrong. She was determined to make him aware of how much he wanted her, and she had more plans for him. One of them was bound to conquer him.

David couldn't believe how brazen Jaunice was. Never in the entire time he had known her had she done anything so . . . interesting. It was all he could do not to throw caution to the wind and make love to her right then and there. But that was what she wanted. She didn't want him; he was no fool. She only wanted what she didn't think she could have. It was a game to her and he was no toy! She would soon learn that little tricks like that wouldn't work, no matter how beautiful she was.

His stomach grumbled and a vision of Jaunice standing in her naked glory distracted him. He had to focus on his driving and his anger so he wouldn't spin the car around and go back to her. She was puzzling, determined and unfair, he decided. If it was the last thing he did, he was going to stay away from her.

David entered the building with a grumbling stomach. He would grab a bite once he settled in, he decided, realizing it was very early and even the cafeteria wasn't yet open. He sat in his office but didn't switch on either the computer or the lights.

Frowning, he thought of Jaunice again, realizing that a few short weeks ago, all Jaunice had to do was show up and he would have been putty in her hands. Now, he was confounded. He didn't know what his problem was. Maybe he was one of those men who played at commitment but when it was time to make the call, he fell through. He sighed. No, he had truly wanted Jaunice to move in with him. He was in love with her at one time. He had needed her every moment of the day and he gave Jaunice every reason to share his love. Was it his fault that she rejected him and left him without looking back? How was he to know she would change her mind two months later? How was he to know that Sionna Michaels would burst into his life and complicate his emotions even more.

Sionna. He sighed thinking of her. A beautiful stranger with eyes that tore into his soul and knew his every secret. That was Sionna. Feisty, strong-willed, yet vulnerable. She stayed on his mind, even as Jaunice flaunted herself before him. He thought of her and knew that she was the barrier between his weakness with Jaunice and his resolve to move on.

He stared at the phone. Feeling a need to release his frustrations and confusion, he left his office and went to the conference room. Joey Michaels had worked on the construction of the addition to the museum before he was terminated. Since then, there had been more adjustments to the plans, and David was suddenly curious about it. He knew instinctively that Sionna wanted more from him than a nice chat about Buerhler. Her abrupt exit didn't make her any less intriguing, either. He wanted to call her, to ask her out again, to see if he was completely crazy or if she was as incredible a woman as she appeared at first sight to be. He wanted Sionna Michaels and was determined to find a way to see her again.

Ten

Sionna was nervous. It was reasonable that her nerves would be on edge. She had been off the job for a while and suddenly she was thrust back into action with a story that could answer some of her own personal questions. With pen and pad in hand, Sionna requested a booth and informed the host that she was expecting Greg Hillman. The host informed her that Greg Hillman was already here and waiting for her. Great! She would have Mr. Eikton's first draft by nine o'clock, that was for sure.

Sionna hesitated a moment at the sight of him, surprised by his short stature. He was no taller than five foot eight. He was a dark-skinned, thinly built man with an air of uncertainty about him. His small eyes were widened by the unassuming eyeglasses he wore. And his greeting was short and cryptic as he turned to her. His voice had a heavy sound over the phone, she thought, as if he were a bigger person. This slender, short man was not what she expected.

"Greg Hillman, nice to meet you at last," Sionna said, extending her hand to shake his.

"Thanks," Greg said, his gruff response setting the tone for their breakfast meeting as he rigidly shook her hand, then released it.

"I've never been here before," Greg said blandly, settling into his seat and looking over the menu.

"No? It's a pretty common spot. And the food is good

and pretty cheap," Sionna said in a pleasant voice, trying to lighten his dark mood and get him to relax.

"Yeah, well, when I'm able to afford food again, I'll try it," Greg muttered.

Sionna looked contrite, and she apologized. "I should have understood that," she said softly.

"It's nothing to be understood," Greg huffed.

His response left Sionna feeling a little uncomfortable. She wasn't sure just how she should approach her questions with him. He was short, tactless and obviously not interested in supporting her questions. She took a deep breath and decided to just dive right in.

"When did you get terminated from Buerhler?" Sionna asked firmly. She sensed that with him she would have to have a no-nonsense attitude or he would simply blow her questions off as trivial.

"Two weeks ago," was his gruff response. "After seven years," he added bitterly, his disposition sullen as he glanced around at the other tables.

Sionna realized that she hadn't even bothered to offer him a cup of coffee, let alone to order breakfast.

"Greg, may I call you Greg?" Sionna asked.

Greg shrugged, responding, "Sure."

"I'm going to wave the waitress over here and let you order. Feel free to order whatever you like, and then we can talk," Sionna said firmly. Waving her hand for their waitress, she continued. "Do you like coffee? Or would you prefer tea?"

"Coffee's cool, thanks," Greg said, the word thanks coming from him as if it were an unnatural act.

"Are you ready?" the waitress asked. She leaned on her left leg, eyeballing them as if they were taking her from a very important chore.

"Greg?" Sionna prompted him.

Greg set his menu down, removed his eyeglasses and rubbed his eyes as if he had a headache. Then, before responding, he replaced his glasses, sat back in his seat and crossed his arms over his chest. Then he said in his same gruff voice, "I'm not hungry. Just coffee."

"Are you sure?" Sionna asked with a slight frown, hoping he wasn't rejecting breakfast because she was buying.

"I'm not hungry," Greg insisted firmly, a hint of irritation edging his voice.

"Okay. No problem," Sionna agreed. "We'll both have coffee," Sionna said to the waitress. The waitress gave them a look as if to say "how cheap," but asked, "Sugar's on the table. Would you like cream?"

"Yes," Sionna answered.

"Be right back," the waitress mumbled before walking away.

"Wow, what's her problem?" Sionna whispered with a light laugh, looking at Greg as if he could relate to her humor. He didn't smile and Sionna was back to being uncomfortable. He was rude and obnoxious and she was beginning to think it was no wonder Buerhler didn't want him working for their company.

"So, Ms. Michaels, what do you want to know?" Greg finally asked after their coffee arrived and he poured himself a cup.

Before Sionna could answer, he continued with a resentful huff. "How about the fact that I was fired without any prior verbal or written notice? How about the fact that I was one of many non-Caucasians fired since this merger? Or would you be interested to know how one of the executives' girlfriends got my job offered to her even before I was told that I was fired?"

"How would you know that?" Sionna asked, interrupting him with an incredulous frown.

"Because I know," was his short reply.

Sionna hesitated, pursed her lips and sat back in her seat with a heavy sigh. She admitted that when she first met the gruff, rude, even brusque Mr. Hillman, she was a little intimidated. But now she was feeling that perhaps he was just a rude, bitter person whose firing was probably justified. Just as quickly as the thought occurred to her, she set it aside. No, he was probably just angry at his loss. He needed to vent and she was going to allow him to do so.

"Greg," she started cautiously. "I can't do a story based on 'because I know.' I need facts. So how do you know that this girlfriend was hired for your position before you were fired . . . I mean terminated? And how did you determine the racial ratio? Through personnel? Your own two-plus-two analysis? How?"

"Are you badgering me?" Greg demanded, frowning as he leaned forward. "Because if this is how you're going to handle my story then I'm walking!" He had gotten loud and Sionna looked around in embarrassment.

"Now just calm down. I'm not badgering you, Greg. I'm just trying to get this story right. I'm a little confused, that's all. You're angry and I need . . . well I just need some facts. Real names, real specific information. Can you help me?" Sionna insisted, although her voice was less patronizing than before.

Greg glared at Sionna with suspicion. He didn't trust her or Buerhler or his lawyer or anyone. He was up a creek, without a job and with few prospects. He was a ball of frustration and just thinking about his problems infuriated him. But he knew he was being unreasonable. He knew he was not helping his case, either.

"Okay. All right. I guess I have been difficult. Let me start over?" he asked. Sionna smiled at him, feeling as if she had just tackled an iceberg alone, without a ship, and won.

"Please do," Sionna agreed.

"I was hired seven years ago. I worked in the information technology and support division. I started as an assistant tech and had three promotions during my tenure. You getting this?" he paused, glancing at her writing pad. Sionna nodded, urging him to continue with a wave of her pen at him.

"I was one of the idiots excited about the merger. I'm an idiot, right? Thinking, man here is my chance to finally get a better position, and what happens? The powers that be singled out me and some of the other long-standing employees and kicked us to the curb."

"And who would that be? Was it by any chance David Young?" Sionna prompted, unable to contain her curiosity about David's role in all of this.

Greg frowned at her suggestion, shook his head and said, "No. If I recall correctly, Mr. Young was cool. He was always checking in on us and making sure we were all right even though he didn't have to. Mr. Young was probably the only original Buerhler employee that I liked, at least at his level. He had your back, you know what I'm saying? Besides, I don't think he worked in that area. No, it was people like Mr. Pfeifer and those other big wheels who worked out the deals of the merger that gave us the boot!"

"So, you're saying that David Young and people like him had no say in who was fired or who kept their jobs with Buerhler?" Sionna probed further.

"Not to my knowledge. David, Charles and Kevin and them, they're designers. That's a whole different kind of management."

"Oh," Sionna murmured. She sat back in her seat, realizing that she had been so involved with his answer that she had been leaning forward. If Greg Hillman was correct, then he put even more holes in Joey's story that David got him fired. It made no sense. Why would Joey make up a lie about David? Unless he was jealous of David Young. The thought had never occurred to her, but after meeting David and hearing Greg and knowing the events that led up to Joey's death, it made sense that his jealousy or envy could have made him feel that David had put him out of work. It was a big mess, that was what it was. A big mess.

"Did Buerhler give you notice or anything?" Sionna asked, trying to focus on Greg's story again.

"Nothing! I'm working my butt off, clueless about their plans. I was coming in on time day after day, then I get called into Donnelly's office, he's the head of personnel no less, and was informed that although my services have been well-performed, unfortunately due to overstaffing, they are releasing me. I get this crap envelope with a scrap of severance pay, a song-and-dance good-bye letter and then I'm booted in the ass," Greg snapped.

Sionna again glanced about her in embarrassment. He was not only loud but cursing, and she hoped no one got the wrong impression. Then, shaking off her embarrassment, she encouraged him to continue by saying, "It sounds like downsizing to me."

"Call it what you like, but it was wrong. Anyhow, I left like a good boy, not making a scene, you know. But I got home and frustration and disbelief just . . . it just kicked in. Man, man, I didn't know I was going to file a lawsuit, I just knew it wasn't right. I called my friend Latasha, thinking she would cheer me up, and looka there. She was fired, too. She was there even longer than I, by the way," he added sarcastically.

"Latasha? Is she filing a claim too?" Sionna asked.

"Yeah, she's filing with me. Also, Mike, Tyrone, that Asian guy Ling, and I know a few others but I can't remember their names. The point is," he added with a hint of impatience, giving Sionna her cue that the interview was coming to a head, "I am not the only one fired, but I sure saw a lot of old-timers kicked out, good or bad."

"Greg, one last question. Do you know why they waited so long to fire you? After all, about a year ago they released several employees right after the merger. As I recall, it was directly related to the downsizing. Was this by any chance related to their continued downsizing?" Sionna asked.

"No! You can call it downsizing and so can they, but they

hired people to fill my old job and the others. So how is that downsizing if you just replace the staff? Uh-huh, this was personal," Greg insisted.

Sionna sighed, then stretched her hand across the table to shake his. He accepted.

"Thank you, Greg. Thank you. I hope all goes well and maybe we'll get to talk again, once you've won," she added with a reassuring smile as she came to her feet. Greg stood up with her, his shoulders visibly slumped as if his outburst had exhausted him.

"Is this going to be in the morning paper?" he asked, shoving his hands in his pockets.

"It's supposed to be. But you know what I think, Greg. I think this story needs to be looked into further. There may be more going on here than meets the eye. We'll see."

"What are you saying? You're not going to do my story?" Greg demanded, confusing her statement as a rejection, meaning the interview had been a waste of his time.

Sionna laughed, surprised that he hadn't understood. "No, of course I am. I just meant, maybe I can get the paper to continue reporting this story until we get to the bottom of everything."

"Oh. Well, thanks," he mumbled.

"Good luck, Greg." Sionna smiled and walked away. She didn't believe Greg had a major case, at least not one worth reporting. But what she had was more information about David. Could it be that David was involved with Joey's firing, just not directly? She doubted it. She usually had a good sense of character and David didn't seem to be capable of being so underhanded. And Greg Hillman didn't seem to think David was the type either. Maybe she needed to meet David again, she thought gravely. It was the only way she could be sure he wasn't the rogue her husband had claimed he was. And he could help her in developing her story about Greg's lawsuit. After all, he had Greg's back, according to Greg.

With a sense of excitement that Sionna chose to contribute to her story, she hurried to her job. She needed to write up her story and then she would have to call David to meet with him again. She was sure he wouldn't mind. After all, he was her only contact at Buerhler. What choice did she have but to call on him again?

Eleven

Jaunice entered David's office with all the flair of a woman of importance. Her confidence and brazen approach left little doubt for Karen who she was and who she wanted to see.

"Hello, I'm here to see David," Jaunice said without pausing as she went directly to David's door and opened it. Karen jumped from her seat and called, "One moment please." Her call was in vain. Jaunice closed the door, shutting Karen out and surprising David.

David looked up at Jaunice's entrance. *Now what?* he thought, instantly annoyed.

"Jaunice, what is the problem? I said I would call you at lunchtime," David bit out, coming to his feet as she approached him.

"And I said I had a flight this afternoon. So we need to talk now," Jaunice retorted.

"Now is not a good time. I have a meeting in a few minutes—"

"Cancel it," Jaunice demanded, standing so close that her body just barely grazed his.

"It's with my boss. I can't. Look," David paused, then sat on the corner of his desk. "I think it's clear to both of us what's happened between us. You don't really want me, Jaunice. You just can't stand to lose. And I have come to agree that we should call it quits. Let's let it go amicably, all right?" David said as reasonably as he could.

Jaunice shook her head slowly, her slight smile showing that she would not make it that easy for him. "No, I will not call it quits. And you are right, I hate to lose. But David," she added tenderly, "I do love you and I do want to work it out. I came here because I wanted to work it out. I didn't mean to embarrass you this morning. I just wanted you so much—"

"Jaunice," David groaned, growing frustrated.

"Wait, I'm not going to go into that, I promise. I just want you to understand how much I have missed you these past two months. And even though I have to get back to New York, I want you to think about us a little more before you give me this song and dance about how you agree with breaking up. Okay. Just think about it and then we could talk."

"Jaunice, I told you last night, I met someone—"

"Who cannot possibly mean more to you than I do, not this quickly. Right?" Jaunice suggested, dismissing the other woman as insignificant.

"Maybe, Jaunice. Whatever. I just want you to cool out, give it a rest," David said.

"Will do," Jaunice said. "As a matter of fact, I had planned to buy you lunch and let you drop me off at the airport."

"I told you I have a meeting, which I'm late for right now," David said.

"Fine. I'm going. I'll call you later." Jaunice smiled and after hesitating for a moment, stood on her tiptoes and kissed him good-bye. David allowed her kiss to linger but did not return her passion. When she was done, he gave her a tight smile and watched her leave. The door had barely closed when he sat in his seat and released a long sigh, grateful that she hadn't caused a major scene.

Jaunice could have kicked herself as she boarded the plane. The entire trip to Virginia had been a disaster. Although she did her best to keep up the pretense that their relationship was not over, she was starting to have doubts about her ability to get David back where she had him.

She sat slumped in her seat, her nerves on edge. It was all she could do not to bite her nails as she wondered just when and how she lost David.

Just two months earlier she had David where she wanted him. He had been panting for her for practically two years and then, suddenly, he wasn't panting anymore. What had she done? She was miserable. She almost had it all. Her dream career in designer fashions, life in the big city with fancy parties and nonstop entertainment, a man waiting for her whenever she fancied a moment's peace. How could she have allowed him to slip through her fingers?

She could have kicked David, too. He was the jerk that let their romance die out. He didn't have to go get involved, mentally if not physically, with another woman. Or maybe it wasn't another woman. Maybe, oh, please no, maybe he was gay!

She sat upright at the thought and stared out the window into the early afternoon sky. The plane would be landing soon and she was glad. She needed to move, to walk, to release her anxieties, to get a clear head. After all, it was ridiculous to think of David as gay. There was no way he could be. She was just reaching for straws because she hated to admit that he was no longer interested in her.

She still didn't want to face the fact that she was losing David, yet she was losing him fast. If she wanted him, she had to make up her mind because time was no longer on her side. Why did he have to be so miserably upright? Why couldn't he have slipped up as she had? And she had been fool enough to make it easy for him by breaking up with him.

"He probably slept with that woman," she thought aloud. The woman in the seat next to her looked at Jaunice with a curious smile.

"Sorry, just talking out loud," Jaunice muttered. A short time later the plane landed and Jaunice jostled through the crowd to meet her ride.

"Girl, what happened?" Patricia asked in a conspiring whisper as soon as she saw Jaunice. Jaunice gave Patricia a smirk and shook her head.

"He met somebody," Jaunice blurted as she grabbed her luggage. Patricia helped her, gushing in disbelief as they went to the car.

"When? How? Not mister goodie-two-shoes! How did you let that happen?" Patricia laughed, her lack of sympathy irritating Jaunice as they loaded Jaunice's luggage in the trunk of the LeBaron.

"I didn't let it happen. I was here, remember? Besides," Jaunice added as they got in the sedan. "He's not admitting to anything more than meeting another woman, but I know he slept with her, too."

"How do you know?" Patricia insisted as she pulled out of the parking lot.

"Patricia, trust me. I just know. He was acting strange. I was standing in his kitchen butt naked and ready for him, and he ran out of the house like a scared rabbit. And David is a *very* sexual man. That's how I know," Jaunice said, feeling a little defeated. Patricia was her girl but she hated Patricia's witnessing her loss before she could even accept it herself.

"Well, I say to hell with him. There's always Jim," Patricia said with a shrug.

"Jim? What am I? Desperate? No way," Jaunice laughed.

"Girl, being picky is going to be your downfall. How old are you? Twenty-nine? Time is running out. What did you say in college? I'm going to be married by twenty-five, a famous designer by twenty-six and two kids by twenty-eight. So which goal are you working on?"

"You are so wrong bringing that up, Patricia. So I missed

the mark. And I'm cool with that. I got my goals, so mind your business," Jaunice said.

Folding her arms across her chest, she stared out the window more affected by Patricia's heartless reminder than she cared to admit.

"I say take Jim up on his offer and at least have dinner with the man. You said it yourself, you're free and it ain't wrong to test the waters, child. Try him on for size. If he doesn't fit, send him back," Patricia suggested.

Jaunice laughed, although she had no intention of going out with Jim, at least not again. She had never told Patricia about her one-night stand with Jim when they were in France. He was another designer of hip-hop clothing and that was their only thing in common. His walk, his speech, his entertainment, his car, everything about him was the opposite of what she wanted in a man. He was too . . . average. Not bad-looking but not fine. Not muscular but not slender. His brown eyes were ordinary, his style a little too loud. And although Jim was almost forty, in a lot of ways he was far less mature than David.

Sleeping with Jim had been a mistake, and although he wasn't a bad lover, they really did not connect, at least not for her. He, on the other hand, kept calling. It was one of those slip-ups that she couldn't even tell Patricia, although Jaunice was surprised that Patricia never guessed. It didn't matter really. She had slipped up before at different shows and none of them mattered. Including Jim. She wasn't interested in him that way. She would have to save him for a rainy day should David not come around and realize what he was giving up.

Sulking with her unexpected problem with David, Jaunice closed her eyes, shutting Patricia out. She may have been hit by a surprise attack but she was not going to lose. David was hers and no Miss Wannabe Mrs. Young was going to change that. David may have sent her packing but she was not going to give up so easily. No, she was going to put on her battle shoes and win her man back. Right after the show on Saturday, she was heading back to Virginia and this time she wasn't packing up and running home just because he was acting like a spoiled child.

Twelve

"Sionna," David greeted her with a big smile as he took her hand and guided her into his office.

"David," Sionna said, entering David's office with an equally bright smile, warmed by his touch. She called him Friday afternoon after gathering all her nerve to make the call. Then she was forced to leave a message because neither David nor his assistant answered the line. She informed him she was working on a story that involved Buerhler and wondered if he would have some time to meet with her Monday morning. When she hung up, she released a deep sigh and waited for his call. When Friday turned into Saturday and David still didn't call, she worried that he wouldn't call and that her aloofness over dinner the other night had turned him completely off.

When she got in Saturday afternoon from shopping, she checked her answering machine and was elated to hear David's voice over the speakerphone. Yes, he could see her Monday morning. Just come by. That was all she needed to hear.

Sionna chided herself for being so excited to see David again. He offered her a seat and she gingerly sat down, crossing her legs and placing her purse on her lap. She needed to calm down, to appear sophisticated, even if she didn't feel that way. She glanced around the office, noting how neat everything appeared, except for the table to her left under the window. It had a wad of blueprints and designs that seemed so out of place with the rest of the space. Her eyes roved from the papers back to David as he sat behind his desk and watched her. His eyes were like a jolt to her system. She had met him twice and found it incredible that he had so quickly roused her senses. What was worse was there was a picture on the windowsill of him hugging a very pretty girl. That picture caught her eyes as she looked away from his gaze. He was committed, she noted in disappointment, finding the woman's picture to be far too sexy to be a sister or cousin.

"Can I offer you something? Coffee?" David suggested.

"No, thank you, I'm fine," Sionna hastily responded, pulling her eyes from the picture to focus back on David.

"I have to admit, Sionna, I didn't think you would call again," David said after a brief pause.

"I wasn't sure you would accept my call after the way I ran out of the Italian shop. I apologize for that," Sionna added.

David shrugged and leaned forward. Tapping his pen on the pad in front of him, he said, "I understand. I was a little pushy there."

"A little," Sionna agreed. "Still, I felt completely ridiculous. You accept my apology?" she asked softly.

"Only if you accept mine," David said firmly.

"I do," Sionna said with a laugh, relaxing beneath his easy acceptance.

"Good. So what's this about Buerhler? How can I help you write the Pulitzer report?" David asked, leaning back in his seat.

"Greg Hillman, a former computer programmer for Buerhler, is suing Buerhler," Sionna started.

"Why?" David questioned her.

"He believes he was fired because he's black," Sionna answered.

"Black? I'm black," David said.

"I realize that. But he is not alone in this case. My understanding is that several other long-standing employees were fired. What I was curious about, David, was how this firing relates to the terminations that took place last year. Do you recall those?" Sionna asked carefully.

David nodded slowly, recalling how a dozen or more employees of On-Site were released after the merger with Buerhler. But he didn't see the connection. "Yeah, I recall."

"So, is there any similarity here? Is Buerhler continuing to get rid of old On-Site employees? Is there a conspiracy, David?" Sionna asked.

"To tell you the truth, Sionna, that's not my area. I could look into it for you, ask around. But I don't know what Buerhler is doing with On-Site staff. I don't believe there is a conspiracy," he added ruefully. "Although I will admit that I thought the worst was over when they released the original management team."

"You mean when they terminated people like Joey?" Sionna asked, suddenly animated as she saw an opportunity to mention Joey.

David paused, evaluating Sionna as if seeing her for the first time. Then he sat straight up and, holding his pen between his hands, he answered, "Was Joey a part of the management team that was laid off?"

"Fired," Sionna corrected.

"When did they release him?" David proceeded to question her.

"A few months after the merger," Sionna answered. "Didn't you know that?"

"No. I didn't even know Joey was terminated. We never got around to seeing each other. I think he may have called me once or twice, but back then everything was moving a mile a minute and I never got a chance to catch up with Joey."

"No?" Sionna asked, dumbfounded again. She had thought at the very least that they had communicated, that something had to have occurred between them for Joey to make the outrageous accusations he had made. She was even more baffled about David and Joey's relationship now than before. "You and Joey never saw each other after the merger?" she murmured, her shock evident in her voice.

David searched Sionna's face, noting her tone with a slight frown. It was as if he were seeing her for the first time, and he suddenly felt miserable. How insensitive of him not to connect her argument with her loss. Deciding that he didn't want to push her into running from him again, he stood up, walked around the desk and took her hands.

"I tell you what," David began tenderly. "Let me check this out for you. Maybe there is something going on that should be brought to light," he added, stuffing his hands in his pants pockets after he released her hands.

Sionna stood up, a little worried by his offer to help her. "You can't, David. You could get into trouble for this," she stated. She would not allow him to risk losing his job to help her, especially when she was investigating him more than she was the company.

"Not a chance. If there is some illegal activity happening in my backyard, it's my duty to get rid of the problem. Besides," he added with a direct gaze at her, "how else can I be sure to see you again?"

Sionna was flattered. "Why not try a traditional tactic, like asking me out?"

"I didn't think you would say yes," David answered.

"You may be right," Sionna said.

"See?" David shrugged.

"Of course, you could be wrong," Sionna said as she laughed, walking toward the door and preparing to leave.

Before she could open the door, David asked, "Would you be willing to have dinner with me, Sionna Michaels?"

Sionna paused at the door, not turning until she was sure the excitement had calmed from her face. Then with a slow, graceful movement, she turned around to give him her full gaze and answered, "I would love to."

"Tonight?" he grinned, pleased as he walked up to her.

"I have much too much to do tonight, but yes, okay," she answered.

"I'll pick you up about six o'clock," David suggested, standing so close Sionna thought he was going to try and kiss her.

She had thought after Joey she would never feel such a strong attraction for a man again. But even Joey had not sparked such energy in her. Feeling a little shy beneath his close scrutiny, she answered in a murmur, "That's fine." Fighting the magnetic charm he exuded, she put her hand on the doorknob and was about to turn it when David's hand covered hers.

"What?" she asked, giving him an uncertain glance.

"Your address. I don't know where you live," he said.

Sionna rolled her eyes in embarrassment, saying, "Oh, I thought you would have gotten it when you had my purse," she said.

"Sure I saw it on your license, but it didn't occur to me to memorize it," David laughed.

"Right," Sionna murmured and released the doorknob. She purposely took a few steps away from him before reaching in her purse to find a pen. A few moments later she had scribbled her address on a piece of paper from her purse, and before he could stop her again, she said good-bye.

Sionna was barely on the elevator before she felt weak from the exhaustion of holding back her elation.

David Young fascinated her. He was so attractive, so take-charge and self-assured. He wasn't Joey by any means, but he was wonderful all the same, different without a hint of brooding. Leaning against the wall of the elevator, she sighed heavily, releasing some of the animated excitement she felt in his presence.

As she thought about it further, she realized that David and Joey actually had very little in common. Sure, they were both about the same height and complexion, but that was where the similarities ended. David was easygoing, funny and quick to smile. Joey had been cool, a man of few words, and Sionna would say he was even more suave. When she weighed the two men, she realized there was no comparison. David was definitely more handsome than Joey had been and probably a little more muscular, but that did not take away from Joey.

Regretfully, Sionna wished that Joey had been able to maintain his dignity in the face of a crisis, a small crisis, she viewed it. That was another difference between the two men. She could never see David losing his dignity over a job. Never. Smiling winsomely, she noted that she had to stop comparing men to Joey. He was forever lost to her, and if she knew her Joey he would want her to move on.

As she stepped out of the building Sionna caught sight of a very familiar face. She walked slowly as she looked directly into the face of the woman who had been so carelessly displayed in the window of David's office. Shocked, Sionna had to force herself not to stop and stare. As the woman passed her, Sionna realized that she had been holding her breath and exhaled deeply. Wide-eyed and feeling a bit shaken at the sight of the woman, Sionna debated returning to David's office and pretending she forgot something just to see who the woman was. But she thought better of it, narrowed her eyes and moved on. She was not going to behave like some love-crazed stalker. Besides, she had gotten so excited from David's asking her out that she forgot to ask him about the woman in the picture.

Holding her head high, Sionna left the building, using all her poise not to look back. She would question him tonight.

Thirteen

"Jaunice?" David called her name in surprise, coming instantly to his feet when his office door opened. At first he had thought it was Sionna coming back, and he was delighted. But seeing Jaunice standing in the doorway, her white suit snugly fitting her, her eyes boldly falling on him, startled him.

"Expecting someone else?" Jaunice asked, watching David carefully.

David walked to the door and closed it before responding. "No, I wasn't," David said.

"Then what, baby, you don't want me here? Am I interrupting?" Jaunice asked, walking up to him and brushing her body against his.

"Jaunice," David groaned, putting his hands against her shoulders to give himself an arm's length from her. "I thought we'd been through this. What's wrong with you?"

"What's wrong with me? What kind of question is that, David?" Jaunice demanded. She had flown back to Virginia with renewed hope that she could make David see that he was still in love with her. She had convinced herself that his lack of interest in her was temporary. She was sure that a few days away would cause him to have second thoughts. After all, it had been more than two months since he had made love.

"You come in my office unannounced and I just don't

like it, Jaunice," David finished, moving away from her until he was safely behind his desk.

"Have you slept with this woman you met, David? Is that it? Is this why you are acting like I have the plague or something? Just tell me the truth!" Jaunice stormed, frustrated beyond reason, her eyes narrowed in anger by his apparent disgust. How dare he treat her as if she were some type of tramp?

"Let's remember something here, you broke up with me. Why should I have to explain anything that I'm doing?" David shot back, irritated with her questions.

"I knew it," Jaunice seethed, taking his answer to mean yes. "So you slept with this woman who you claim to have just met. Why don't you just be a man and say it, David. You've probably been with her all along and were waiting for me to call it quits," Jaunice accused.

"What?" David frowned. Shaking his head, he sat in his seat and looked at her as if she were a stranger. "Do you realize how you sound? How ridiculous that statement is. I gave you every reason to trust in me, Jaunice. And you were so blind and so determined to have it your way, you never once thought about how you were hurting me, how I felt when you just decided we weren't working out. So lay off me about seeing other women," David said firmly.

"I hurt you. I realize that," Jaunice whispered, suddenly calming down. She sat on the edge of his desk, and, caressing his face with her fingertips, she said in a gentle voice, "That's what this is all about, isn't it? I hurt you and you want me to suffer because of it. Well, you've won because I'm suffering. Just say you'll give me a chance to talk it out, David. Just tonight and I promise, if you still feel the way you claim you're feeling, then I'll leave you alone."

David sighed, tired of fighting with Jaunice. "I can't tonight."

"Oh please, David," Jaunice begged, smoothly slipping from her seat on the desk into his lap. She wrapped her arms about his neck, sensing that he was weakening. "I promise I just want to talk. Over dinner. We need to talk, David. You at least owe me that," Jaunice added, working on his sympathy.

"You're right, I owe you that much, but not tonight," David sighed, moving Jaunice from his lap and coming to his feet.

"Why not tonight?" Jaunice demanded, glaring at him as he walked away from her.

"Because I'm committed for the evening," David blurted, frustrated with the conversation.

"Committed? To whom? Oh, let me guess, your new girl-friend," Jaunice snapped.

"She's not my girlfriend. In fact, she's the widow of a friend of mine," David said.

"I don't understand this, David," Jaunice muttered.

"A friend of mine died about a year ago and his widow and I bumped into each other recently. She's working on something that I'm trying to help her with and I promised her dinner tonight."

"Oh, how sweet. Consoling the widow," Jaunice sneered, sitting on the edge of his desk and rocking her leg back and forth in agitation.

"Jaunice," David said with obvious exasperation. "You're being childish."

"Oh, please. You've been acting like a lovesick puppy and I'm childish? I just want the truth. You sent me packing like a madman over your friend's widow, the same someone that's keeping you from making love to me. And why? So you could get closer to her, and now the truth comes out."

"The truth is I didn't send you packing," David retorted, his anger exploding in a rush of words. "You left me. Remember?" David demanded.

"I left because you were pushing me, David. I wasn't ready for what you wanted. And you kept insisting we get married—"

"I stopped asking months before you broke up with me," David interrupted in denial.

"Well, so, I knew that it was still on your mind. You were unfair and now, just because I needed a little time, you start dating another woman. This is so unfair," Jaunice whined, her eyes wide with unshed tears.

David stared at her, uncertain of what to say. Jaunice never cried. At least it was a rare occasion to see tears in her eyes. Could she really be that hurt? Feeling guilty, he wondered if maybe he was being foolish? No, he wasn't being foolish, he was just plain tired. He wanted to get to know Sionna and that was that. Sionna was beautiful, intriguing, exciting. He had spent two years with Jaunice and up until a few months ago, he thought himself madly in love with her. He had given her his all and she didn't want it. Now he just wanted her to leave him alone.

"I don't mean to be unfair, Jaunice," David said carefully.

"Then what's going on with you and the widow?" Jaunice demanded, her eyes suddenly dry.

"Nothing . . . I told you. Her husband died and she just wants some answers. And . . . we have a date tonight. There it is," he said gruffly, taking a seat in frustration.

"David." Jaunice said his name with such pain that he couldn't look at her. She sat down, her demeanor showing how bewildered she was. When he told her he had met someone else, she suspected it was more serious than he had let on, but she would never have thought it was serious enough to truly put a dent in the love David felt for her. Suddenly, she realized just how possible it was that she had lost him.

"You left me, Jaunice," David groaned, tired, wishing she would go away.

"Are you sleeping with her?" Jaunice demanded, ignoring his statement.

David knew he didn't have to answer Jaunice, but he felt

he owed her at least that much. "We are barely even friends, Jaunice, let alone lovers."

"Then you haven't made love to her?" Jaunice insisted on a direct answer. She had to know. She had to keep her pride intact.

"I haven't even kissed her," he said softly, thinking of Sionna with a yearning he didn't realize he was expressing. "No. We haven't made love," he answered, seeing Jaunice's scowl.

"Why haven't I ever heard about this friend of yours?" Jaunice demanded.

"You have, you just don't recall. His name was Joey Michaels. He used to work here, or rather for On-Site. Sionna and I never even met until a few days ago," David added at her dubious frown.

"And all of the sudden, sparks flew between you, is that it?" Jaunice hissed.

"No, Jaunice," David answered, exhausted by her sarcasm. "Look, I have a meeting, Jaunice. We can talk later." Then he opened the door.

Jaunice stood, feeling humiliated by his dismissal of her. "Tonight, David?" she asked sweetly, her eyes wide as she stared up at him.

"I can't," David answered uncomfortably.

Jaunice stared at the floor, looking pitiful.

David groaned. "Look, maybe I can for a few minutes. We can talk. I . . . give me a call before five," he said grudgingly. He wasn't used to Jaunice's new humbled, even vulnerable demeanor. And he found he didn't like it. Whatever it took, he determined it was time to end their bond.

Jaunice perked up. She had him, she was sure of it. "Okay. I'll call," she murmured demurely. Then with a slightly lowered head, she left his office and could feel his eyes on her as she headed down the hall. A slight smile curved her lips. She felt confident that all was not lost. David

Young still felt something for her and she was determined to make him aware of it. In the meantime, she had a call to make to Mrs. Sionna Michaels.

Fourteen

David took a deep breath the moment Jaunice was gone. She exhausted him. She didn't know what she wanted, David decided, sitting down at his desk in frustration. He picked up a pen and tapped it against his desk. He needed to think. To clear his head.

Sighing heavily, he picked up the phone and dialed Sionna. He wasn't going to break their date, he decided firmly, he was only going to meet with her later. He needed to hash things out with Jaunice. Send her away. Let her know she couldn't bounce in and out of his life like a basketball. He wasn't in love with Jaunice anymore, of that he was certain, but he had to put an end to their relationship. Otherwise, she would never stop hounding him. He just wished it was something he could do later, but it couldn't wait. He wasn't comfortable with the idea of having dinner with Jaunice and then seeing Sionna. As he dialed Sionna's number, he knew he was going to break their date, and he prayed it wouldn't be the wrong decision.

Sionna sat in stiff rejection as David's voice filtered through her bedroom. His excuse for breaking their date was the traditional "Something's come up." Ignoring her impulsive desire to cry, Sionna carefully hung her black dress back up in her closet. She put her black heels back in their neat place on her shoe rack, then slowly released her hair from the rollers she had just finished setting.

She was replacing her jewelry because she couldn't decide whether to wear her gold chain and pendant or silver one, when she began sobbing. She couldn't believe she was crying over a broken date. As the sobs poured she began to laugh, realizing how emotionally foolish she was behaving. What did she expect? He was Joey's best friend. He probably felt he was doing Joey an injustice to date his widow. Or he could even be wary of her motives. After all, she was trying to uncover a story on his company. Taking a deep breath, she gathered her distraught emotions and went to the bathroom and splashed cool water on her face.

Oh, how her sisters would laugh if they knew she had cried over being rejected. She smiled at her face, feeling foolish and awkward.

"You have a right to be emotional, Sionna. You've been through a lot these past few months and it's all right to cry," Sionna said loudly, trying to convince herself she was behaving rationally.

Feeling a little better, Sionna went to her bookshelf, found one of her favorite novels and curled up in the bed. She wasn't going to dwell on David or Greg Hillman's case or anything about the present. She was going to escape, relax and find some sense of peace, if only for a few hours with a good book.

She was barely out of the first chapter when the phone rang. Groaning, wishing whoever it was would hang up before she answered, Sionna rolled over and picked up the phone.

"Hello," she said in a voice that could have been mistaken for just awakening. A small part of her expected to hear David on the line, but she refused to admit to it and get her feelings hurt again.

"Sionna Michaels?" the feminine voice demanded.

Sionna frowned and sat up, answering with her own question.

"Who's asking?"

"Jaunice Sumner. David Young's fiancée," came the firm answer. Sionna stood up, unpleasantly surprised. Fiancée. Wife to be. The woman in the picture. What did she want?

"Hello, Mrs. Young-to-be. And how may I help you?" Sionna asked with all the dignity she could muster. She was not going to be caught up in an over-my-man argument. No way.

"You can start by not mixing business with pleasure, at least not with my man."

"You're not serious," Sionna scoffed. "This is just too corny."

"Maybe, but you get the point. I love David and I've given him two great years. He loves me too, even if he is a little confused these days. I don't need you confusing the situation more. Are we clear on this, Ms. Michaels?" Jaunice asked haughtily.

Sionna actually smiled, more amused now than angry. Was this woman serious?

"Let me get it straight. You're calling me to warn me away from David, right?"

"Right," Jaunice answered stiffly, not liking the amusement in Sionna's voice.

"Are you a huge, muscular woman?" Sionna asked, almost unable to control her laughter. She would teach this woman to call her again.

"No! What in the world . . ." Jaunice snapped, annoyed, not understanding Sionna's line of questioning.

"Are you into kickboxing or wrestling?" By now Sionna was openly laughing and Jaunice was fuming. How dare this woman laugh at her call? But before Jaunice could curse Sionna for being so nonchalant, Sionna continued. "Oh, wait, I know. Maybe you are a professional boxer. That's it. Now that's a scary thought."

"Just stay the hell away from David!" Jaunice hissed, then hung up the phone. Sionna burst into even more laughter.

Jaunice was fuming. That hussy. That creeping, slip-through-your-back-door hussy had insulted her. Sionna Michaels was just lucky Jaunice wasn't a fighter, or she would have run over to Michaels's house and given her a good uppercut.

Furious, Jaunice glared into the mirror. She was going to make sure David didn't leave tonight. At first, maybe, just maybe, she could have understand Sionna's loneliness, but now, after the way she had made fun of Jaunice, Sionna Michaels didn't have a chance with David. Not a chance.

Sionna sat on the edge of the bed, spent from her laughter. She couldn't believe what she had done. But she was caught off guard. Jaunice Sumner. So he was engaged. That was why he called off their date. That was the something that came up. Of that, she wasn't surprised. What she was surprised by was the call itself. She had never received a call from the other woman before. It was a very strange thing.

Sighing, Sionna picked her book up again and after a moment of staring at the blurred pages, she tossed it aside and walked downstairs. She was hungry. It was way too early to be in bed anyway.

She turned on the television set and listened to the news as she began chopping vegetables and preparing dinner. After all, she thought with a rueful smile, dinner was off. She was humming, enjoying her moment of triumph against Jaunice. She knew full well the call was meant to upset her, but she had turned the tables on Miss Sumner and showed her just how tough a Georgia girl could be.

"She can have David Young," Sionna muttered. She was just finishing carefully straining her pasta when she heard the news reporter on the television mention Buerhler industries. She nearly dropped the pot, so hastily did she race to turn up the television set.

". . . after six claims of wrongful termination, Buerhler has agreed to settle out of court. Steve, what's the weather going to be?"

"Well, Marlene, more of the same . . ." the weatherman began, but Sionna muted the television set as she raced for the phone and immediately called Mr. Eikton.

"Shoot!" she swore when his voice mail came on.

"Mr. Eikton, what's going on? They settled the case. Is this still a story? Have you heard from Greg Hillman? I'm at home. Talk to me. I have to know what made them settle. Bye." Sionna rushed on. After hanging up, she quickly searched for Greg Hillman's number and called him. Again she received no response and she left the same message.

Then she hung up the phone and sat back in front of the television. She flipped through station after station, trying to find news coverage that hadn't already reported on the lawsuit. But she was too late. She glanced at the phone, for a moment tempted to call David, but she thought better of it. She wasn't worried about Jaunice, but she didn't want to appear desperate and looking for an excuse to call him. He was one heartbreak she could easily get over, of that she was determined. But in the meantime, she was curious about the lawsuit, and any bit of information that could help to bring her closer to understanding her husband's suicide was welcome.

Sighing heavily, she stared at the television set in disappointment. She had no choice but to wait on a response from Mr. Eikton or Greg Hillman or David Young.

Fifteen

David wasn't sure if he could deal with the drama. Jaunice was supposed to call but instead she showed up in his office again. He didn't like what she was doing, but he knew that once Jaunice made up her mind, there was no stopping her. He had thought about it all day. He was going to end this foolishness today, tonight, this moment. Standing, he showed as much patience for her as he could.

"I'm here," she said with big bold smile. David cocked his head to the side and considered her.

"You look exceptionally beautiful," he said.

Jaunice's smile grew even bigger. She loved compliments, especially since she had designed the midnight blue dress she was wearing. She had pinned her long hair into a curl pile on top of her head and wore just the right amount of makeup. She felt pretty and was determined to wipe all thoughts and images of the insipid Sionna, as she imagined her to be, from David's mind.

"Thank you, David. You look handsome as usual," she added, walking up to him and holding her face up as if expecting a kiss. David stared at her sweet mouth a moment, then sternly walked away from her. He wasn't going to be pulled in so easily.

"Thanks."

"So where are we going?" Jaunice asked sweetly, although she was reeling with disbelief that he had so blatantly shunned her. Maybe he was more infatuated with that Sionna than she had calculated. Or maybe, maybe he was truly no longer in love with her. She stilled her panic, refusing to be weak in the face of adversity. No, she would win David. Of that, she was determined.

"Nowhere special. I had planned to talk to you at the house," David answered carelessly, ignoring the fact that she had taken so much care to dress for him. He was angry. Angry with himself for breaking his date with Sionna. And for what, a woman who was enjoying the hunt more than the capture? He wanted to call Sionna, beg her to forgive him for being an idiot. But he knew that to call Sionna now would be a mistake. Nevertheless, when it was over and once Jaunice got the picture, he was going to call Sionna and explain the entire situation to her, regardless of how embarrassing it was going to be.

"David. I insist that you stop acting like this," Jaunice hissed as they entered the elevator. David frowned at her as though he'd forgotten she was there, so engrossed was he with thoughts of Sionna.

"Like what?" he asked.

"Cold, that's what. I don't like it when you act this way," Jaunice said with a pretty pout. David considered her again and thought how once that look would have melted him and he would have done anything for her. But now, it only annoyed him.

"Jaunice. I'm tired, it's been a long day and I . . . let's face it. I wasn't expecting to spend the evening with . . . this way," he corrected, not wanting to be completely callous with her.

Jaunice's face was crestfallen. He was being a complete ass. She had shown up unexpectedly many times before, but that never resulted in this behavior. He was hurting her feelings. Couldn't he see that? she thought bitterly.

"Perhaps I should just go back to my hotel," she murmured.

David sighed again. She was exasperating. He stared at her and as they exited the elevator he relented, murmuring, "No, don't do that. Let's get a bite and we can talk, like adults," he added.

"No, David. No. You . . . I'm just bothering you and I'm sorry. I have been pushy," Jaunice murmured again, feeling a surge of energy at his weakening.

"You're not bothering me," David said with an edge to his voice. "I just don't want to confuse things and how it is between us, Jaunice. I need—"

"Wait for that, David," Jaunice whispered, stepping to him in her familiar way. "Wait until we're seated at our Little Italian Shop and then let's talk. Okay. Please," she added when he started to reject the offer.

"Fine, Jaunice. Fine," he grunted. Together they left the building and Jaunice could have floated. She had him. Call it how he wanted, but she just knew she had him.

The restaurant was crowded to capacity and they had to wait almost twenty minutes before being seated. During that time they didn't speak a word. David stared out the window, brooding. He should be with Sionna, laughing and enjoying the evening, not sulking with Jaunice, trying to end a relationship that was already over.

"David, come on," Jaunice urged him, tugging at his elbow while the host waited for them to follow him.

Within moments they were seated and Jaunice was pleased by the romantic seclusion their seat gave them in the back of the restaurant. David was uncomfortable with it.

"Brings back memories, doesn't it?" Jaunice murmured in her huskiest voice. David nodded.

"I wish it could be how it was, David. I wish you still loved me," Jaunice murmured so softly he wasn't sure he heard her correctly.

"Jaunice," David sighed, unprepared for her heart-wrenching confession. Jaunice put her forefinger to his lips, hushing him.

"Don't say it, David. I know you don't love me anymore. And I understand," she said hastily. "I put you through a lot. Not wanting to give up my career to marry you—"

"That's not what I asked you to do," David rushed in defensively.

Wide-eyed and innocent, Jaunice said, "Well, then, maybe you just wanted me to change careers. I don't know what you wanted. I just know . . . wait, hear me out. I just wanted a little time to clear my head. To think about what was really important to me. Do you have any idea how much it hurts to be tossed aside just because my career was important? No, don't explain anything—"

"Come on, Jaunice. You know you've been playing me like an idiot for two years, or at least this last year. I never asked you to give up your career. I wanted you to keep doing what you were doing but to add marriage to our arrangement. That was all. I was willing to be your husband in a long-distance relationship as long as you would have loved me. You chose to give it up, not me," David insisted.

"I did not give it up, as you say. I came here last week and look at you, lovesick over another woman," Jaunice said, waving her hand over his head.

"I'm not lovesick and you broke up with me over two months ago. Was I supposed to twiddle my thumbs and play Romeo? Come on," David mocked.

"Yes. Yes. You were supposed to love me so much that you were willing to give me time."

"I gave you two years!" David grated between his teeth, leaning forward.

"I needed more time!" Jaunice grated back.

David sat back, tired of the conversation. He tapped his glass of water, then asked, "So now what?"

Jaunice looked away from him. Forming her words carefully, she responded, "We try again."

He shook his head vehemently, considered her for a moment, then shook his head again. "Try how? Are you trying to give up your career? I don't think so."

"Yes," came Jaunice's flat and completely unexpected answer.

David paused, surprised. Then he narrowed his gaze and pursed his mouth in deep thought. "Why now? Because you can't stand the thought of me with someone else?" he demanded.

"Yes, as a matter of fact, that's exactly why now," Jaunice responded. Why lie? she thought. It was far more effective to tell him the truth.

Again, David sat back and contemplated her. She was willing to give up her career for him. Her precious designing career. She would never be happy. She would always blame him for her failure. And besides, it would be like he was asking for far too much and it was never what he expected.

"I'm flattered, Jaunice. Really, but you don't have to do that," he said softly, subdued.

"But I do. I have thought it all out and it can work. I can turn your basement into my shop and I can continue to do my designs, and with the help of FedEx, I'll never be late for a deadline," she added with an excited laugh.

David didn't laugh. It was too sudden, yet too late. He didn't want Jaunice to turn her life upside down for him, not like this. There was nothing left between them and he had no intention of changing directions now.

"Jaunice, it's not a good idea," David said firmly. "Let's leave things as they are. It can't work between us, I'm sorry."

Jaunice considered David. Her vanity refused to believe that he was bowing out for good. He still loved her, she was certain of it. It was in his eyes, she silently declared. And she had no intention of giving up her career so drastically, but she did have every intention of getting him back. So she put on her sweetest smile and said in a voice that would have melted the coldest heart, "I'm hearing you, David. So let's switch gears. Tell me about your widow friend."

Sixteen

It was late and Sionna found herself unable to sleep yet again. In a short time, David had managed to invade her thoughts. When he broke off their date it was bad enough, but when Jaunice Sumner had called him she had gone from amused to tearful to downright angry.

He had played her. And like a desperate idiot, she had allowed it. She had all but forgotten her anger over Joey's death and David's role in it. She had all but forgotten her frustrations with being lonely in just a few short meetings with David.

Aggravated with herself for being so stupid, she donned her biker shorts and tank top and went into the basement. She was going to work out, release some energy until she was so exhausted, all she would be able to do was sleep. She barely made it into the basement when the doorbell rang. Frowning and glancing at the clock, she wondered who was visiting her at so late an hour. Curious, she raced back up the stairs and went to the front door.

She peered out the window. With a racing heart she recognized David's form softly silhouetted against her front door lights. She hesitated, but not wanting to appear foolish, she swiftly opened the door and stared at him.

He looked boyishly charming with his hands tucked into his jeans pockets and a rueful self-mocking smile across his face.

"Hey," he muttered.

"Hey yourself," Sionna responded.

"It's late, I know. But I wanted to come by," David began, feeling foolish as the words came out of him.

"So you came by," Sionna said sarcastically, a smirk across her face as she considered him. Had he been rejected by Jaunice, was that why he had come over? She hoped not. She hoped that if anyone was rejected, it was Jaunice by David.

"I needed to talk to you . . . about Jaunice Sumner," David said as if reading her thoughts. In his experience, he found it far easier to tell a woman up front about another woman than to try and pretend she didn't exist. And as far as he was concerned, Jaunice was the past. Sure, she wanted to revive what they had, but David knew, especially after dinner tonight, that their relationship was over.

"Jaunice?" Sionna repeated, watching him with daring eyes, wondering if he had any idea that the woman had called her only hours earlier.

"My ex-girlfriend," David answered.

"Why would I care about your ex-girlfriend. I've barely had dinner with you yet," Sionna said coolly. David grinned, realizing where she was going after he had broken off their dinner engagement.

"Can I come in?" he asked so politely that Sionna laughed.

"Oh, why not?" she responded in a sardonic voice, stepping aside to allow him entry.

David noticed her tone but ignored it. He stepped into her foyer and waited for Sionna to offer him a seat. Amused by his suddenly polite demeanor, she waved her hand for him to take a seat in her living room. Sionna watched as he sat in what used to be Joey's favorite chair. For a moment she envisioned Joey sitting there, smiling, watching her. Shaking her head, she forced the melancholy from her mind and sat in the chair across from him. Now was not the time to brood.

David caught the look on her face and he glanced at the chair. "Nice chair," he murmured.

"It used to be my husband's favorite spot," Sionna responded.

"Oh," David muttered, a little uncomfortable. He wanted to stand and sit somewhere else but then he would have felt foolish. Releasing a heavy sigh, he dismissed the chair and considered her.

"How are you?" David asked, looking for a point to start. Sionna laughed with a slight scoff.

"I'm fine. Did you expect otherwise?" she asked. Her voice held a sharper edge than she had intended.

"No. I . . ." David began.

"Look, David, let's cut the small talk. You came here to tell me you have a girlfriend, oh, excuse me, I mean a fiancée by the name of Jaunice Sumner. Right? So fine, I can handle that. I don't know what she did to anger you enough to ask me out in the first place, but I'm a big girl and I can handle a rejection, especially so early in our relationship," she added caustically.

"I came here, yes, to admit to Jaunice but not the fiancée part. I don't know where you got that from, but she is not my fiancée," he added.

"I got it from her, and according to her, you two are engaged," Sionna said.

David frowned, confused. "You got it from her? Look, never mind." He went on, "I like you, Sionna. A lot. I want to get to know you. I'm sorry we keep having bad communication about ny intentions, but I swear Jaunice is the past. I don't know when you two talked, but I put that to her loud and clear tonight."

After a quick glance at the clock over David's head, Sionna cocked her head to the side and asked with a slightly disbelieving smile, "And just how did you put it to her, David?"

"Oh, come on," David huffed, leaning back in his seat to consider her with a frustrated expression.

"No, really, I'm curious how you put it to her, as you put it. Is she asleep, David? At your place? Or is she on her way home as we speak?"

"She's asleep." David's answer was honest, and before he could explain, Sionna released a disbelieving laugh.

"Do I look desperate to you? Just what kind of a game are you running, David? Because it's sorry, I have to tell you."

"Let me explain," David sighed, realizing that from the moment he had arrived he had been fumbling and making mistakes in every word he used.

"Oh, please do explain, explain," Sionna murmured.

"We broke up about two months ago. She and I realized that we have completely different goals and expectations in a relationship and so we called it quits. Then, the day you came into my office, Jaunice decided to pop up as well. She wanted to rekindle our relationship, but it was too late because by then I had already met you."

"David, that's sweet. Unbelievable, but sweet. I just don't believe one word of it. What I do believe is you got caught trying to play me and Jaunice and, left with no choice, you come running over here to try to amend the situation before I slam the door on you," Sionna explained, sure that she was right.

David laughed, shaking his head in disbelief. If he had lied, she would have believed him. He could have thought of many ridiculous lines to run, but he chose to tell the truth, because for him the truth was all he needed. He was attracted to Sionna and did not want Jaunice. How to get Sionna to believe it, he didn't know. He only knew he wasn't going to give up that easily.

"You don't believe me," he stated incredulously.

"No, not at all," Sionna said flatly. He stood and so did she. Thinking he was about to leave, she took a step forward.

At her movement, David reached for her and before she could think about what was happening, he was holding her in a sweet embrace.

"I promise you," he whispered, his lips nearly grazing hers, "I am not lying. I know Jaunice called you. I didn't know what she said to you, but I had to see you when I found out . . ."

"David," Sionna whispered, trying to end his confession, uncomfortable at the close contact and how weak it made her feel.

"I had to break off our date, Sionna. I had to make sure Jaunice knew it was over between us, completely. I had to let her know that there was someone else."

"This is way too much for a man who hasn't even been on a real date with me," Sionna whispered, fascinated by his statement and his intense gaze.

"I know, and I kept thinking, David, this is crazy, you don't even know Sionna Michaels. She's your friend's widow. You can't have any future with her. I kept thinking, what if I didn't try? What if I was a damn fool and just let you walk right by without at least trying. And not Jaunice or Joey's memory or our strange beginning can stop the reality that there is something between us. Isn't there?" he asked so carefully that Sionna thought he was trying to hold back an emotional moan. Entranced by his words, she nodded and her response was all David needed. The next moment, he was kissing her, something he had wanted to do the first night he had dinner with her.

The kiss seemed to last forever, and when he pulled away they were both breathless. Sionna just wanted to melt against him. She had to admit what he had said was true. There was a strong attraction that she sensed from the very moment she met him.

Still, she was torn now. Was he a schooled Casanova playing her, or was he for real? She had just lost her husband, his best friend back in college, and the last thing she needed was another emotional roller coaster. Gathering her wits about her, she pulled out of his arms and took a deep breath.

"This last week has been a whirlwind for me, David. You can't play with me, David. I cannot handle boy-meets-girl games. Not yet, not now," Sionna murmured, choosing her words carefully.

David nodded, understanding. It was a shaky moment for both of them. One way or another, they were both risking everything to test water that could be no more than tepid. David, looking at Sionna, felt it was worth the risk.

"I'm not playing a game. And I don't want to rush you, either. But I guarantee you this, I have more to offer than a good story for your paper and I'm determined to prove it. Just, please, give me a chance," he added emphatically.

Sionna walked back to him and felt oddly comforted when his arms encircled her again. "I guess I'm just going to have to trust you," Sionna murmured, pursing her mouth for his kiss.

David didn't disappoint her. His kiss was wonderful, invigorating and left her melting. He wanted to hold her all night, to caress her tender body against his, but he knew it was too soon. Grudgingly, he released her and took a step back. He stared into her eyes and before she could say another word, he murmured, "Good night, Sionna."

Seventeen

Jaunice rolled over in frustration. Again she found herself confined to the guest room. But this time, David had not only rejected her kiss, he had left her lying there like an idiot in her newly bought lingerie. He had dropped her off at the house, saying he had to go and that she knew where everything was. Dinner had not been successful. Nothing she said or did moved him and she was completely flustered by it all. And she had made the ultimate mistake. Frustrated with him, she had blurted that she called Sionna and told her about them. David was furious. Before she knew what was happening, he stormed from the house and she knew he had gone to Sionna.

It was late when he came home and she could have slapped him silly when he returned looking like a pleased cat, whistling like a refreshed man. Bitter, frustrated that none of her charms were working on a man that just a few short months before could barely be in the same room with her without begging to make love to her, she questioned her attraction. Had she lost it? Was she fat?

She jumped out of the bed and raced to the bathroom, quickly observing her body from all angles. It was like a nightmare and she was growing enraged. Her anger built up, she stormed from the bathroom. Yelling, "David!" in a fierce voice, she approached him in the living room.

David walked out of the kitchen, a beer in one hand and

the remote control in the other. He was frowning at hearing her yell his name.

"What the hell is wrong with you?" he demanded as he sat his beer on the coffee table.

"What's wrong with me? Please, what's wrong with you? Where have you been?" Jaunice demanded as if she and David had not just agreed to rethink their relationship.

"Jaunice, you know where I've been," David said coolly as he sat down and flicked on the television set. Gasping in irritation, Jaunice stormed to the television set and turned it off.

"I am talking to you! You could at least tell me the truth." Then before David could answer she gasped again, stamped her foot and screamed, "You were with that Sionna! How dare you do this to me? You could have at least waited until I was gone back to New York."

"Was it an act tonight, Jaunice, this 'tell me about your friend' line? Tell me something, when does it end? When is the ordeal over?"

"Ordeal!" Jaunice was enraged. She put her hands on her hips and glared up at him with storming eyes. "Ordeal, huh! I've been that horrible? I tell you what, David Young. You won't ever have another woman like me. And certainly not in that sappy girl Sionna. Have her. Enjoy your new-found love because frankly, you are not the man I want anymore. Be gone," she hissed. She began racing from room to room grabbing her belongings. She had had enough. She was taking every item she had ever brought into his home.

David shook his head, not knowing if he was more amused at her bravado or sorry for hurting her. He sat still, listening to her pack her bags. He didn't want to move. He didn't want to stop her, but he couldn't just let Jaunice walk away in anger. If there was a chance they could salvage their friendship, he felt the time they had spent together deserved at least that. Setting his beer on the coffee table, he entered his bedroom, where she was rummaging through the drawers, and watched her in sorrow from the doorway. She glanced at him in a huff of frustration as she crammed all her belongings that had accumulated over the years into her two suitcases.

"Jaunice, it doesn't have to be this way," David began.

"You made your choice and I've played the fool long enough," Jaunice spat out.

She couldn't believe David had fooled her. She could have laughed at how stupid she was, thinking that he loved her. Finally getting her suitcases shut, she whisked them off the bed and stormed past David. He opened his arms as if to ask what he could do to help. She ignored him, set her bags in the living room, then brushed past him again and went back to the guest room and dressed. A few minutes later she stormed past David again and got her purse from the foyer table.

She grabbed her keys and was about to leave the room again when she spotted her picture on his dresser. With a smirk his way, she snatched the picture and stuffed it under her arm. She was about to grab her bags and leave the house when she thought better of it. With her best haughty voice, she demanded, "Please bring my bags to the car." Then she left.

David obliged and carried her bags to her car. She unlocked the trunk, then waited as he settled her bags inside. The moment he closed the trunk, without so much as a glance his way, she sped off and went straight to the airport.

David dragged his feet back into the house. He wished it had been different, but he believed it was for the best that they were finally through. Agitated with the drama that had just taken place between himself and Jaunice, he pulled out some of the designs from the firm, hoping they would distract him. He would just work until he was too tired to do anything but fall out. As he looked over old designs, and

new designs, he stumbled onto the Smithsonian old designs
and this time, after taking a closer look, he couldn't believe
what he saw.

Eighteen

Jaunice was fuming. She was so angry she could spit. She was not going to let David treat her like some airheaded idiot. If he ever loved her there was no way he could have dismissed their relationship so easily. So it had been a few months between their last visit and when she broke off their relationship. She needed space, but now she seriously regretted the game she had started. Her competitive spirit awoke in her and she began to calculate the best way to get David back, if only to prove a point. At the airport, she checked into a hotel room. Sitting on the edge of the bed, she glared out the window, then decided she would wait a week. Next week was David's company party. She was on the guest list, and if she wasn't, she would see to it that she got on it. At his party, she'd make him know just how desirable and wonderful a catch she was. That Sionna was going to have nothing on her and when David finally got to see them side by side, he would know just what kind of an idiot he was.

Picking up the phone, she called her girlfriend Patricia in New York. The phone rang forever and she was just about to hang up when Patricia's sleepy voice answered.

"Hello," Patricia whispered.

"What is Jim's phone number?" Jaunice immediately asked. She couldn't come back to Virginia without a date on her arm.

"Who?" Patricia questioned, rubbing her eyes before glancing at the clock.

"Jim the designer. I need to call him," Jaunice said impatiently.

"In the middle of the night? He's going to think you're crazy," Patricia scolded.

"Just give me his number, Patricia," Jaunice hissed, now pacing the floor between the bed and the window.

"Hold on," Patricia conceded. A moment later she returned to the phone and ran off Jim's phone number.

"Thanks," Jaunice said, then before Patricia could ask what happened between Jaunice and David, Jaunice hung up the phone.

"Good-bye to you, too," Patricia said testily, then lay back down and fell asleep.

Jaunice hesitated only a moment before she dialed Jim's phone number. He answered on the first ring and Jaunice knew for sure that he was just too desperate for her.

"Jim," she managed to say in a cheerful voice. "I'm glad you're home. Let's talk." Then she smiled, sat on the bed and began to invite him as her guest to the Buerhler Architects company party.

Nineteen

Sionna lay in a state of uncertainty. How could she date David? How could she so quickly be involved with another man? What would Joey think of her forgetting him so quickly? Feeling a strong sense of guilt, Sionna tossed and turned. She felt strange, as if someone were watching her. With nervous energy, she switched on the lights and began to walk about the house. If dating David was going to cause her stress, she wasn't sure he was worth the worry. But she really liked him. They had a keen spirit and it was going to be difficult to walk away from him. He was just so . . . nice.

Needing to calm her anxious nerves, she went to the kitchen and switched on the small television set. She turned on American Movie Classics and began watching the 1958 movie *Indiscreet,* which had obviously been playing for a while. As Cary Grant and Ingrid Bergman got to know one another on the screen, she searched the refrigerator. She took out the carrots, celery, onions and green peppers and began cutting them and bagging them. When she was done dicing the onions and watching the breakup of Cary and Ingrid, Sionna realized the mistake she had made in trying to get over her jitters by watching an AMC romance.

She sighed before she cleaned off the counter and washed her hands. She switched off the movie and, feeling exhausted, headed for the living room. She glanced at Joey's old chair and thought again that she had to get rid of that chair. She curled up on her sofa and continued to watch *Indiscreet.* The lovers were just beginning to reconcile when the phone rang and Sionna jumped. She hesitated a moment before hurrying to the phone.

"Hello," she murmured, hoping against hope that the caller was David. It wasn't.

"Have him, Ms. Thang. I don't want him anymore. You two belong together," stated a bitter female voice that Sionna instantly knew was Jaunice. Sionna stood back on her heels, grounded only by her calculation that David must have officially broken up with Jaunice to have caused this call.

Still she played dumb and said, "I beg your pardon."

"Oh, don't beg. It's unbecoming. I'm on standby at the airport and you should know that David has just played us both. Where I thought he was making up with me, he was also trying to get with you. So have him. He's all yours. I can't be any man's fool. Have a great life, Sionna Michaels." With that the phone clicked and Jaunice was gone. Sionna glanced at the clock. She hadn't realized it but she had stayed up all night.

Don't let her get to you, Sionna said to herself as she hung up the phone and walked with heavy feet up to her bedroom. As the sun was rising, Sionna laid her tired head down and fell asleep, at last.

"David, Mr. Foster would like to see you," Karen whispered, sticking her head in David's office. David glanced up, shuffled some papers to the side and nodded.

"I'm on my way," he said.

Karen backed out and quickly took her seat. Working with David was definitely a dramatic experience. Jaunice Sumner in particular. She made constant calls, all of which David refused to accept. Karen suspected Jaunice was being rejected and was not at all pleased by it. As David walked by her, Karen watched, curious how a guy who seemed so nice could be so callous.

Karen's phone rang again and in a professional voice she answered, "Buerhler Architects, this is Karen.

"Karen," the familiar voice gushed. "I'm so glad you answered and not David."

"Really?" Karen said in disbelief, rolling her eyes heavenward as she watched David disappear down the hall. "And this must be Jaunice, again," Karen added.

"Yes. As a matter of fact, Karen, I was hoping that I could talk to you. You see, as you can probably guess, David and I broke up recently," Jaunice began.

Karen smirked while murmuring a sarcastic, "No?"

"Yes. And I had planned to go to the company party next week," Jaunice continued, oblivious to Karen's tone.

"Uh-huh. Well, as David's assistant, it is not my place to get involved with what's going on between you two. I suggest you be patient and give him a chance to call you back."

"He won't call me back!" Jaunice shrieked, near hysterics. "I mean he hasn't so far. I just need your help in a small way."

Karen paused, considering that Jaunice could be emotionally disturbed and that was why David was so obviously distracted this morning. Then she recalled the way Jaunice had strutted into David's office a few days earlier, and she knew there was no way that Jaunice Sumner was emotionally disturbed. Feeling a pang of sympathy for her, Karen asked, "What do you need?"

Jaunice could have jumped for joy. She was truly worried that Karen was going to be coldhearted or too loyal an assistant to help her. She needed to be at the party. She needed to shake things up, and she was certain that Sionna Michaels would be there on David's arm. Well she would show them both what a mistake they made with her.

"I was hoping you could ensure that my name gets on the guest list," Jaunice asked with such sugar in her voice

Karen had to flinch. She couldn't say no yet she feared losing her job if David found out.

"I can't," Karen murmured, uncomfortable with saying no, especially considering Jaunice's hysteria.

"Oh, please. I need you," Jaunice begged, very disappointed. "I have clients there and David and I forgot when we broke up how important this party is to my career. It could cause me to lose my house," she lied.

"I would, really, but I can't," Karen insisted, too concerned about her own job to be moved by Jaunice's sob story.

"If you're worried about David knowing you got me on the list, I won't tell him. He probably won't even see me," Jaunice laughed, trying to sound lighthearted. She grew anxious at Karen's response. It was her last chance to prove to David that she was the woman he wanted. What she would do with him when she won, she wasn't sure.

Karen continued to hesitate. The party wasn't that big a deal to her. It was more for networking and she was quite comfortable in her role as an assistant. She could tell the coordinator she was going and put Jaunice down as her guest. She could do that, she thought, softening to the idea.

"I'll have to think about it," Karen said.

"When can you let me know?" Jaunice pursued.

"I don't know," Karen rushed on.

"I need to know right away, today. I don't live there so I have to make arrangements, since David won't let me stay with him. Please say yes," Jaunice pleaded.

"I can't. I simply will have to let you know . . . I guess today sometime," Karen responded, then before Jaunice could insist again she hung up the phone. Just as she did, David returned, his eyes full of distraction as he passed by her desk. She waited several minutes after he had settled in before knocking cautiously on his door.

"Hey, Karen," David said, turning from his gazing out the window to consider his assistant.

"I don't mean to disturb you, David, but I wanted to ask you a quick question about the company party next week," Karen said.

"Oh, yeah? I forgot about it," David said, lightly remembering even as he said it that he had originally invited Jaunice.

"Yes, well, I just wondered, since it's my first time going, if it's a small intimate affair or something more elaborate. You know, like a lot of people."

"A lot of people. It's usually more than just staff. Our clients, their clients, etc. You'll probably get lost in the shuffle of people, so if you don't like crowds, it's not the place to be," David added with a laugh.

"Crowds are fine with me. I guess we'll probably not even see each other in the crowd, then, huh?" she laughed, although she was a nervous wreck. David shrugged and gave her a considerate smile.

"There's no telling. But I hope you will be there. You'll have a good time. Did you need anything else?" he asked when Karen hesitated again.

"No, no, I'm fine. Thank you, David," she said, then hurried back to her desk. She knew she was going to be a coward and let Jaunice coax her into putting her on the party list. The poor girl sounded so desperate, how could she say no?

Once Karen left, David went back to his pondering. Last night he had found Joey Michaels's old layout of the Smithsonian and found it curiously lacking any doors in the underground rooms, only ceiling exits. Although he was grateful for the distraction from his guilt at the way he and Jaunice had ended, he was intrigued by Joey Michaels's work. It was some of the finest he had seen. It definitely warranted a question or two about why he had been terminated. And why were the plans not being used? The last he checked, the Smithsonian was still contracting the firm.

When he asked Mr. Foster about the plans, Mr. Foster

seemed completely unaware of the project changes. Further, he could barely recall Joey Michaels's role in the plan layouts. David himself couldn't remember one conversation where Joey was mentioned on the Smithsonian project. He wondered if the project meant anything, and even deeper, if the failed contract was the real reason Joey had committed suicide. It was so illogical. He couldn't believe that Joey would sweat something so trivial as losing a contract. Everyone he knew in the business had lost a contract before.

Confident that there was more to Joey Michaels's termination than met the eye, David sat in contemplation at his desk. Determined to fill the blanks between Joey's termination and suicide, David began searching the contractors' database for any information related to Joey. After a quick query, he sat back in fascination at the ton of activity that Joey had been involved in for the company. As he reviewed the files, it occurred to him that he didn't see any mention of the Smithsonian project. With a frown, David did a second query on the files found, using the keyword Smithsonian. He was confounded that not one of the files mentioned the Smithsonian and thus, it appeared that Joey Michaels never had a relationship with the project. David knew it to be otherwise, after all Charles and Stan had found a copy of Joey's old blueprints, which included the Smithsonian project.

David paused for a moment then decided to do a new query on the Smithsonian. As he suspected, within moments dozens of files came up. But his query for Joey Michaels failed. In effect, the company showed no connection of any kind between Joey and the Smithsonian project and David's curiosity was fueled even more. For whatever reason, David was confident that Joey was somehow omitted from the Smithsonian project with deliberate precision. He just couldn't understand why.

Sionna Michaels may have been grasping for straws with

her discrimination case, but there was one thing for sure, someone didn't want Joey Michaels's relationship to the Smithsonian known. It was a clear cover-up and he was going to find out why. What reason did Buerhler have to hide Joey's relationship to the project, David wondered. He was determined to find out. Besides, Sionna deserved to know the truth about Joey.

her the conclusion over, but there was one thing not clear. If someone up in Charity Jones Ministries really contributed to the contribution Joey did, it was at the Center up and she was going to be hopeful. When she mentioned Buerhler however, Joey's recommendation the project Data described. He had disregarded Warren and Charity Jones described to know the truth about it.

Twenty

Sionna headed downtown feeling pleased with herself. When she awoke her first thought was of David. The thought of him had warmed her all over and even Jaunice's irate call could not put a damper on Sionna's good mood. Of course she had questioned how much truth was in Jaunice's call, but the more she thought of it the more certain she was that Jaunice and David were over, and that was all that mattered.

She really liked David. He had an air of genuine kindness about him that she was drawn to. He was the type of man she needed to help her get over Joey. As she pulled into the parking lot of her job, she was silently thankful that the case was closed with Buerhler Architects and that she could shift gears and begin her life without the shadow and intrigue of the relationship between Joey and Buerhler.

After a quick glance over the parking lot, she spotted Mr. Eikton's car. It was a shabby powder blue sedan that had to be thirty years old. She had no idea what make the car was, and she always intended to ask Mr. Eikton what it was, because it was in such bad condition the nameplate had fallen off.

Amused, she hurried into the office and headed straight to Mr. Eikton's desk. The *City Desk* office was as quaint and predictable as any local small-town paper could be, except they were in the city. It amazed Sionna the first time she entered the office of the *City Desk* that anyone would have bought space so small. There were seven desks in the small space. The office was a hubbub of chatter on the phone, keyboards and the local news station playing on the television set mounted on the far corner wall. There was an old Coca-Cola soda machine and an even older candy machine beside it. They marked the entrance to the ladies' and gentlemen's restrooms. The place smelled of ink and old papers.

What was most interesting about the office was that the designer had thought it would be creative to add three steps leading up to a small area of space that allowed just enough room to position a desk there. And it was there that Mr. Eikton had chosen to put his office. The designer also added a rail on both sides of the steps. Although the space was compact, placing his desk there was effective in distinguishing him and his status from the other staff.

As soon as she entered the office, Mr. Eikton looked up. He was on the phone, loudly arguing with one of his other reporters, and Sionna smiled affectionately at him. He was gruff on the exterior but she knew he was all heart.

"Well, what do we have here? Sionna has returned and just in time. I hear you lost that story with Buerhler because they settled out of court," Mr. Eikton said loudly, pausing his conversation on the phone to consider Sionna.

"As a matter of fact, they did," Sionna beamed, pleased to be no longer on the story. She dropped her purse on her desk as she approached him and halted on the second step to give Mr. Eikton her full attention.

"So it's over?" Mr. Eikton asked, his voice so calm that Sionna paused.

"Yes," she responded hesitantly. Her hesitancy was warranted. At her reply Mr. Eikton became livid.

"No, it isn't over, Sionna," Mr. Eikton said. "You need to follow up. How many times have I said to you reporters that follow-up is key, key, key. Now get to your desk and get Hillman on the line. And follow up," Mr. Eikton ordered.

A moment later he turned his attention from Sionna and immediately continued to yell at the person on the line.

Sionna gulped back a response, wanting to scream that she had no interest in following up. Instead, she rolled her eyes in exasperation and said in a lighthearted murmur, "I'm glad to see you, too," as she headed for the familiar overwhelming clutter of her desk.

With a heavy sigh, she sat in her seat. After a moment of looking over the mess she had left on her desk, she began searching her purse for Greg Hillman's phone number. She would close out her story with Greg beaming about his successful win and then it would truly be over, for what it was worth.

"Greg here," he answered within a few rings.

"Mr. Hillman, this is Sionna Michaels. I wanted to congratulate you on winning your case. I was hoping I could get a comment or two for our paper to finish the story," Sionna said brightly, hoping that his comments would be short and sweet and that would be that.

"Yeah, well I ain't got much to say. I still don't have a job and twenty grand doesn't go far." His voice was sulky and Sionna couldn't blame him as she realized the settlement was definitely less than his original claim for five hundred thousand dollars.

"I thought they settled for five hundred grand?" Sionna probed.

"Nah, it's a shared settlement and my part after legal fees and all that was twenty thousand dollars. It's enough to hold me while I get another job, but you know how hard it is to find a job when you really need one? That's all right. That's all right."

"So you're saying that the money they paid was not sufficient."

"Not even close. I made three times that amount in a year. Now I'm being forced to relocate or push some other brother out of a job."

An important message from the ARABESQUE Editor

Dear Arabesque Reader,

Because you've chosen to read one of our Arabesque romance novels, we'd like to say "thank you"! And, as a special way to thank you, we've selected four more of the books you love so well to send you for only $1.99.

Please enjoy them with our compliments, and thank you for continuing to enjoy Arabesque...the soul of romance.

Karen Thomas
Senior Editor,
Arabesque Romance Novels

3 QUICK STEPS
TO RECEIVE YOUR "THANK YOU" GIFT
FROM THE EDITOR

Send back this card and you'll receive 4 Arabesque novels!
These books have a combined cover price of $20.00 or more,
but they are yours to keep for a mere $1.99.

There's no catch. You're under no obligation to buy anything.
We charge only $1.99 for the books (plus $1.50 for shipping
and handling, a total of $3.49). And you don't have to make
any minimum number of purchases—not even one!

We hope that after receiving your books you'll want to
remain an Arabesque subscriber. But the choice is yours to
continue or cancel, anytime at all! So why not take us up on
our invitation to receive 4 Arabesque Romance Novels, with
no risk of any kind. You'll be glad you did!

Call us
TOLL-FREE
at 1-888-345-BOOK

THE EDITOR'S "THANK YOU" GIFT INCLUDES:

- 4 books delivered for only $1.99 (plus $1.50 for shipping and handling)
- A FREE newsletter, *Arabesque Romance News*, filled with author interviews, book previews, special offers, and more!
- No risks or obligations. You're free to cancel whenever you wish... with no questions asked.

BOOK CERTIFICATE

Yes! Please send me 4 Arabesque books for $1.99 (+ $1.50 for shipping & handling, a total of $3.49). I understand I am under no obligation to purchase any books, as explained on the back of this card.

Name _____

Address _____ Apt. _____

City _____ State _____ Zip _____

Telephone ( ) _____

Signature

Offer limited to one per household and not valid to current subscribers. All orders subject to approval. Terms, offer, & price subject to change. Offer valid only in the U.S.

AN090A

Thank you!

Accepting the four introductory books for $1.99 (+ $1.50 for shipping & handling, a total of $3.49) places you under no obligation to buy anything. You may keep the books and return the shipping statement marked "cancel". If you do not cancel, about a month later we will send 4 additional Arabesque novels, and bill you a preferred subscriber's price of just $4.00 per title (plus a small shipping and handling fee). That's $16.00 for all 4 books for a savings of 33% off the cover price. You may cancel at any time, but if you choose to continue, every month we'll send you 4 more books, which you may either purchase at the preferred discount price. . . or return to us and cancel your subscription.

THE ARABESQUE ROMANCE CLUB: HERE'S HOW IT WORKS

ARABESQUE ROMANCE BOOK CLUB
P.O. Box 5214
Clifton NJ 07015-5214

PLACE
STAMP
HERE

heart&soul's got it all!

Motivation, Inspiration, Exhilaration!
FREE ISSUE RESERVATION CARD

YES! Please send my FREE issue of HEART & SOUL right away and enter my one-year subscription. My special price for 5 more issues (6 in all) is only $10.00. I'll save 44% off the newsstand rate. If I decide that HEART & SOUL is not for me, I'll write "cancel" on the invoice, return it, and owe nothing. The FREE issue will be mine to keep.

Name _____ (First) _____ (Last)

Address _____ Apt.#

City _____ State _____ Zip _____ | MABQ |

Please allow 6-8 weeks for receipt of first issue. In Canada: CDN $19.97 (includes GST). Payment in U.S. currency must accompany all Canadian orders. Basic subscription rate: 1 year (6 issues) $16.97.

"I'm sorry your win is so disappointing." Sionna was sincere, feeling bad that she could do nothing to help him.

"Me, too. Hey, I gotta roll out. I'll see you." He hung up and Sionna slowly set the phone back on the cradle. Certainly twenty thousand dollars was nothing to scoff at, but she could understand his feelings, especially after what Joey had gone through.

Before she could dwell on Greg Hillman, her line rang and Sionna jumped. The office was a buzz of activity around her, yet the phone's shrill ring had unnerved her. Feeling foolish, she glanced around to see if anyone had noticed how on edge she was as she answered the phone.

"Sionna speaking," she answered carefully, curious about who was calling her.

"You don't call your mother anymore? You've had me worried out of my mind. All of us in fact," Rose fussed the moment she heard her daughter's voice. "And you didn't even tell me you were going back to work. You had me worried sick." With that Rose caught her breath and Sionna immediately spoke.

"I'm sorry. I didn't mean to worry you. A lot has happened in the past week and I just . . . well I've been busy."

"Busy how? You're on leave. What are you doing in the office anyway?" Rose demanded.

"I decided the leave was too long, like you said. I needed to get back out there and live," Sionna responded.

"So you're back at work. Great. Just when I planned to send the twins to stay with you for a day," Rose murmured.

"A day? Why so short?" Sionna asked.

"I wanted them to stop through on their way to New York. They're checking out universities up there and I wasn't too thrilled with their spending the night in New York," Rose responded.

"They can still come up here, Mom. I would love to have them keep me company. I wish it was more than just one night because I miss you all," Sionna said.

And just as she spoke she realized that having her twin sisters around could prove very interesting. They were bound to find out about David, if he was as sincere about getting to know her as he claimed. She wasn't sure if she was prepared to tell her mom yet that she had met a man. She worried for the first time what her mother would think if the twins told Rose about David and that he was a friend of Joey's. Shaking her head, Sionna refused to worry over something that had not yet happened. She missed her family and if the twins wanted to visit her, she was all for it. Besides it was for just one day.

"Are you sure? Now that you're working you may not want to deal with two teenagers," Rose said.

"Mom, please, I can handle them. Besides, it's just one night, how bad can they be? At any rate, how did you know to call me here anyway?" Sionna asked after a moment's pause.

"A hunch. You didn't get those reporter instincts from a tree," Rose laughed. Sionna laughed too, but before she could respond Mr. Eikton's gruff voice caught her attention.

"That had better be Buerhler or Hillman you're chit-chatting with," Mr. Eikton squawked as he strolled past Sionna's desk, his scruffy eyebrow raised inquisitively.

"Mom, I got to go. I'll call you tonight. Love you," she said, then quickly hung up the phone and raced after Mr. Eikton.

"What is it, Sionna Michaels?" Mr. Eikton demanded as he forced ten dimes into the soda machine.

"There's no story there. Hillman settled for twenty thousand dollars after expenses and he's as satisfied as he is going to be. My contact at Buerhler says it was not discrimination, that it was due to management changes. There's no story," Sionna repeated at Mr. Eikton's dubious expression.

"I tell you, Sionna, I am highly disappointed." He sighed and Sionna grew worried. Instantly she feared that he was about to discharge her. Holding her breath, she waited as he continued.

"You came back too soon. I think you need a few more weeks. A month maybe. Then give me a call," Mr. Eikton said before turning back toward his desk. Frowning, Sionna grabbed his shoulder, halting him in midstride.

"Wait, Mr. Eikton, you're . . . you're not firing me, are you?" she asked fretfully.

Mr. Eikton paused and stared at her with a stern expression. Then he burst into peals of laughter and Sionna could have pushed him in irritation. "Why would I fire my favorite reporter? No, I just can see you're not ready to come back yet. You're not using that fiery reporter instinct that made me hire you in the first place. When you get your fire back, then I want to see you. Don't worry Sionna, your job is safe," he added, patting Sionna fondly on her shoulder.

Sionna was relieved, wondering how she could have doubted Mr. Eikton's intentions. Then she frowned again, realizing he was right. Once upon a time she would have made a serious story out of Greg's termination. But how could she explain her confusion and the emotional havoc she was experiencing because of Buerhler. The best thing she could do for herself was to leave Buerhler alone and focus on her life.

"I guess you're right," she confessed.

"Of course I'm right. Now go on, get going and I'll see you in a few weeks, right?" Before she could respond, he gently shoved his way past her and sat down behind his desk.

Sionna hid an amused smile at his gruff exterior as she went back to her desk, grabbed her belongings and hurried from the building. It was late September and she loved the warm breeze that swept over her the minute she left the building. After a brief pause to fully feel the breeze, she got in her car and immediately rolled all the windows down.

Driving away, she smiled winsomely. She was relieved.

Relieved not to have to pursue Buerhler again, not to have her constant anger and depression that followed her after Joey's death, relieved to be able to enjoy the basic part of living again. And one part of that basic living was dating, and she couldn't wait to see David again. A tinge of guilt paused her and she wondered how Joey would feel if he knew she was interested in another man, particularly David Young. He wouldn't like it, she concluded ruefully. He wouldn't understand that she felt a natural bond to David, a natural connection that she initially tried to deny. The problem was, there was no denying what she was feeling. Just thinking about David stirred butterflies in the pit of her stomach. It was a pleasurable feeling that she had to admit she had not felt with Joey.

Joey had been special to her too, but he was gone and she couldn't live her life around what would have been. She was confident she was making the right decision to give David a chance to get to know her and to get to know him.

It would be interesting to see how well David handled the twins. They could be a nosy bunch, and being her little sisters, they were sure to be nosy about David. She grew concerned for a moment, hoping they would understand that her attraction and interest in David was not wrong or by any means disrespectful of Joey's memory.

"I'll sit them down and explain things. Besides, David and I may not even hit it off," she said aloud as she pulled into her driveway. She was unlocking the door when she heard the phone ringing. She was sure it was David. Excited, she hurried inside the house and caught the phone before he could hang up.

"Hello," she answered breathlessly.

"Sionna? Did I catch you at a bad time?" David asked at hearing her breathless hello.

"No. I just got in," Sionna reassured him as she sat her purse on kitchen bar, then slipped out of her heels.

"I was just calling, hoping that we could try that date again," David said, deciding to just jump right in.

"I would love to," Sionna said quickly, then wished she had paused. It sounded so desperate to say yes to a date so quickly.

"Great. Is six thirty all right?" he asked, sounding a little abrupt to Sionna's ears. She looked heavenward, surprised that he meant tonight.

"I . . . sure. Six thirty works fine for me," she said.

"I'll pick you up then. Talk to you later," he responded, then hung up.

Sionna slowly hung up the phone and worried for a moment that maybe David was a fickle man and planned to tell her that he and Jaunice had made up and were back together. Irritated that he would dare to ask her out just to tell her something about his relationship, she dismissed the entire notion. She wasn't normally paranoid and she wasn't going to give that Jaunice person the pleasure of making her that way now.

David hung up the phone and stared at the memo in front of him. He had impulsively called Sionna the moment he read the memo. It was the information he was looking for and he was very disappointed at what he had discovered. He could understand now, at least to a small extent, how Joey could have felt so humiliated that he would rather face death than face the world.

Joey Michaels was a fraud. A thief in the most common way. And he had been caught stealing ideas from the junior designers. David shook his head as he again read the memo accusing Joey of having stolen the Smithsonian plans as well as countless other ideas from fellow architects. Apparently he had been stealing for years and it had finally caught up with him when he stole from the wrong person, the son of the former president of his company, On-Site Associates.

Joey had copied the idea for the museum site in Colorado and turned it into his own creation for the Smithsonian. When it came across Edgar McHughly's desk, Edgar was instantly alerted to the similar landscaping and dimensions that were so unique to his son's style. When he questioned Joey, Michaels denied it. But Edgar was positive, so he had Joey investigated. It wasn't until the acquisition was signed off with Buerhler that Joey's full indiscretions were exposed. By then Joey was confident that he was in the clear. It must have come as a shock to him, David thought, when Buerhler management approached him and the next moment he was quietly ushered from the offices of Buerhler Architects.

David recalled sadly how he had anticipated meeting up with Joey, but those first few weeks he had been so tied up he hadn't a moment to think about renewing old friendships. Between Jaunice's waning interest and the obligations of the job, David had no time to reunite with Joey. By the time word got out about Joey's suicide, his widow had already buried him and David had only been able to send flowers of condolence. Again caught up in his job and his failing relationship with Jaunice, he became distracted. When Sionna approached him it was both shocking and exciting to discover she was Joey's widow. A beautiful widow. A woman of mystery if ever there was one.

Taking a deep breath that expanded his chest, David set the memo from Edgar McHughly aside. He would tell Sionna about Joey, but he didn't like it. Still, he had several hours before he would pick up Sionna and he had a ton of work to get through. The last thing he needed was for Mr. Foster to think he wasn't up to his job.

Shaking off his pensive mood, he called Karen from his intercom.

"Yes, David," Karen responded.

"Let Kevin and Charles know I'm on my way," David said. Grabbing his reports, he left his office, careful to turn the memo regarding Joey Michaels facedown.

Twenty-one

Sionna considered every stitch of clothing in her closet with stern deliberation. Nothing she had fit the mood she was in. She felt demure yet sexy. Sweet yet feisty. Subdued yet animated. She felt free.

She flipped through her formal dresses with growing disappointment. Most of her dresses were black and without much style, but she didn't feel like wearing black. She had a nice pair of white slacks but she didn't have a top that fit the weather and the style of the pants. Of course she could just wear a suit, but it seemed so professional, so uptight for a date.

She weighed her options carefully. She needed to relax, to be herself. Realizing tonight was not the night for formal wear, she went to her dresser and searched her jeans drawer. She chose her denim blue jeans and immediately she knew she had hit upon the look she wanted. She went to her sweater drawer and found a shell pink short-cropped chenille sweater that was a favorite of hers.

Confident that she had found the look that fit her mood, she quickly laid her outfit out, then began preparing her toiletries. She took a long hot shower, taking care to use her favorite Victoria's Secret fragrance. Afterward, she towel dried her hair and carefully put on lotion until she was as soft as a newborn baby.

Then she carefully began to dress, choosing her underclothes with as much as care as she had chosen her outfit.

Although she didn't plan to make love to David on their first real date, she was honest enough to know that things could spark between the two of them, and if they did, she wanted to be prepared.

Time flew by. It was almost six o'clock and Sionna nearly went into a panic. She had not yet done her hair or makeup. Swiftly she plugged in her curlers and fixed her hair. She styled it and hated it, so she styled it again.

"Ugh," she groaned, hating how wild her hair looked. She grabbed the brush and began brushing her hair until it fell into full bouncy curls and circled her face. Confident that the style was working for her, she quickly applied eye shadow and mascara. She was looking for her pink lipstick to match her sweater when she heard the doorbell. A glance at her clock and she could see that David was early. Did that mean he was anxiously waiting to see her too? She hoped so.

She turned in slight panic, her semicircle around the room leading her nowhere. Then she opened the vanity drawer and nearly fainted with relief when she saw her favorite Revlon lipstick. Grabbing it, she went downstairs, afraid that David would think she wasn't home even if her car was in the driveway. Nearly five minutes went by after he rang the doorbell.

When she entered the foyer she called, "Just a minute," then quickly put on her lipstick while glancing in the mirror hanging on the wall. A quick adjustment of her hair and sweater and finally she was ready to open the door.

David was staring out into the street, patiently waiting for Sionna to open the door. He wondered if she had forgotten about their date. But the moment he turned and saw her, he knew she had not forgotten. His lips curved into a bright generous smile that showed his appreciation for the care she took in dressing.

"Wow," was all he could say, and for Sionna that was plenty.

"Hello to you too. I'm so sorry I took so long answering the door," Sionna added, stepping aside to welcome him inside.

"I thought you had forgotten. I was very disappointed," David teased, a whiff of her perfume pleasing his senses as he entered the house.

"Trust me, David, I didn't forget. I have to admit there was drama in my getting ready for tonight," Sionna laughed, her honesty catching him off guard.

"Yeah?" David asked, entranced by her declaration. "How so?"

"Nothing that I want to tell you about, that's for sure," Sionna stated with a charming smile. David laughed, nodding.

"Uh-huh, I see. Keeping secrets already," David said.

"No," Sionna responded, knowing full well he was teasing. "I just feel some things are best left private."

"I give up. I won't ask about your drama. So are you ready?" he asked. She looked so good, he felt he could stand there staring at her forever, but he wanted to give her so much more.

"Certainly. I need to get one thing, I'll be right back," Sionna said. She ran up the stairs and quickly grabbed her purse, her makeup and her perfume. Slipping them into her purse, she hurried back downstairs and presented David with a bright smile and said, "I'm all ready."

"This is nice," Sionna murmured as she and David were escorted to a secluded seat in the restaurant Butterfly Valley about half an hour later. Sionna immediately liked the cozy quaintness of the restaurant, and the small stage had her intrigued. As she sat in her seat she took in the ceiling lights that illuminated the stage. Was it for a band?

"Was this a random selection or have you been here before?" Sionna asked David as the hostess walked away.

"Random. I heard about this place from a friend but I never got around to coming out here. I thought you would enjoy a little entertainment with your dinner," he answered.

"So there will be a performance. Wonderful. Do you know what it is, who's playing?" Sionna asked, enthused about the whole idea.

"I believe the schedule out front said poetry. I think that should be cool," David said with a smile.

His tone was a little dry and Sionna thought it was strange. Sure, she barely knew him but that didn't mean she couldn't tell he wasn't his usual charming self. Reaching over, she held his hand and looked into his eyes, determined that he would not look away, then asked, "Is everything all right? There isn't something you need to tell me, is there?"

David shook his head with a rueful smile, certain that Sionna was referring to Jaunice. She had nothing to worry about with Jaunice. "There's nothing wrong. Maybe I'm a little tired . . ."

"Oh. You could have called me. I would have understood," Sionna quickly murmured, feeling a little guilty that she had dragged him out on a work night and that he was tired on top of it.

"No. I wanted to be here. I want to hear all about you, Sionna Michaels. How you are, what you do, what you like. I need to know these things if I am to ever get a chance to impress you," David said, a wolfish smile making him even more handsome.

Sionna sat back in her seat, impressed by his words and confident in his sincerity. Of course she wondered if there was a slight chance she was a rebound for him, if it was possible that he still wanted Jaunice and was using his interest in her to ease the pain of their breakup. She wasn't usually insecure, and if her hunch was right about Jaunice, David was sincere in stating that he didn't want Jaunice.

She smiled at him, a little smile she was sure left an aura of mystery around her.

"I would love to tell you about myself but I must confess, there isn't much to tell you."

"Sure there is. Where do you come from, Sionna. Who were you before you were Sionna Michaels.

"Sionna Sloan."

"And you are from where originally?" David probed further.

Sionna grinned, knowing he was going to get a laugh out of her small town in Georgia.

"I don't know if I want to tell you. It's so small where I'm from," Sionna grinned, feeling a little shy beneath his curiosity. He was so involved in her world and she found it fascinating.

"I want to know all about you," David said in a husky voice that caused Sionna to shiver all over. She hoped he didn't notice. It would be embarrassing for her to have him know how much she liked him.

"Atlanta, Georgia," she answered.

"Hum, yet minimum to no accent. How interesting. And you left Atlanta because you fell in love with Joey?" David probed. Sionna smirked and shook her head.

"Not quite. Actually I met Joey about two years ago."

"You're kidding," David whistled, a little surprised because he had thought they were together much longer.

Sionna nodded, looking away from him and into space as she reflected, "Yeah. We met while I was going to work, where I work now. He was getting his suit out of the cleaners and I was trying to put mine in. He was cute, too. I thought instantly that I would love to know who he was. And I believe he felt the same way because he paused . . ." and so did Sionna as she closed her eyes for a moment and recalled Joey's first words to her. She opened her eyes and felt a little choked up, not sure if she wanted to laugh or cry.

David considered her in silence, feeling guilty that he

had encouraged her to rehash emotions that she obviously wanted to control. "Then he asked me if I came here often, to the cleaners," Sionna explained with a slight laugh, although she was trembling with emotion.

"I'm sorry to bring him up. It was rude of me," David apologized.

"No, please, I need to get used to talking about Joey. I guess it doesn't get easier."

"Not overnight," David agreed, sitting back and considering her with compassionate eyes.

"No, but it's been a year, David," Sionna said dryly. "You know, Joey was special. He was very cool and in the beginning very thoughtful. I think we or at least I fell in love that very first date. You know how when you meet someone and you realize that all the lonely moments you ever had were over? You suddenly feel a burst of energy and expectations that no one can ruin for you. Because that person is just right for you. He was not perfect, yet he fit me perfectly. You know?" Sionna rambled. When she was finished she realized that tears had somehow managed to slip through. Embarrassed, she hastily wiped the tears aside.

"Joey and I had great times in college. I was broken up when I found out about his suicide. If someone had asked who was stronger, me or Joey, I would have without question said Joey. He handled all the burdens of college way better than I did, including his temper, especially his temper. I think now maybe he should have allowed his temper to express itself. Maybe—" David started, but Sionna cut him off.

"No, let's not do this. Let's not make this date a memorial to Joey. There's nothing we can do about what he did. Certainly nothing that could explain it. Because we knew him from our own perspectives, not his," Sionna interrupted firmly, becoming more and more choked up as David spoke.

David nodded in agreement, tapped his fingers on the table and turned around and waved for a waiter.

"Hungry?" he asked Sionna as the waiter approached.

"Definitely," Sionna replied.

"As I told you, it's my first time here so I can't recommend anything on the menu. Good luck," David laughed.

"Oh, thanks," Sionna said, then thoroughly considered the menu.

A few minutes later they both ordered. David crossed his fingers and Sionna laughed as the waiter took their order back to the cook.

"It can't be that bad," Sionna said.

"I don't know. I'm used to having intoxicating aromas or something to pique my interest," David warned.

"Yes, well, if the food isn't good maybe the entertainment will be a lot better," Sionna suggested.

David shrugged and they both fell silent.

"All right, so now your turn. Tell me about David Young. Who is he and why is he so special?" Sionna asked.

"This could take all night" David joked.

"I don't have anywhere to go in the morning," Sionna said.

"All right, let's see. I was born in Alexandria, Virginia. My mom was a seamstress and maid, and my dad was a janitor. They scraped and scraped every dime they had to send their oldest son of six to college. But I was the traditional athletic type," David said with a laugh. "And I got a scholarship on my athletic skills to Syracuse. I was supposed to play basketball—"

"Basketball? Are you tall enough?" Sionna asked, surprised. David laughed heartily.

"Yes. Basketball, although portrayed as a game that requires height, is really about skill and maneuvering, and I had what it took, thank you," David added with a wide grin.

Sionna shrugged sheepishly, saying only "Oh."

"Anyway I got the scholarship and it helped a lot. The

money my dad had saved for me I used to get a cheap used car and it kept food on my table and clothes in my closet. So there I was, expecting to play ball, and I found myself sitting and warming the bench every game. Literally. I couldn't believe it. I found out later on that I was not the player I thought I was. That I was all right but not the stuff that stars are made of, and I was promptly informed that I had better start thinking of another career. So, living in Alexandria and all, what better career could I go for than architecture? At least that was the plan, design and layout. I did my dues and got an internship with a builder in Buffalo, New York. Things got great and my career took off. Next thing I knew I was a junior designer at Buerhler in New York and that was that."

"Was it disappointing not to ever get to play?" Sionna asked.

David paused to drink from his water before he answered her with a rueful grin, "Yes. It was absolutely a disappointment. But"—he shrugged—"I got over it. And the more I learned about architecture, the more I got over basketball. I love the business I'm in and I plan to open my own firm ten years or so down the road. So you know some disappointments are blessings in disguise."

"That's big of you, really," Sionna responded. "You seem to have had an exciting life. Living in the city, going to college in New York, being on a major college basketball team, then getting the dream job. I'm impressed."

"You call Alexandria, Virginia, the city?" David asked with an amused smile.

"Where I'm from, all of this is the city," Sionna explained. "When I got the job with the *City Desk* paper I was so excited, thinking I was big-time. Then I met Joey, who as you know was a New Yorker and definitely used to city life."

"You are big-time in my eyes," David complemented.

"You're too kind," Sionna smiled, feeling a flutter of

activity in her abdomen that was in no way related to hunger pangs. He excited her senses and brought her a joy she thought dead with Joey, and she wasn't sure what to do.

"Ah, the poets, at last," David murmured, turning slightly in his seat to watch the stage as the lights dimmed and the form of a very somber young woman appeared on the stage. Sionna looked up and watched, intrigued by the young white woman's expression. A sudden keystroke came from a piano that Sionna could not find anywhere in the room. Sionna blinked, happy not to have jumped because she would have felt foolish. But the sudden sound had caught her off guard.

"I bend over for you. Like a rose in the wintry breeze." The young woman began to speak, her voice sharp, bitter and loud. Sionna found her strange and frightening.

"I gasp in your presence. You being all perfection. I know what you think. What you see. What I am to you. But I still hover in your shadow because your light is far brighter than mine. I bend over for you. Like a dog without a dream."

Sionna gasped at the last statement, sorry for the woman, shocked by the depiction.

"I know that I am nothing. Comparing myself to you is like a fool fighting the night. I am you when my eyes close. I know you more than I know me. I bend over for you. Like the wild woman without love. I search your eyes and find myself. Defeated. Bruised. Lost. I am what you make me. I am nothing at all."

Then a piano key struck and Sionna was amazed at the bluster of applause. The poem had been awful, morbid and everything Sionna wasn't. Her eyes caught David's and he shrugged as if to say he had no idea what that was about.

"Take your eyes off the street." A sudden booming male voice filled the room and Sionna came to attention. "Take your eyes off the sky. But look, over there, at that mirror. What do you see? How do you expose yourself? Are you and I so high that we cannot see? Stop, fool, stop. Am I not warning you of my rage? Can't you hear the bitter gunfire? I will not be tormented, or hurt, or feared, or weak . . ."

"Are you getting this?" Sionna whispered, leaning over the table to David. He chuckled and whispered back, "I guess."

Sionna sat back in her seat, stunned as poet followed poet. By the sixth poet she was exhausted. They had drained her of hope, she decided, and with a wistful look at David she hoped he sensed her lack of pleasure in hearing those tormented souls invade the stage. David looked at her and caught her hopelessness. Without a word, he pulled out his wallet, waved for the waiter and paid for their dinner. When the waiter returned with his receipt, David stood up and helped Sionna to her feet.

"Are you ready?" she asked.

"If you would rather stay through the program," David teased.

"Oh, no. I'm ready," she laughed, and they hastily found their way out of the dark dining hall. The moment they were outside, Sionna laughed in disbelief.

"That was unbelievable. Who told you about this place?" Sionna asked in amazement as David opened the car door for her.

"A guy on my job. He said it was great. So either he's nuts or we just caught a strange night," David said as he laughed, starting the car.

"Strange indeed. I was ready to slit my wrist and get it over with." Sionna laughed and then she paused, instantly recalling that Joey had committed suicide. Suddenly it was no longer funny. Suddenly she realized those poets may at any time feel just as lost and hopeless as Joey had. And she felt sorry for them.

"Yeah," David agreed, although he too thought of Joey at her words. Again they fell silent and David wondered when they would be able to talk normally without Joey's memory invading their affair. He sighed and Sionna glanced at him.

"Tired?" she asked.

"No. Are you?" David asked, glancing her way to consider her. Sionna shrugged. She wasn't tired at all. In fact, she felt energized enough to go dancing.

"Not at all," Sionna responded.

"So where to, then?" David asked, giving her the option on how they would finish the night.

"Dancing," Sionna stated. David laughed and shook his head.

"Oh, no. You're not getting me in a club. I can't dance and I'm in no mood to look the fool," he said.

"Everyone can dance," Sionna insisted, refusing to accept his lame excuse to avoid dancing.

"Yeah, right. Have you been out lately? You have some young kids who can burn, but that's it. Most people on the dance floor do not know what they're doing. I am not going to be added to the list."

"Fine. Suit yourself," Sionna said with obvious disappointment.

"I know something you may appreciate," David said after a few minutes passed between them. Sionna perked up, curious.

"And that is?" Sionna probed.

"The Potomac. It's a beautiful view from Alexandria and I know the perfect spot. How does that sound?" he asked, pleased with himself at the idea.

"Sounds romantic," Sionna murmured, sitting back more snugly in her seat as she considered him.

"It is, but I promise I'm not up to anything. I am just having a wonderful time with you and I'm not ready to end the night yet. Besides, it's one of my favorite places and I want to share it with you," he added carefully.

Sionna laughed, then sat up straight and gave him a rueful grin. "You are a smooth one, aren't you David? You say the right things, behave the right way. I'm going to have to really keep my eye on you."

"And beautiful eyes they are," David murmured in a husky voice, glancing at her after he stopped at the red light.

Sionna flushed, caught off guard by his words and the sudden change in his voice. "Thank you," she finally breathed. She shifted in her seat and looked out the window.

"Be right back," David said as he pulled into the parking lot of a liquor store. Sionna nodded and waited patiently as he left her in the car. Watching him disappear into the store, she felt cozy and warm all over. He was wonderful. She didn't want to think about how quickly she was falling, and she knew she was falling for him.

She didn't want to consider what people would think about her relationship with her husband's old college friend. And she certainly didn't want to consider what Joey would think. He was, after all, the reason she was sitting beside David tonight. If Joey had not been so adamant in his belief that David had ruined his career, Sionna would never have sought him out to rip a sorrowful confession from him.

It was odd how fate had turned out. She had done a complete circle from hating and despising David to finding herself falling head over heels in love with him. She paused, wide-eyed at the thought that she could be loving David. As she watched him exit the liquor store, she realized that if she weren't careful, he would have her heart. She wasn't prepared for that, for the guilt it would bring her to know she loved the very man her husband once confessed to hating.

Their moments together were stolen from the beginning. She couldn't allow herself to become dependent on David. She would give her time, her laughter, possibly even make love to him, but she was determined not to lose her heart over him. The moments they were sharing weren't meant to last forever, she firmly decided, although as she watched him return to the car, instinctively she knew she could give him her heart.

Feeling a high from being in his presence, and a low from knowing she could never be free of the guilt Joey's memory placed upon her, Sionna sighed as he started the engine. She would just forget about Joey for the moment. She was going to enjoy the moment with David and worry about her conscience another time.

"I hope you like Alizé. I thought we could have a drink at the waterfront," David suggested as he pulled out of the parking lot.

"Sounds like a wonderful idea to me," Sionna agreed, feeling almost giddy at her decision to be free of guilt.

David glanced at her, the lightness in her voice catching his ear. She was very beautiful, he thought. And unlike Jaunice, Sionna was genuine, funny and pleasant. He wasn't always being prepped for how to act, what to say, how to make love. He glanced again at Sionna, sensing that she would be a passionate lover. Realizing he was being presumptuous in considering her lovemaking abilities, he focused on his destination, although a hint of a smile curved his full mouth.

He wanted to make love to Sionna, that he couldn't deny. But he wanted to be sure she was making love to him and not the memory of Joey. He was not going to pretend his time with Sionna was not directly a result of Joey. And Joey's memory was very much a part of who Sionna was. It was a disappointing realization, but he had to accept that fact.

David frowned, thinking that even more unpleasant than Joey's memory was what he had done. His lies to Sionna and how he had used everyone around him. And when his back was against the wall, instead of being a man and confronting Sionna with his predicament, he had lied to the woman and made her feel a warped sense of guilt at his disillusionment.

David fought with himself on what to tell Sionna. He could show her the memo from Joey's old boss or he could allow Sionna to continue to wonder what haunted her husband into committing suicide. Either way it would hurt Sionna.

"Wow, this is pretty," Sionna gushed as she stepped out of the car.

"I'm glad you can appreciate it," David said as he went to the trunk and pulled out a cooler. He set the cooler on the hood of the car. Sionna watched as he opened the cooler and pulled out two shot glasses and a bottle of water. He poured a little water into each glass, swished it around for a moment, then poured the water onto the ground.

Sionna asked, "Is that how you always clean your dishes?"

"The glasses are clean. I'm just giving them a quick rinse," David stated, giving her a hurt expression.

"Okay." Sionna conceded with a smile.

When he was done rinsing the glasses, he opened the Alizé and poured them both a glassful. Sionna accepted her glass with a teasing, "Are you hoping to get me drunk, Mr. Young?"

"Absolutely," David confessed just as teasingly.

"Then I will stay on my guard. Besides, isn't this illegal, drinking in public?" Sionna queried.

"Absolutely," David laughed, then purposely downed his entire drink. Sionna grinned although she didn't follow suit. She sipped from her cool drink, enjoying the mellow atmosphere of the waterfront.

"I've never really been to the waterfront. I've driven by many times," Sionna confessed.

"This is the unpopular side. In fact, I don't think this is an official waterfront spot. If it weren't so dark I would walk you down the path to a small beach I discovered."

"It sounds really nice," Sionna murmured as she moved away from the car.

"Do you want to walk a bit?" David asked.

"No, this is just fine," Sionna answered, looking back at him. As she glanced at him, she caught the expression in his eyes. She caught her breath. His gaze was so magnetic and full of admiration that she felt warm all over. Feeling awkward, she turned away from him, a hidden smile tugging her mouth, pleased with his obvious attraction to her.

She took a deep breath, rejoicing in the calm of the night even as she felt the first taps of raindrops. She could hear the cars speeding by just over their heads on the Wilson Bridge. There were hundreds of twinkling lights that lit up the houses and the waterfront as far as the eye could see, and in the darkness, they were like little playful dancers.

The water sparkled from lights and the half moonlight. Sionna was turning to tell David how wonderful it was when she realized he had come to stand right behind her. She caught her breath and stared into his eyes. He stared down at her, and before he could stop himself their lips caught in a tender, searching kiss.

As Sionna returned his kiss David grew bolder and wrapped his arms about her. He pulled her to him as his kiss explored the sweetness of her mouth. Sionna tingled all over. Her body was a buzz of excitement as he pressed her even closer to him. The raindrops came faster and harder, matching their growing passion for one another.

Sionna gasped for air even as she was melting inside with pleasure, falling like a feather into his charms. She didn't want to fight it, to resist her feelings. She only wanted him to go on kissing her, filling her with his passion.

"Do you want me to stop?" David asked, feeling his desire grow and wanting to find control before passion took possession of him.

"No," Sionna whispered, staring boldly into his eyes.

Unable to resist her soft brown gaze, David threw caution

to the wind and without hesitation lifted her off her feet and carried her back to the car, both of their drinks going unnoticed as the glasses fell to the ground. She snuggled against his broad shoulder as he bent over, still holding her, and opened the back door of the car. He laid her on the seat and immediately his mouth found hers. And, as if they had not paused, his kiss picked up where it had left off.

He hadn't planned to make love to Sionna, at least not yet. He wanted to tell her about Joey, to clear the air between them, but her big eyes beguiled him and he was left with only one thought: to possess her.

His kiss quickly became an exploration as his tongue tasted the sweetness of her flesh. He explored her chin, her sleek neck, her collarbone, and Sionna could barely stay still. His left hand found its way under her sweater and Sionna shivered when he cupped her breasts and began to fondle her nipples until they hardened with desire.

She was reeling with desire and began to breathe heavily. Her uncontrolled breathing excited David. He wanted her, but reason stopped him, bringing him to his senses. He didn't want to make love to her like this. It was wild and passionate, but it wasn't right. Groaning because it took every ounce of control he had, he removed himself from Sionna. Her eyes were still closed in anticipation of his next move. Watching her so willing beneath him, it took all of his energy not to remove her jeans and make love to her.

When he didn't continue caressing her, Sionna's eyes opened in surprise. They were dark with unfulfilled passion. He was staring down at her and she was baffled. What was wrong? With an expression that Sionna couldn't fathom, he backed out of the car.

"David?" Sionna murmured, getting out of the car to follow him. By now it was raining hard. David didn't seem to notice the rain. Grabbing her purse off the front seat, she tried to shield her head as she followed him. He was standing in front of the car, staring out over the river. He turned around and considered her with a gentle smile.

"Yeah?"

"I hope . . . I hope you realize this is not normally how I behave with men," Sionna said hesitantly.

David's expression was thoughtful. He walked to her. Placing his hand under her chin, he searched her face slowly, taking in her confused gaze with a hint of amusement.

"I know you don't," he said with confidence.

Sionna had braved his searching gaze, not wanting to lower her gaze in a coyness that didn't come naturally to her.

"I don't normally make love to beautiful women in the back of my car, either. I owe you an apology," he added in a suddenly disgruntled voice.

"Why?"

"You and me. I wanted to take it slow, give you a chance to be comfortable with me. I know Jaunice is or was an issue, and then there is Joey. I just . . . well I didn't intend for things to happen so fast. You're a beautiful woman, Sionna," David added, considering her with another passion-filled glance.

"David," Sionna said in a reassuring voice. She reached up to gently stroke his cheek. "I'm a big girl and fully aware of what I'm doing. And I didn't even finish my drink, thank you," she added with a sheepish grin. "I wanted you to make love to me and I guess I didn't care where. Don't feel bad if we don't make it—"

"That's not what I was getting at," David rushed in.

"I understand that, but I repeat, if we don't make it, remember that I chose every moment with you. And so far, I've enjoyed them all," she added sweetly.

"You sound as if you never plan to see me again," David muttered, a little confused. Her words were those of a woman saying good-bye. He was determined that this evening was not going to be a one-night affair. He was too attracted to her beyond the usual physical needs. She had a kindred spirit and he had to at least explore the possibilities of their connection. He wasn't going to let her kick him to the curb so easily.

Sionna laughed, shaking her head. "No, oh, no. That is not it at all. I just don't want you to feel an obligation to me as if I'm a kid. I knew full well what I was doing and I was comfortable with it. It's up to you. I . . . I like you a lot," Sionna added, hesitating only for a moment.

She didn't want to come on too strong for him. After all, he was right. The woman he claimed to love just a few short months ago was still, like it or not, in his life, even if he was trying to get her to see otherwise. She was preparing herself for the realities of life.

He owed her nothing but she would love to have him.

David was relieved. A little confused, but relieved. He glanced around them and contemplated his next move. Sionna's purse had done little or no good in keeping her safe from the rain. And he was soaking wet as well.

"I better get you home," he observed.

Sionna shrugged. She hadn't felt so free in months and she had David to thank for that. She was enjoying his company, his lovemaking, his honesty. She was enjoying the romantic tension that the rain encouraged between them. She couldn't ask for a better setting.

Packing up his cooler, he found the glasses and put them in the bag with the remaining Alizé, then helped Sionna into her seat. She couldn't resist a peek into the back seat, and she grinned. If someone had walked by, they would have looked completely foolish. Ah, but he was a wonderful kisser.

Twenty-two

"What's tomorrow like for you?" David asked as they pulled into Sionna's driveway. She pursed her lips and tilted her head to the side before answering.

"Let's see. I'm back on leave. It's Mr. Eikton's opinion that I'm still too distracted to do a good job. Oh, my twin baby sisters are due in town. That's all," Sionna reported.

David cut off the car and gazed at Sionna. She was adorable. Her spunky personality, her habit of pursing her lips as if she were ready to be kissed, it all drew him to her. He didn't want to leave. Impulsively he reached for Sionna and kissed her. She returned his kiss and relished every moment of it. When he finally released her, she smiled up at him.

"May I come in?" David asked, his voice so polite Sionna laughed.

"Come in?" she asked, mocking him.

"Yes," David confirmed, knowing she was teasing him.

Sionna grinned. She took his hands and stroked them for a moment, then planted a kiss in both of his palms before saying, "Absolutely."

David smiled, knowing she was imitating him.

They entered the house, each very aware of the other and what was to come. Sionna locked the door, then watched David. He shuffled his feet, seemed a little uncertain, then walked into her family room and paused.

She knew he was waiting for her. She wouldn't disappoint him. She wanted him and she knew he wanted her. This time the setting was appropriate and she wasn't worried about the consequences.

She started toward him, prepared to pull him into her arms this time, when the vision of Joey's chair caused her to halt. David saw her hesitation and followed her gaze.

She was staring at a suede blue chair and he recalled she had said it was Joey's favorite chair. He was disappointed by her reaction but not surprised. Joey was a memory to be reckoned with, of that he had no doubts.

"Are you all right?" David finally asked. He approached her and turned her face until she was looking at him. He wanted to ease her mind. Unfortunately, he realized that everything surrounding her would always bring Joey to mind. It was more than just the chair, he decided, but the entire house and there was nothing he would be able to do about it.

"Can you do me a favor?" Sionna asked.

"Whatever you need," David responded.

"Throw that chair out, please," Sionna pleaded, nodding her head toward it.

"No problem," David said and immediately picked it up and walked to the front door.

Sionna opened the door for him, stepping aside to give him room to exit. A moment later he was setting the chair beside her garbage cans. Sionna was relieved, not realizing just how much of a burden that chair had created in her life. It was the strongest memory and association she had of Joey, and it was time to let it go.

When David returned, she whispered, "Thank you."

"My pleasure," David commented.

He meant it. Anything to ease her mind, especially from thoughts of Joey. Joey. He sighed softly, feeling it was time he informed her about Joey. He needed to tell her what he knew not only for his own peace of mind, but hers as well. It was why she came to him in the beginning. He was sure of that, even if she would never confess it.

"I've been wanting to do that for quite a while," Sionna murmured. She wrapped her arms about herself as if she were cold.

David hesitated at the door. Watching her, he grew concerned that maybe she would prefer some privacy. "Maybe I should go. You seem a little tired," he suggested, although everything in him wanted to stay and hold her and comfort her.

Sionna emphatically rejected his suggestion. She escorted him inside and closed the door.

"Absolutely not. I'm fine. A little chilled from the rain, and I'm sure you are, too. Can you start the fireplace while I get us some dry clothes?" she asked so definitively that David couldn't see himself turning her down. Not that he wanted to.

Sionna raced upstairs. She was barely in her room before she began discarding her wet sweater and jeans and replacing them with an oversized T-shirt and terry cloth floor-length robe. She pulled her hair back in a ponytail and washed her face. Feeling a little better, she went into Joey's remaining clothes and found a shirt and shorts for David. She then got Joey's robe out of the back of the closet and hurried back downstairs.

When she arrived, David was on one knee prepping the fireplace. His cloths were clinging to him in a miserable way, but he didn't seem to notice. Hearing her arrive, he glanced behind him. He paused from stoking the fireplace and considered her green robe and warm plaid slippers with an appreciative grin. Sionna noted his amusement and showed him with bravado the robe she brought for him.

"Don't laugh. If I recall correctly, you got a little soaked yourself. So here you are, a robe, a dry shirt and a pair of comfy shorts. The bathroom is down the hall," Sionna said, dropping the clothing over his shoulder.

"They all look a little small," David commented dryly, holding up the shorts for emphasis.

"Don't brag. Go get dry," Sionna scolded him. As he walked away, she headed for the kitchen. "Do you prefer coffee or tea?" she called out to him.

"Brandy," David called back before he closed the bathroom door.

"Brandy? I don't have any brandy," Sionna muttered, looking about the kitchen as if she were lost. Giving up, she prepared her coffeemaker.

As the coffee began to brew, Sionna for a moment became lost in time, thinking how if nothing else in the end, she and Joey at least still enjoyed a cup of coffee together. She recalled how in those few short months they were married, Joey had changed from an attentive, loving man to an irritable, disagreeable grouch who complained or brooded incessantly. She couldn't do anything for him no matter how hard she tried. He just didn't want to be bothered with her. In hindsight she resented how guilty he made her feel. It was as if she had cost him his job. He had no pleasure other than his moments in the darkness of their living room. She was going to completely remake that room with bright, cheerful colors that represented life and love.

She pulled two mugs out of the cabinet with a heavy sigh. It was as if she had never really known Joey at all. She had to admit, though, that they had met and married fairly quickly. Their love affair lasted less than a year. And in that time, she grew up. She at least had Joey to thank for that.

"The shorts aren't that bad, I guess," David commented, walking back into the family room.

Sionna playfully rolled her eyes at him and laughed. "Oh, good. Then you can turn on the stereo in comfort."

"Sure." He glanced around him for the stereo system. He spotted it in the living room, hidden between the television set and VCR in the entertainment center. He opened the glass door, found the remote control and turned it on. Instantaneously he jumped.

"Man!" he called, surprised by the sudden blare of loud music.

Sionna burst into laughter, barely able to speak at the look he gave her. "I'm so sorry," she said. "One of my favorite songs was on earlier and I just forgot how loud I had it. I'm sorry," she said again, although she couldn't stop laughing.

David narrowed his eyes at her laughter, but found himself laughing as well. He must have looked pretty funny, he realized as he turned the volume down and changed the station. When he was comfortable with his music selection he went back into the family room and sat on the floor, his back leaning against the sofa.

Sionna regained her composure and quickly poured them both a cup of coffee. After adding her favorite flavored cream, she joined David. She considered his position on the floor, a bit taken aback. He wasn't wet anymore, so he could have sat on the sofa, but he did look comfortable. With a shrug, she sat beside him on the floor and handed him his coffee.

"This smells great. What do you have in this?" David asked, taking a deep whiff of the pleasant aroma.

"It's gourmet coffee and French vanilla cream. My favorite," she added, pleased that he had noticed.

He took a sip and nodded his approval. "It's good. Perfect. As if you already knew me," he added. The look he gave her left Sionna flushing. She stared into the fire, not wanting to drown in his magnetic gaze. David considered her with a slight frown, then took another sip of his coffee. She looked so vulnerable staring away from him and he found himself wishing he didn't know anything about Joey. Again he considered how he was going to tell her about Joey. She deserved to know.

He was choosing how he should begin when Sionna released a small laugh. He looked up and asked, "Now how I am amusing you?"

"It's not you. I just realized how crazy I must seem to you," Sionna murmured.

"How so?"

"I came to you like a nut, prepared to wring a confession from you. Then, well, it was just completely crazy," Sionna confessed. She gave him a sheepish look and David thought she was even more adorable.

"I was always curious about that. I never believed that line about investigating Buerhler, although when you came back with the Greg Hillman case I started thinking maybe it was real," David said.

"Oh, it was. It just happened after the fact rather than originally," Sionna exclaimed.

"I don't understand," David said.

"I wanted to meet you, to find out who you were. Joey said a lot about you before he died and frankly, David, none of it was very good," Sionna confessed, amazing herself as she spoke. She had no intention of ever explaining the truth to him, but she felt compelled to make him understand.

David frowned, surprised by her confession. Joey didn't have good things to say about him? Then why would she want to meet him?

"Why not? What *bad* things could he say about me?" David asked with a light laugh, although his question was very serious.

Sionna set her coffee on the coffee table and then considered David carefully. She was debating just how much to tell him, and seeing the bafflement in his face she decided to tell him very little.

"He thought you took his job. That was all. He was upset about it, but I think now he was probably confused."

"Very!" David huffed, annoyed to find out that Joey had bad-mouthed him. For crying out loud, he hadn't even seen Joey since Joey left New York. That was years before the

Buerhler merger. "Joey's job was to bid. You know that, don't you?" he asked, looking at her firmly.

"Yes. But I also thought that was your job until I met you. That was why I came to your office. To find out if what Joey said was true. But the moment you began explaining your job, I knew I made a mistake and wished I had never come to your job," Sionna said.

"Hmm, I'm glad you did," David said, recalling their first meeting with a light smile, his frustration over Joey's description of him gone.

He wanted to say more but he knew it was too soon. Then he would look crazy. How could he say to her that he felt completely connected to her. That even Jaunice, whom he had been crazy about, had never made him feel so completely satisfied? It was too soon and that was that.

Sionna held back a winsome sigh. She wanted to explain herself further, but decided against it. She wanted to make him understand that she wasn't fickle and prone to go from one extreme to another, the way she had the first few times they met. Her common sense told her to leave the matter alone. A man didn't want to hear a bunch of sob stories and excuses, at least not on a first date. So she switched gears.

"Maybe I shouldn't ask, but I'm curious. How did you and Jaunice ever get together?"

David laughed and Sionna felt compelled to explain her question.

"Seriously. From the calls, she seems very high-strung. And look at you," she added with a wide grin. "You're relaxed, at ease. I can't imagine you behaving like her or finding her, oh, I don't know, compatible?" Sionna finished, feeling a bit awkward beneath his mirthful gaze.

David scooted into a more comfortable position and considered Sionna, trying to decide how best to answer her.

"You don't have to answer that. Actually we can talk

about something else," Sionna suggested, believing his hesitation to be discomfort at talking about Jaunice.

"No, it's a good question. I was trying to remember how Jaunice and I hooked up. I think it was a chance meeting. One of the building grand openings. She was a guest of a friend of a friend or something like that. She loved the building design and I happened to be the designer. Her friend introduced us and next thing I knew I thought I was in love."

"And now?" Sionna couldn't help but ask. David shrugged, finding his next answer far easier.

"I'm free," he declared.

"Free?" Sionna probed, not understanding him.

"Yes. You have no idea how it feels to want someone so bad and know that the feeling isn't mutual. That was me and Jaunice. I think she was just thrilled off how much I wanted her and I was infatuated with her seeming lack of interest."

"She played you," Sionna murmured in a matter-of-fact voice.

"You're right," David agreed. He set his coffee on the end table. Leaning his arm onto the sofa, he stared deep into Sionna's eyes. "I think I was always aware of the game. But my pride, my ego, got in the way. And instead of winning her over, I made a fool of myself. I think I didn't know what love was any more than Jaunice did. I wanted her bad, but she never touched me, you know. She never moved my spirit. If anything, she exasperated my patience."

"You're saying you never loved her?" Sionna asked.

David released a chuckle and shook his head. "I wouldn't lie and say I never loved her. I think I was never really, truly in love with her. I think I needed her."

"Why?" Sionna was curious.

"I don't know. But when she broke up with me, I felt a certain relief that I hadn't expected to feel. But I was also hurt."

"You were hurt that it was over, but relieved to be free of the pain," Sionna suggested.

"You may be right."

"I was definitely in love with Joey," Sionna murmured after a few moments of silence passed between them.

"A once-in-a-lifetime love," David commented. Sionna nodded her head in agreement.

"Almost. I think the worst thing is that I never really knew him."

"You married him," David said gently.

"Yes, I did," Sionna agreed, "but we only knew each other two months before he proposed impulsively one night and I said yes just as impulsively. He was so handsome and cool and suave. I liked him and I guess I trusted him."

David sat up straight, surprised by her confession. Two months. And how long were they married? If he recalled correctly it was only for a few months as well. No wonder, he thought, enlightened. Joey had played Sionna as well. Here she was thinking Joey had lived and died a perfect angel, a man who succumbed to grief caused by other people's interference, when in fact Joey had been a sorry architect and a thief, and had used poor judgment. David's only question was how Joey had managed to fool Sionna about his character right up to his death.

"I guess true love has no time boundaries," David finally said philosophically.

"Yeah," Sionna muttered.

"So you went to work and got kicked out," David commented. Again there was a brief pause in their conversation. Sionna laughed and David smiled, loving her easy laughter. She had no false attitudes or haughty comments that kept him on the defensive. He could easily fall in love with her, he thought. Realizing where his mind was headed, he shook his head to clear it.

Sionna didn't notice as she began to explain about her

job. "Mr. Eikton felt I was not ready to get back to work. Do you want to know why?" Sionna probed.

"I'm dying of curiosity," David responded.

"Your company settled. No story, I said to Mr. Eikton. He said that's because I wasn't into my job and needed more time to recoup. So you see," Sionna continued in a triumphant voice, "I wasn't kicked out, I was lovingly told to rest. And this time, I intend to."

"So you're going to do what now that you have no story? Lie around all day?" David inquired, leaning forward and staring at her with an amused smile.

"No," she insisted. "I'm going to enjoy the day. Visit a few museums. Oh, my sisters are coming tomorrow and I'll get to spend a few days with them."

"Sisters?"

"I have baby sisters who are twins. They are nineteen and my mother felt it was time I had a little company," Sionna explained.

"I take it she doesn't know you're dating," David inquired.

"I didn't think to tell her," Sionna answered, realizing that she hadn't mentioned David in any sense to her mother or family at all. She wondered what the twins would think. One thing was for sure, she wasn't going to inform them of Joey's accusations. They would think she was crazy.

"I'm just teasing," David said, sitting away from her. "Why would you tell her about a guy you just met. Of course, unless you were madly in love with me at first sight," he added, his playful tone mixed with a curious glance at Sionna. She looked intently at him.

"I didn't embarrass you, did I?" he asked at her silence.

"Why would I be embarrassed?" Sionna asked in reply.

"From the truth," David suggested, leaning forward. Sionna didn't move nor did she lower her eyes. Without a word she boldly invited him to kiss her. David sensed it but didn't respond, preferring to bide his time. Instead of kissing her, he sat back against the sofa and took another sip from his coffee, his eyes resting on her in thoughtful consideration.

Sionna smirked at him, tilting her head to the side as she returned his scrutiny. She knew he was determining the best approach and she found it funny. He didn't know her if he thought she was going to wait for him to make the first move. Feeling giddy with the knowledge that he wanted her just as much as she wanted him, she leaned forward and found his mouth.

David was a little surprised, but responded enthusiastically. He gingerly set the coffee aside and pulled Sionna into his arms. Their kiss deepened. It was an exploring kiss, as if each wanted to know each other's deepest secrets.

As he kissed Sionna, he realized his kiss was more than just passion. Their kissing was a discovery. David groaned, consumed with the soft feel of Sionna in his arm.

As his mouth explored hers, she gasped and tossed her head back in ecstasy. His mouth fit to her skin like satin as it trailed a blaze of fiery pelts over her tender flesh. His grip held her as though he were afraid to lose her. It was firm and possessive, and Sionna reveled in his strength, excited by his growing desire.

He wanted her and nothing else mattered, not for him, not for her. She leaned back and pulled off her robe. He helped her, kissing her neck as he did so. Sionna rose and pulled her T-shirt over her head, exposing her bare breast to his passion-filled gaze. David paused for a moment, his eyes drinking in the vision of her perfectly full breasts before he put his hands to her face and ravished her mouth once more. Sionna's hands held onto his arms as his mouth tasted every part of hers, the corners, her lower lip, her upper lip. Then he nipped her chin before running his tongue over her jawline up to her earlobes. He nibbled on her ears, tasting the sweetness of her flesh as his hands stroked her soft skin. Sionna gripped his back, holding on as he laid her back against the floor and gently removed her shorts.

She was trembling, unable to hold back her excitement as his hands stroked every part of her body. His fingertips lightly caressed her smooth shoulders, the gentle protruding of her collarbone. They circled her breasts before tenderly pinching her hard nipples, only to leave them bare as his hand stroked her abdomen and crept down to the small mound of hair that secreted her most precious treasure.

Sionna gasped as his hand gently parted her thighs, and a moment later he touched her, rubbing her gently until she was moist and warm with desire. She grabbed his hand, afraid she would have an orgasm before he could enter her. David understood her silent gesture and traced his hand back up to her abdomen, then found her breast again. This time his mouth joined his hand and suckled her breast until she sighed his name in pleasure. As if by a will of their own, her hips moved slowly side to side, enticing David to mount her. He didn't hesitate as he easily stripped and gently straddled her.

"Sionna," he murmured, giving her a chance to reject him. With eyes glazed with desire, she peered at him, a half smile greeting him.

"Make love to me, David," she murmured, and a moment later with the condom firmly in place, she felt his manhood enter her ever so slightly.

She lifted her hips, encouraging him to fully enter her, but David was patient. Gently, he penetrated her, careful not to fill her even as her body urged him to do so. Sionna gasped, grabbed hold of his buttocks and pressed down, but David remained firm. Even as her reaction excited him, he continued to hold back, stroking just within the walls of her cushion until she was writhing with insatiable desire.

He continued to tease her, slowly entering her then retreating until she was brimming with ecstasy. Just when she thought she could not hold back, when her legs trembled ever so slightly and her body melted against his, he plunged deep into her, causing her to gasp. Her breathing became heavier.

She moved her body with his, encouraging him to take her fully. She held onto him, holding onto his back as if she thought she would fall. David groaned, moving deeper and harder with each movement of her hips. He reached under and squeezed her buttocks, then, supporting himself on his knees, he lifted her to him and held her against him as he shoved into her with growing force. Sionna held on, moving with him in the same fluid motion, following his lead without thought. He shifted his weight, turning around until her back was against the sofa, then he gently lifted her onto it. A moment later he swung her left leg over his shoulder and entered her again, moving deeper and more forcefully with every moment. Sionna sunk into the sofa, her hands gripping the arm of the sofa over her head as she lifted her hips in unison with his movements.

He was firm and filled her completely. He began to sweat and Sionna felt the soft petals fall to her abdomen, causing her to shiver with pleasure. Her reaction excited him, and David released a deep grunt as his body fell against hers in a spasm of ecstasy. Spent and exhausted, David rolled off Sionna and fell against the floor. Sionna laughed lightly and peered down at him. David looked at her and pulled her down with him. She squealed but didn't resist as he wrapped one arm over her and put his other arm over his forehead. He closed his eyes, a pleased smile curving his mouth as he fell into an exhausted sleep with Sionna beside him.

Twenty-three

Sionna awoke with a start. She stared down at David, feeling overwhelmed. When she first awoke and felt his body beside her, Joey's image instantly came to mind. Realizing it wasn't Joey was a relief. She didn't want it to be Joey. It was incredible that for the first time she had awoken without a deep craving to see Joey just one more time.

Carefully she came to her feet. David had pulled the pillows down from the sofa while she slept. He lay comfortably next to the sofa and was snoring lightly. Sionna walked to the kitchen, glanced at the clock and gasped in surprise. It was four A.M. After they had made love she had only meant to lay her head down for a moment. She couldn't believe they had slept for so long.

Shaking her head, she left the kitchen and walked lightly to the front door. As she always did in the middle of the night, she checked her locks. Feeling secure, she turned off the bathroom light, then hastened upstairs. She went into her bathroom and took a short shower. Feeling refreshed, she pulled on another T-shirt before opening the linen closet. She grabbed a blanket then took her pillows from the bed and headed back downstairs.

After a brief perusal of David lying in an exhausted sleep, she lay beside him again. Covering them with the blanket, she cuddled beside him. He rolled onto his side and pulled her closer to him until her body curved with his.

Sionna closed her eyes. She was curious to know if he

recalled where he was or who he was holding. As if he could read her thoughts, he planted a kiss on her forehead and whispered, "Good night, Sionna."

When Sionna awoke again, it was after seven. She immediately sensed that David had moved. Her eyes popped open. He had replaced the pillows on the sofa and was no longer beside her. She sat up, holding the blanket to her chest as she looked for him through sleepy eyes.

She heard the shower in the bathroom shut off and the door open and she looked up. David walked out of the bathroom, his body still wet as he pulled on his robe. He saw her watching him and paused. Incredible, he thought. She was just as beautiful in the morning as she was the night before. Sionna returned his appraisal, hoping she didn't look a mess but realizing it was too late to do anything about it.

"Did you sleep well?" she finally asked as David continued to stand watching her.

"Believe it or not, I did. I must have been exhausted," he commented, finally moving toward her.

"I'm sure," Sionna agreed with a mischievous smile. David caught her tone and grinned.

"I'm hungry. Would you like to go out for breakfast?" he asked, pulling on his pants. Sionna stood up, wrapping the blanket around her.

"No, I have food here. I can cook," Sionna declared.

"And I can help," David offered.

"All right. What will it be? Eggs, bacon? I can flip some pancakes."

"No pancakes. At least not for me."

"Too filling?" Sionna asked, putting the container with the pancake mix back into the cabinet.

"No, I'm just not feeling like pancakes," David said as he laughed.

Sionna gave him an odd look, then shrugged, saying, "Okay."

Together they bustled around her kitchen. David was as comfortable as if he were at home. As they sat at the table, Sionna brushed against David. His touch was like an electric shock and it fascinated her that she could feel so ignited by him. She sat down carefully, hoping he hadn't noticed her reaction to his touch. It was all too silly, reacting that way.

David did notice. He held back a grin, not wanting to embarrass her. "You have a nice house."

"Thank you," Sionna said.

"Who's the builder?" David inquired.

"I don't know. I moved in with Joey after we got married. We never really got around to buying a new home," Sionna responded.

"I see," David muttered, feeling foolish for asking. They had enjoyed a wonderful evening together, connected like a bee to honey, and made passionate love. Still, Joey managed to invade their space. Feeling a slight frustration over the ever-present memory of Joey. David wolfed down his food and got up from the table. Sionna looked up, concerned by his sudden movement.

"I've got to get to work," he said. He picked up his plate and took it to the kitchen. Sionna stood as well and followed in his direction even though she was not done eating. She didn't feel very hungry. What was wrong with him? she wondered as she scraped her leftover food into the trash.

David paused after cleaning his plate. He cocked his head to the side and considered her. How could he compete with Joey, a ghost of perfection. He could shoot Joey's character down, tell Sionna the truth about him. But he didn't want to win her that way and now was not the time to bring it up. He should have told her before he made love to her.

"Can I call you later?" he asked, a frown creasing his forehead until his eyebrows nearly touched.

Sionna stared at his frown and nearly laughed. Did he

expect her to say no? She actually did laugh and David's frown increased.

"David," she began. "Are you worried about last night? If you are, don't be. I would love for you to call again, to see you again," she said brazenly.

David's frown instantly disappeared and his stance relaxed. He pulled her to him, unable to resist holding her once more before he left.

"I was a little concerned. You're not exactly shy," he chuckled. Sionna grinned sheepishly and, raising her eyebrows, asked, "Would it make you feel better if I were?"

"No. I like you the way you are," he said firmly, then planted a kiss squarely on her mouth.

"Good. I'm not good at changing," Sionna giggled.

"I'll call after lunch. I had better get going before I'm called into Mr. Pfeifer's office." With that, he hastened to the front door. After he opened the door, he paused, looked at Sionna and blew her a kiss.

She held that kiss all day.

After he left, she grabbed the pillows and blankets off the floor and began straightening up. She went upstairs and stared at the bed. As she put her pillows back on the bed, she wondered if she hadn't unconsciously avoided inviting David to her bedroom for the shame of tainting the memories she had of making love to Joey.

"Nah," she huffed. It was a coincidence and completely unintentional.

Joey was gone. He was a brief and beautiful moment in her life, but she could not and would not stop living because she lost him. As wonderful as Joey had been, David was . . . well he was special.

She wanted to get to know David. To understand his ways, his habits, his likes and dislikes. She wanted to peek into his mind and discover why he so often frowned. Was it just a habit or was he really engrossed in thought? Those were things she just needed to know. Call it curiosity, call it journalism, call it love. She laughed aloud, feeling rejuvenated just by thinking about David.

He had said she wasn't shy and he was right. She wasn't. She tried to be coy and sweet, and play the games that girls once played. She learned way back in high school that she was made of blunt blood and couldn't control herself. Her personality used to get her into trouble, both in school and at home. Her mother had said she needed a class on how to be feminine. But Sionna graciously declined, stating that the earth was full of variety for a reason. There were men out there who would find her unpretentious kisses appealing. And she was certain David was one of them.

She lay across her bed and stared up at the ceiling, a smile playing across her mouth as she replayed their evening together. She was just about to recall his first passionate kiss when the phone rang.

"Hello," Sionna answered hastily, half expecting it to be David even though he had just left.

"Sionna," a girlish voice called. "We're here."

"Terri?" Sionna asked, trying to guess which of the twins she was talking to.

"My own sister doesn't know me. It's Tracy," Tracy said.

"You deliberately disguised your voice. Otherwise I would have known it was you," Sionna accused her in a cheerful voice. Tracy laughed.

"We're at Union Station. You're on your way, right?" Tracy asked.

"I'm just jumping in the shower, then I'll be right there," Sionna answered.

"Where do you want us to wait? In the food court?"

"No. It's way too crowded down there. There's a bookstore, B. Dalton, on the main floor. Be there in about"— Sionna glanced at the clock—"forty five minutes. Okay?"

"We'll be there. See you."

Sionna raced through her shower. She wished the girls weren't so young. The eight years between them made it difficult for Sionna to feel comfortable telling them about her infatuation with David.

She dressed and left the house. She was running behind and knew that Tracy and Terri would give her the blues when she arrived. They were notorious for their uptight attitudes. She parked the car and raced for the escalators. It was crowded and she tried to politely get through the mounds of people without knocking anyone down. When she finally reached B. Dalton books, she knew the girls would be at the end of their tether. They were leaning against the wall, pouting with their arms crossed in front of them.

They were very much twins, from the way they stood to their twin bags they carried. Tracy was wearing a plaid shirt and jeans. Terri had on a jean dress with a white T-shirt beneath it. Tracy was slightly taller than Terri, but they were both tall, almost five nine. Their hair was cut close to their face in the Halle Berry cut that was the rave several years back. And they were pretty girls. Both had big dark brown eyes, full, pouty mouths and flawless skin.

They were adorable, Sionna thought, ignoring their obvious irritation at having to wait nearly a half hour longer than she had told them.

"Hey," Sionna called, coming up to them with arms wide open. The girls looked up in unison, both refusing to smile. Sionna took a step back, considering them with a crooked smile.

"What? I'm sorry, all right. I thought it would take a lot less time," Sionna explained, forcing the girls into a group hug.

"Sure. Sure," Terri huffed, pulling free. Tracy followed suit. Sionna sighed, remembering instantly how stubborn and easily upset the girls were.

"All right, then let's go. I can see how this visit is going to be," Sionna grumbled, then turned to head back up the escalators.

Terri and Tracy followed her. They were a stubborn pair, Sionna thought, but she refused to let them mope around her.

"How's Mom? I miss you guys. I wish you would get over being mad at me," Sionna said as they approached her car.

"Mom's fine. She's always worried about you, though," Terri answered, ignoring Tracy's angry glance.

"Oh," Sionna commented, unlocking the door.

"Yes. She didn't want you to marry Joey so quick anyway. And then you're up here all alone," Tracy finally spoke.

"Mom said that?" Sionna asked with a surprised glance at the girls as she drove out of the parking lot.

"She said you've always been too abrupt in your decisions. Or something like that. She told us to take our time and make sure that the man we love is level-headed," Terri said.

"You know, girls, right now I don't like you two very much," Sionna muttered, glancing at both of them with narrowed eyes.

"Sorry, it's what she said," Tracy insisted.

"I'm not abrupt or headstrong. I am honest with myself and I loved Joey. He was perfect for me," Sionna declared, now irritated with the twins.

"Mom said he was great, Sionna," Terri said, wanting to console her sister. Sionna may seem to be strong and in control, but Terri always found Sionna to be sensitive and loving. She wasn't mad at Sionna anymore and was sorry that she and Tracy had even brought up anything their mother said.

"He was," Sionna confirmed, glancing at them with a bright smile. "And I miss him. I do. And if I had to do it again, I would."

"That's how I want to love a man. I want it to be romantic and beautiful like you and Joey were. To meet a guy and know that he is perfect for you. A well-lit match," Terri said in a dreamy voice.

Sionna and Tracy peeled with laughter. "Well-lit match?" Tracy asked.

"Planning to start a fire, Terri?" Sionna chimed in.

"All right, maybe that's not how I meant it. But I want to feel special. Like there is no other man out there for me. So confident in him that I could marry him without a moment's hesitation and without looking back. Like you did with Joey. You know. You knew him so well. You were one, right?" Tracy added.

Sionna nodded slowly, although hearing Tracy talk about Joey like that could have been better applied to David. She felt connected to David like that, not to Joey. She and Joey were a great love. She sincerely believed that. He was someone she had found exciting, but she was never truly connected to him. The moment there was a problem, just a few weeks after they were married, he shut down on her and kept his pain from her. No, it wasn't the great love the twins imagined, but Sionna was not going to spoil their idealistic opinion of her, either.

"Do you think you'll ever marry again?" Tracy asked as they pulled up to the house.

"I certainly hope so," Sionna answered. They got out of the car. Sionna opened the trunk and handed them their bags.

The girls paused and stared up at the house. It was a beautiful house, but the girls found it lacking the warmth of the South. In Georgia they lived in a three-bedroom house. It was a simple house with beds of roses and greenery meeting visitors from the moment they pulled up to the driveway. As for neighbors, there were only a few and they were hidden by the trees. Here, Sionna's neighbor was just a few steps away.

"Coming in?" Sionna asked, watching them from the doorway when they stood gawking at the house.

"Are you going to move?" Tracy asked, following Terri inside the house.

"I haven't decided. I like this house, you know," Sionna responded.

"It's kind of creepy knowing someone who died lived here," Terri muttered, setting her bag at the stairway.

"Dad died in Mom's house. You two still live there," Sionna reasoned. She went into the kitchen and prepared a pot of coffee.

"That was different," Tracy said, sitting at the table and staring out the window. There was a cute lake a few feet beyond Sionna's backyard but not a soul in sight. Terri released a loud yawn, then went to the bathroom.

Sionna ignored Terri and considered Tracy with a warm smile. "How so?" she asked.

"It was Dad," was Tracy's answer.

Sionna paused, sat in the chair next to Tracy and said, "I see."

"I'm just saying that it's different because Dad inherited that house. Living there is a tradition," Tracy tried to explain.

"I see," Sionna repeated. She patted Tracy on the shoulder, then went back into the kitchen and prepared a cup of coffee.

"I want some," Terri called, coming back to the family room. She switched on the television set and plopped onto the sofa.

"Since when do you drink coffee?" Sionna asked, although she got another cup for her sister.

"Since I enrolled in Syracuse," Terri declared. Sionna nearly dropped the mug and released a loud whistle.

"You didn't," Sionna laughed.

"We both did," Tracy chimed in. They were all laughing. Sionna was too proud.

"My baby sisters are going to college in New York. I am so impressed. Does Mom know? Because the way she explained it to me, you two are just looking at colleges." Sionna asked.

"Yeah, well we didn't want to tell her yet. We wanted her to think we were looking so she didn't feel, you know, slighted," Terri said carefully. Sionna nodded, understanding completely how the girls felt. Their mother had certain steps she felt everyone should take. She was structured and disciplined, and she felt everyone should be the same. Sionna was sympathetic to her sisters and didn't judge them at all.

"Well, hey, I understand and am just proud you are off to school. You go girls." She went to give them each a hug. She was giving Terri a bear hug, which caused Terri to complain in annoyance, when the phone rang.

"I'll get it," Tracy said and grabbed the line. "Hello."

"Sionna?" David asked, not recognizing her voice. He was staring out his office window and frowned at the phone as if it were a strange thing.

"Just a second," Tracy said.

"Who's that," Tracy whispered as she handed Sionna the phone.

"This is Sionna," Sionna said, taking the phone and walking a short distance from her sisters. They stood watching her, knowing instinctively it was a call she didn't want them to hear.

"Miss me yet?" David asked with a big smile the moment Sionna picked up the phone.

"Yes," Sionna answered. A grin she couldn't wipe away was plastered to her face.

"Then you'll have dinner with me tonight?"

"Oh, I would love to, but my sisters are here," Sionna answered, disappointed to have to turn him down.

"Is that who answered your phone?" David asked, hiding his disappointment with a question.

"Yes. That was Tracy. Hey, why don't you come by and I could introduce you to them," Sionna suggested. "That's of course if you have time."

"I'd love to meet them. About seven, all right? I can bring dinner with me," David agreed.

"Seven is great."

"Italian or Chinese?" David asked.

"Just a moment," Sionna whispered. "Would you prefer to have Italian for dinner or Chinese?" Sionna asked, turning to Terri and Tracy.

"Who's that?" Tracy asked again, not answering Sionna's question.

"Don't you worry about it. Now what do you prefer?" Sionna insisted.

The girls looked at each other, then together they chimed, "Italian."

"Italian is the winner," Sionna told David in a bright voice.

"I'll see you later," David confirmed, then hung up.

Sionna hit the off button on the phone and walked casually back to the kitchen. She felt Terri's and Tracy's eyes on her, but she ignored them, wanting to keep the feeling of David's voice for as long as she could.

"So who was that?" Tracy persisted.

"A friend," Sionna finally answered.

"A friend? So soon?" Terri demanded, her hands on her hips.

"Yes, a friend. And it isn't so soon. Besides, sometimes things just happen," Sionna responded carefully. She sat on the couch and within moments the girls sat beside her. Terri was on her left and Tracy was on her right.

"What things just happen?" Tracy whispered, dying of curiosity about her sister's obvious affair.

"Nothing," Sionna said, tight-lipped.

"Nothing, my foot. You're not in love again, are you?" Terri inquired, managing to sound shocked.

"What does he look like? Is he handsome? I bet he's handsome," Tracy murmured, enthused about the whole idea.

"He's probably a Joey look-alike," Terri said in a dry tone.

"I hope not. Say he isn't a look-alike, Sionna," Tracy pleaded.

"He's not a Joey look-alike," Sionna said.

"Then why are you with him?" Terri asked, trying to sound like an adult.

"I am not . . . we're just dating," Sionna stated, trying not to get too hyper with the girls. They were excitable, and if she weren't careful they would make her the same way.

"Dating?" Terri repeated, giving Sionna a dubious look.

"Dating," Sionna repeated firmly, then stood up. The girls looked at her then at each other. They knew she was holding back.

"Sure," Terri shrugged, turning in her seat to stare at the television.

"Right," Tracy muttered, disappointed not to get the full scoop. She crossed her arms and pouted.

"You two need a life. College is going to do wonders for you. Thank you for your curiosity," Sionna added with a grimace at both of them.

She sat at the table and picked up her coffee. Sipping it, she stared out the window. She was happy to have the twins but she wasn't sure if she was ready to explain her love life. How could she explain something she wasn't clear on? She liked David a lot. She had a very positive feeling about them. They had made love and it was beautiful. But she also knew that making love did not make a relationship.

She didn't want to do what she had done with Joey and put more into their relationship than she was ready for. After all, Joey had taught her that you never really know a person. That could work both ways. Fly headfirst into a relationship and worry about the consequences later, the way she did with Joey, or take it easy and let nature take its course. However she and David turned out, she was confident it would be right for both of them.

Twenty-four

Jaunice packed carefully. The party was at the end of the week. She needed to be prepared. She called that jerk Jim but suddenly he was tied up, busy. Right! She had to make that last-ditch effort. She never imagined that she could be so desperate. But suddenly she realized how much she actually wanted David. How much he meant to her. It was fun, yes, but somewhere along the line she had fallen in love with him. The least he could do was give her a chance.

Fighting back tears of frustration, she zipped her suitcase. The doorbell rang and she cursed. It rang again before she could get to it.

"I'm coming!" she yelled in irritation.

"What is the problem?" Patricia asked the moment Jaunice swung the door open.

"Uh! I'm so irritated. I can't do this. I'm not going to sit here and take that woman taking my man," Jaunice shouted, slamming the door as Patricia entered her apartment.

Patricia giggled, tickled by Jaunice's statement. "If I recall it correctly, he wasn't your man. At least not to you. Just a few months ago, I remember you laughing about how stupid he was and how tired you were of him. So what's this? Are you in love with him now?" Patricia teased as Jaunice went back into her bedroom.

"It isn't funny, Patricia. It isn't funny," Jaunice groaned, finally winding down from her tirade.

"I know, honey. But you did bring it on yourself. For crying out loud, the man wanted to marry you and all you could do was play games," Patricia pointed out to her.

"I was biding my time. I wasn't ready. I was confused. I thought I had more time. Who knew he was a bastard?" Jaunice seethed. She stamped her feet in frustration, then sat in a huff on the edge of the bed.

Patricia looked at Jaunice's defeated, slumped shoulders and took mercy on her. She sat beside Jaunice and gave her a short hug.

"It's all right, honey. You know I understand. I'm just giving you a hard time. You go down to Virginia and stake your claim. You're beautiful and remember, he loved you first. That girl ain't got a chance. Especially when he sees you in that red dress you bought for the party. You'll win him back. I'd bet my next paycheck on it," Patricia said as she comforted her.

"You think so, Pat?" Jaunice asked, giving Patricia a wretched look.

"Yeah, I do," Patricia reaffirmed.

"Then I had better get going. The last shuttle is at nine o'clock."

"That's why I'm here, to chauffeur you to the airport and to help you win back your man," Patricia said, coming to her feet and helping Jaunice with her bag.

"Let's go," Jaunice said, glancing around the loft to make sure she hadn't forgotten anything. Confident that she hadn't, she and Patricia went to the car.

"You're going to make me miss my flight," Jaunice complained, aggravated at the casual pace at which Patricia was driving.

"It's a shuttle. You can take the next flight," Patricia retorted, refusing to speed up.

"I don't want the next flight, Patricia, it'll be nine o'clock by then. I want this one," Jaunice huffed, frustrated again.

Patricia didn't appreciate Jaunice's desire to get back to

Virginia. For the past two years she had witnessed Jaunice play the fickle lover to David, cheat on him on a whim and treat him no better than a doormat. Now suddenly Patricia was supposed to believe that Jaunice was in love with the man. Patricia held back a smirk. It was hard for her to accept that in one visit, David had finally managed to cause Jaunice to fall head over heels in love with him. No, this was about competition and Jaunice's desire to win. Whatever was wrong with Jaunice, it certainly wasn't love. Infatuation, maybe. An unhealthy determination to win, yes. But Patricia could not believe it was true love. And even if it were, there was nothing she could do about traffic.

"Okay. The traffic is breaking up," Patricia said.

"About time," Jaunice hissed.

"Oh, as if it's all my fault," Patricia suggested in indignation.

"You were late getting to my apartment," Jaunice accused.

"You weren't ready!" Patricia rebuked.

"You drive like a turtle and I was ready," Jaunice continued.

"You could have taken a cab," Patricia snapped, giving Jaunice an irate glare.

"Oh, nice. Very nice. I'm going through major changes and all my best friend can do is argue with me. Very nice," Jaunice grumbled, crossing her arms in front of her chest. She glared at Patricia and narrowed her eyebrows so hard that they were almost one. "You are truly the epitome of that old saying, 'With a friend like you who needs an enemy.' "

"Now that was harsh," Patricia murmured, a little hurt by Jaunice's statement.

Jaunice considered Patricia's hurt look and grimaced. Patricia was right. It was a harsh thing to say. Grudgingly, she uncrossed her arms and, turning her attention to her window, whispered an apology.

"I'm confused right now, Patricia, and everything is annoying me. I'm sorry. You didn't deserve what I said. Friends?" Jaunice asked with an uncertain smile. Patricia gave her a sidelong dubious glance before shrugging and easily slipping back into a good mood.

"Friends. But you better be nice to me from now on," Patricia declared, then grinned. Jaunice didn't return Patricia's good humor. She remained silent the rest of the ride, heaving a huge sigh of relief when they finally arrived at the airport.

"Take it easy. Have a safe flight. Call me when you check in. Oh, and I'll make sure your designs get to the shop by Friday. Be safe," Patricia rambled quickly, following Jaunice to the gate. Jaunice was nodding. After she gave the attendant her ticket, received her stamp and heard the intercom call the passengers aboard to their seats, she turned around, gave Patricia a fierce squeeze and whispered, "Wish me luck."

"I will," Patricia murmured and waved as she watched her friend board the plane. She stood there until the attendants closed the door, then, with a worried frown, she left the airport never once believing that Jaunice would get David back. She had become a desperate woman and men did not find desperation attractive in women.

Twenty-five

David was feeling like an idiot. The more he thought about Sionna the more irresponsible he felt. He should have told her about Joey, especially after her confession about him, however bizarre that was. He had several chances last night to tell Sionna about Joey. He should have told her. But he held back. As he stared out his office window into the freeway, he became lost in the vehicles speeding by.

He thought of Sionna and Joey and the things she had said about him. It was obvious that Sionna had known very little about Joey when she married him. And Joey had apparently been very good at giving the impression that he was a saint. How he managed to pull the wool over someone like Sionna, who seemed to be a good judge of character, David couldn't fathom.

Nevertheless, he knew that eventually he would have to tell Sionna the truth. The sooner the better, he reasoned, although his company's annual party was just a few days away. Would she be comfortable coming out with him if she knew?

He doubted it.

He wanted to invite her, to walk into the room with her on his arm. And he wanted Sionna to be relaxed, at ease. Of course, he could just not go at all. He laughed aloud, knowing it would be questioned if he didn't show up.

"Charles is on the line for you," David heard Karen's

voice announce over the intercom. He glanced at his watch. He had a meeting at four o'clock and then he planned to swing by his house to change before he met with Sionna. He had better stop the daydreaming before time slipped by him.

"David?" Karen's voice called again.

"Let Charles know I'm en route," David said firmly, pressing the intercom button to respond.

"I have the designs from Kevin. Do you want them?" Karen asked.

"Umm, yes. I'll grab them," he added.

He closed the blinds to his window and pulled off his jacket. He was about to sit down at his desk when he recalled Karen's words. He needed the blueprints.

Karen looked up when David came out the door. He glanced over her desk, then at her, and he asked, "The designs?"

Karen calmly picked up the manila folder on the corner of her desk and handed it to him. David accepted it, turned to walk back into his office, then turned back to her.

"Thank you, Karen."

"Just doing my job, David," Karen said, giving him a cool look. David looked confused by her expression but then hastened back into his office. He closed his door, sat at his desk and began reviewing the designs. For just a moment he paused and wondered why Karen had looked at him so distantly. He had no idea what to think. It could just be one of those women things, he thought. Shaking his head, he shrugged and hastened over the information in front of him.

Sionna lay staring at the ceiling. She had long since grown tired of the girls and their chatter. Plus she was tired. She had excused herself to lie down for a nap. But she found she was unable to sleep. She was torn. Torn between guilt and pleasure, and she wasn't sure which was stronger. She hadn't delved deeply enough into Joey and David's relationship. She hadn't asked enough questions about why Joey was so angry with David. Now that she knew David, it seemed so illogical that Joey's accusations could have any truth to them. But she was also reasonable enough to know that she could very well be blinded by her attraction to David.

They needed to talk. To clear the air. If they were going to have any hope at all for the future she needed to be comfortable that he had absolutely no hand in Joey's suicide. She at least owed Joey that respect.

She sighed, turning on her side and staring at the clock. It was well into the afternoon. She wished she had never walked into David's office. With a rueful smile to herself, she knew that wasn't true. In fact, she wished she had walked into David's life before she had ever heard of Joey. Then things would be different. The guilt would be gone, the shame, the uncertainty.

Again she heaved a heavy sigh. Since David had entered her life in these past few weeks, she had found herself consumed with thoughts of him. Even Joey did not have that effect on her.

"I have to stop doing that," she muttered, turning her face into the pillow. She didn't want to keep comparing the two men. She wanted to separate them, to leave Joey in peace and meet David with a hope of the future.

Groaning in frustration, she squeezed her eyes shut, repeating the words sleep, sleep, sleep, until she thought she would go crazy.

"Ugh!" she grunted, sitting up and tossing the pillow across the room. Giving up on the hope of getting any sleep, she went back downstairs.

Terri and Tracy had made themselves comfortable in the family room. When they heard Sionna coming down the stairs, they glanced up at her with curious eyes.

"I thought you were so tired?" Terri asked, watching her older sister plop in the chair across from them.

"I am. I can't sleep. Are you watching cartoons?" Sionna asked in disbelief. The girls laughed and said yes in unison.

"I would think two young women such as yourselves would be watching the news or something. I have cable. Find an adult program," Sionna suggested.

"I know many adults who watch cartoons, Sionna. For instance, our Dad I seem to recall watched cartoons all the time," Tracy pointed out.

"What a poor excuse," Sionna blurted. "Fine, watch what you like," she added, coming to her feet and leaving the room.

"Where are you going?" they asked in unison.

"Back upstairs. You two gave me the sedation I needed to get some sleep. Wake me up at five thirty," Sionna added as she dragged her way back up the stairs. She walked into her bedroom, bent down and picked her pillow off the floor by the door then lay back down. This time, sleep came easily.

Twenty-six

David was growing more and more frustrated with Charles. The man was making their meeting unnecessarily long. David kept glancing at the clock. It was almost six o'clock and he hadn't had a chance to go home yet.

"Come on, Charles. What's wrong with these details?" David insisted, staring at the specifications that Charles kept harping on.

"See this curve. It's not logical. Why would a designer put a stairway in a circular set like this smack between the elevators. I not only do not like it, but I think it will cause structure issues. I'm surprised that you didn't pick it up in your review," Charles added doggedly.

Charles wasn't going to give in. If David didn't care about his job, Charles did. They had gone over seven designs submitted for this project and all of them had major flaws that Charles felt David should have noted.

"What is wrong David Young?" Charles questioned with an astounded gape at David.

"I thought it was unique," David muttered, looking at the designs in resentment.

He could have kicked himself. He was so focused on Sionna that he hadn't noticed the mistakes and downright idiotic ideas depicted in some of the designs. He was just thankful that he and Charles reviewed the concepts before he was to meet with Mr. Pfeifer. He wasn't usually that way either. Even when he was going through changes with

Jaunice, he never got so distracted from his work. If anything, his issues with Jaunice made him a more firm director.

"I think you better go through these designs again, David. When you're more focused, we can get back together," Charles suggested, his instincts telling him David was definitely not himself.

"You're right. Give me a few days. I can have some updates and suggestions by Monday morning."

"The buyer is looking for a concept by next Friday. Is that enough time?" Charles asked, concerned that it would be another week before they could lock down a concept.

"I'll make it enough time. Tomorrow and Friday I'll just work on the designs. And if necessary, I'll skip the party Saturday as well," David added, a little relieved at the idea of not having to attend.

Charles laughed heartily. Coming to his feet, he remarked, "Yeah, right. Miss the company party in your position and I'm just curious who'll get your office."

"It's not that serious," David mocked, stuffing the designs back into the folder.

"Maybe not for you. But I would come anyway. Stick your head in, say a few words of hello, and then you leave. If I were you, that's what I would do," Charles added, adjusting his jacket just before he opened the door.

"Uh-huh. I'll remember that," David replied. "Thanks for the advice," David added as he escorted Charles from his office.

When he settled back at his desk, he pondered Charles's comments. Charles was right. David had been completely unfocused. He could not stop thinking of Sionna. Maybe he was afraid it would be another Jaunice situation and she would turn out to be all wrong for him. He shook his head, knowing there were no similarities between the two women. No, he was enamored with Sionna. And making love to her had only made him even more infatuated. He grinned, swiveling around in his chair. He slammed his feet on the floor when his eyes landed on his window. It was dark outside! He glanced at his watch and could have wrung Charles's neck. It was nearly seven o'clock.

Running to the door, he opened it and saw that Karen was gone. Swearing beneath his breath, he grabbed the phone and called Sionna.

"Hello," her familiar voice answered, and David could feel his blood race.

"Sionna, it's David," he said a little breathlessly.

Sionna instantly smiled, loving the sound of his smooth voice. "Hello, David," she said. "What's going on?"

"I got a little sidetracked. Can I push our date back a little, to about eight thirty?" he asked.

Sionna shrugged. "Sure. I think the twins can wait until then to eat."

"Great. I'll see you then." He hung up and Sionna held the phone to her chest.

She would have let him make it ten o'clock. She didn't care. She just wanted to see him again. And she loved the fact that he so obviously wanted to see her again. The sound of laughter caught her attention and Sionna blinked.

"What's that? Is he listening to your heartbeat?" Tracy laughed, pointing at Sionna holding the phone against her bosom. Sionna flushed, hating that the twins had witnessed her dreamy behavior that was worse than acting like a teenager.

"All right, all right. So I'm busted," Sionna said as she laughed, setting the phone down. She leaned against the kitchen sink, considering her two sisters with a wavering smile.

"Is he still coming over?" Terri asked.

"Yes," Sionna answered.

"Are you in love?" Tracy demanded, her voice edged with excitement. Terri frowned at the thought, but Sionna laughed.

"I don't think so. But," Sionna added, giving them both a thoughtful look, "I really do like this guy a lot," she murmured. The twins moved closer. Terri sat up on the counter next to Sionna, and Tracy leaned against the refrigerator.

"Is he gorgeous? Like Joey was?" Tracy asked, her eyes wide with curiosity.

"More so, believe it or not," Sionna answered truthfully.

"Why do you like him so much?" Terri asked, fascinated that her sister was in love yet again.

"I'm not sure, to be honest. I just know that he's extremely nice . . . no, interesting. He flirts with me, which I love, then he's considerate and spontaneous."

"How long have you known him?" Terri asked, mentally calculating how long to the day Joey had been dead.

"I've known him for months. But I just met him a little over two weeks ago," Sionna answered.

"Two weeks!" Tracy blurted in disbelief. "All this 'he's so wonderful' in just two weeks. Even we know better than to fall for a guy after just meeting him."

Sionna shrugged, accepting Tracy's outburst as youthful inexperience.

"You slept with him, didn't you? That's why you're in love, admit it. My girlfriend's mom, she says a woman sleeps with a man, has an orgasm and thinks she's in love. The man just thinks he had a wonderful night," Terri commented dryly, giving her sister a disappointed look.

"I'm sure your friend's mom is experienced enough to know. However, whether I slept with David or not has nothing to do with how I feel," Sionna said, not liking Terri's statement.

"Yes it does. It's clear that you don't really know him. So sex has to have been involved," Terri insisted. Tracy stared from her twin sister to her big sister in wide-eyed fascination.

"Mom is going to hit the roof," Tracy gushed.

"No, she's not. Because you two are going to keep David

to yourself. At least until I'm ready to tell her about him. Understand?" Sionna demanded.

"Aha!" Terri blurted triumphantly. "You slept with him!"

"That is none of your business. Just be on your best behavior when he gets here," Sionna said firmly, although she was holding back a mischievous grin.

She wanted to blurt to the girls, "Of course I slept with him," but she knew that would be a bad influence on them. No matter how much they tried to hide it, she knew she made a huge impression on them and they were always competing against her. She didn't want them competing in the sex department, so she kept her most private moment to herself.

"He doesn't snore, does he?" Tracy whispered. Sionna rolled her eyes and left the twins in the kitchen, studiously ignoring their giggles as she began straightening up the house.

"Shouldn't he be here by now?" Terri asked, looking at her watch pointedly.

"What time is it?" Sionna called, vacuuming the living room.

"Almost nine," Terri complained, meeting her sister in the hall.

Sionna shut off the vacuum and frowned. She went to the window and stared out into the street. She didn't see any cars coming.

"Did the phone ring? I couldn't hear over the vacuum," Sionna said, walking into the kitchen to check the caller ID.

"No, the phone didn't ring. He isn't coming," Terri stated sharply. She was irritated and disappointed. As far as she was concerned, this guy was a jerk. Her sister had been through enough, losing her husband. She didn't need some jerk playing with her mind.

"He's coming," Sionna muttered.

She refused to accept that she had been stood up. And she refused to call him as well. He was coming, she thought, almost defiantly. She finished vacuuming, then hurried upstairs to change. She was pulling on a black casual dress when she heard the doorbell ring.

"Sionna!" Tracy called, refusing to open the door until Sionna came downstairs.

David grinned, his amused expression showing through the screen door. Sionna raced down the stairs, instantly apologetic when she saw that her sisters had not allowed David to come inside.

"What is wrong with you two?" Sionna scolded, pushing past them to allow David to enter. His hands were full, but his grin broadened as he took in the two girls' thorough examination of him.

"I am so sorry David, they're teenagers," Sionna explained as she helped him with his bags before guiding him toward the dining room.

"We're nineteen and I'm Terri," Terri said sternly, putting her hand out for David to shake as soon as his hands were free of the food.

"That's still a teenager, Terri," Sionna insisted.

"Hello, Terri," David said, giving her hand a thorough shake.

"And I'm Tracy. You must forgive Sionna for being so rude not to introduce us," Tracy added, giving her sister a knowing wink. Sionna's expression was stern as she glared at Tracy.

"Happy to meet you both," David said. They all stood around the table, then Sionna took a step back and clasped her hands.

"I'm sure the girls are hungry. I'm starved. Terri, Tracy, wash your hands then join us," Sionna said, guiding the girls toward the bathroom.

"My hands are clean," Terri insisted, narrowing her eyes at Sionna.

"Then wash them again," Sionna hissed.

"Wow, they are a handful," Sionna said, turning her attention back on David.

"I'm sure you're loving every minute of it. They are adorable," David commented. They stood looking at each other, both with a hint of a smile.

"It's not too late for you, is it? I apologize for making you wait so long," David added, finally pulling his gaze from her.

"The twins are cool and you know I'm not tripping. Here, let me get some plates," Sionna said as David began to take the food out of the bags. It was still hot and the aroma caught her senses with a pleasant kick.

"Where did you go?" Sionna asked as she reached into the cabinets and pulled down dishes.

"The Little Italian Shop," David answered, sitting at the table.

"I should have known. The food smells delicious."

"It sure does," Tracy chimed in as she came back to the table and sat beside David.

"So, did you wash your hands?" Terri demanded of David the moment she was at the table.

"As a matter of fact, I didn't," David said. Excusing himself, he went to the bathroom to wash his hands.

"He is gorgeous!" Tracy laughed the moment he was out of ear shot.

Sionna flushed, glancing at the bathroom door that David had left open as he washed his hands. She was certain he could hear them, so she didn't respond.

"He's late," Terri complained. Sionna considered her baby sister with a curious lift of her eyebrow.

"Is something wrong, Terri? You seem just a bit irritable," Sionna said in a sardonic voice. Terri looked offended but before she could answer, David returned.

"No," was her short reply. She sat at the table and waited for Sionna to finish setting the table. Tracy followed Terri's suit, a little confused by her sister's behavior. As they ate, she kept tossing curious glances at Terri, wondering what could be the problem.

"Are you girls enjoying your visit?" David asked. He was piling lasagna onto his plate and didn't notice the look on Terri's face. But Sionna noticed and gave her sister a swift kick under the table.

"Hey," Terri grumbled, glaring at Sionna.

"It's all right. But Sionna is supposed to be relaxing. Mom sent us up here to be slaves, I guess," Tracy answered.

"Of course, I am so neat I didn't need any help at all," Sionna gloated.

"And that's why we're leaving tomorrow," Terri added testily.

"That's not why, Terri. You two were coming for a quick visit en route to New York. That's what Mom said," Sionna said defensively.

"Yeah," Tracy agreed.

"Whatever you say," Terri moped.

"Sionna didn't say what you do? So, what do you do?" Tracy asked, choosing to ignore her sister's sour mood.

"I'm an architect," David answered.

"An architect? Like Joey was?" Terri demanded, giving Sionna a shocked look. Sionna's food caught in her mouth and she coughed, realizing she didn't think of the logical connection they would make to Joey's career.

"Yes. David actually works for the firm that bought On-Site, Joey's old company," Sionna explained.

"Really? Did you know Joey?" Tracy asked innocently.

David hesitated, glanced at Sionna, then nodded. "As a matter of fact, I did. We went to college together, and although I never actually ran into him at Buerhler, we worked together for a few weeks as well."

"How interesting," Terri commented, eyeing her sister with growing concern. Sionna was using David to get over Joey, Terri concluded. It made sense. He was an architect.

He was good-looking, like Joey. He was tall, like Joey, and he was pleasant, like Joey. It would be horrible if he turned out to be weak like Joey, too, Terri thought sadly.

"Have you ever been married before?" Tracy asked.

"No. I haven't crossed that threshold yet," David answered wryly.

"Why not? You're not that young," Tracy indicated.

David laughed and Sionna shrugged, giving David another apologetic glance.

"No, I'm not. But when I get married, it's going to be a very special woman and until a few weeks ago, I hadn't met anyone who fit the bill," David responded smoothly, easily forgetting his repeated proposals to Jaunice as his eyes fell on Sionna. Sionna flushed, feeling warm beneath his adoring gaze.

"A few weeks ago as in when you met my sister?" Tracy asked blandly. She seemed completely unaware of how inappropriate her question was. But she was curious and so was Terri. They both paused from eating to consider David as he answered.

"That's exactly right," David said without hesitation.

Again Sionna felt a warm flush and she wished she had not invited David over while the girls were there. They had the incredible ability to say any and all of the wrong things. It was embarrassing, but she was determined to brave it out to the end.

Terri and Tracy gaped at David, then looked at each other and burst into giggles. They silently agreed that David was an interesting character. From then on they treated him like a man who had received their stamp of approval.

When the girls finally tired, they dozed off to sleep on the sofa. Sionna and David still sat at the table and spoke softly.

"They're adorable girls," David murmured, looking from the twins to Sionna.

Sionna rolled her eyes heavenward before whispering a tart, "That's because you don't know them."

"They can't be that bad," David chuckled, leaning forward to take her hand. Sionna's heart thumped at the contact, but she kept talking, hoping to appear normal.

"They are. They have always been way too in tune to me," Sionna muttered, although the glance she gave the girls was filled with affection.

David noted her affection. Stroking her hands with the heel of his thumb in an almost hypnotic motion, he stated, "How can anyone not be in tune to you? You're a very sincere person. Not to mention adorable as well."

"I guess it runs in the family," Sionna responded with a flirtatious smile.

David paused, considering her with open admiration. She was a beautiful woman, the kind of woman he could believe in and love forever. He wondered how she felt about him. Could she love him, so soon after losing Joey? He wanted to believe she could. Holding a groan, he looked down at her hand and paused. He hadn't noticed it before, but it occurred to him that she was still wearing her wedding band. He released her hand and sat back in his seat.

Sionna felt suddenly bare without his touch. She held back a shiver and wondered why he had stopped. She was enjoying his touch. Staring into his eyes, she reached for his hand and asked, "Has anyone ever told you that you have the magic touch?"

She was flirting with him, giving him her sweetest smile. David felt chagrin at her comment. He was acting like a kid, being flat-out foolish. It was very likely that she simply never thought to put her wedding ring away. And who ever said a widow was expected to get rid of her ring? But he couldn't help not liking how obvious her attachment to Joey still was.

"Not lately," David finally responded, unable to hide his disappointment at the sight of the ring.

Sionna considered him and was about to ask what was

wrong with him when Tracy yawned and stretched. Sionna gave David an apologetic glance, then got up and went to the twins.

"Hey you two. Come on. Off to bed with you," Sionna said, gently nudging them awake.

"I should be going, too," David suggested once the girls were upstairs. Sionna glanced at him, a little disappointed by his suggestion. But with a brave smile she nodded.

"It is a little a late," she murmured, walking up to him until they were right in front of each other. David looked down at her, a hint of a smile curving the corners of his mouth. He didn't want to leave. He wanted to hold her all night, to make love to her again. But the twins were upstairs, and although they were asleep, he knew he wouldn't press Sionna to risk their discovering them together.

"I had a great time," he finally said. He bent over and grazed her cheek with a soft kiss. Sionna held back a slight shiver, amazed yet again at how animated she became at the barest touch from him.

"I'm glad. The twins can be a bit much," Sionna commented as she opened the front door. He was about to leave the house when he recalled that he had forgotten to invite her to the company party.

"Sionna," he said so hastily that Sionna paused, certain he had hurt himself.

"What's wrong?" she gasped, grabbing hold of his arm, her eyes wide with fear.

"Nothing. I'm sorry if I scared you," David apologized, seeing her anxious expression. "I just forgot to ask you something," he added.

"Oh," Sionna murmured, relieved. She leaned against the door, put her hand to her heart and asked, "What did you want to ask me?"

"Buerhler's annual company party is Saturday night. I was hoping you wouldn't mind being my date," David said so humbly that Sionna nearly laughed.

As she stared up at him, she understood his humility. It was because Buerhler had fired Joey and for her to go to the party could be painful. Sensing his consideration of her feelings, and thankful for how thoughtful he was, Sionna ran her hand across his cheek and gave him a sweet smile. "I would love to be your date, David. You have to promise me one thing, however," Sionna added.

"Sure," David responded, curious.

"Don't introduce me as Joey's widow. Let me just be Sionna Michaels. Okay?" Sionna said.

David considered her, taking in every detail of her face. In that moment she was truly the most beautiful woman he had ever known. She had no idea how elated her request made him feel. He understood that she was Joey's widow, he understood that she loved him and that Joey's memory would never completely leave her. But her being able to express her independence made David feel as if he had a fighting chance.

"David?" Sionna asked, frowning slightly when he didn't respond. She wondered if he thought she was being cold to dismiss Joey. How could he understand her need to let go of her attachment to Joey. It was sudden, yes, but if she was going to Buerhler's party on the arm of David, the last thing she needed was to be introduced all night long as Joey's widow, the man who had committed suicide over losing his job at Buerhler.

"Absolutely," David said firmly at her inquiry. "I won't think of you as Joey's anymore," he added softy.

Sionna flushed beneath his gaze, but she held his gaze. She maintained her composure as he slowly leaned forward. And it was only when she felt his mouth press against hers that her eyes fluttered closed. She stood perfectly still, melting beneath his kiss, a kiss that seemed to immobilize both of them. Though their only contact was the passionate kiss, Sionna's entire body was aflame. When he finally pulled away, his mouth brushed against her cheek until he reached her ear and whispered, "Sweet, sweet Sionna. I want to love you."

The softly spoken words left her even more breathless, and she felt weak. "Yes," she whispered instinctively, her breathing heavy with contained excitement as her eyes popped open.

"Mmm, you tempt me," David groaned, nibbling against her ear. "I won't cause you regret." Before she could say anything, he continued, "Good night, Sionna."

"Good night," Sionna whispered, wishing she could insist that he stay, knowing that with the twins upstairs, she wouldn't dare encourage him further. She watched him as he got in his car, waved and drove away. When he was gone she went back inside, feeling warm and cozy inside after his long, breathless kiss.

Twenty-seven

Jaunice was furious. She sat in her car staring at David's house for hours. She couldn't believe he had brought her down so. He was supposed to be madly in love with her! He was supposed to be feeling rejected! Instead he was running around making love to that woman! And she had seen Sionna Michaels. She was nothing to brag about, Jaunice thought jealously, although an honest part of her insisted that Sionna was very pretty and definitely could compete against Jaunice even on a bad day.

She could have cursed. David was hurting her feelings and he didn't have even the decency to care. Feeling a sense of loss, almost defeat, she flipped open her mirror and took a reassuring look at herself. She patted her hair and wiped under her eye. She was still beautiful, definitely worthy of David's attention and love.

She didn't even know why she was making such a fuss over David. He wasn't all that. So he had a great job and a nice house. But she had seen better-looking men. And definitely he was not the hottest lover she had ever had. Again she told herself that she should leave, give it up and stop worrying over him.

Winking at herself in the mirror, she grinned, flashing pearly white teeth, then started the ignition. She was going home. She had just turned the key when a familiar car pulled into David's driveway. She paused from shifting the car into drive. She found herself holding her breath as

David turned off the car, got out, turned on his alarm and went inside.

Feeling suddenly breathless, Jaunice took several deep breaths. She watched as the lights came on in the house. A few minutes passed, then all but one light was turned off. The house seemed still. She watched, waited and held her breath. But nothing happened.

She opened her mirror again, considered herself again, and swore under her breath. She had come too far to give up now. Snapping her mirror shut, she turned off the car and left it. She was at his front door when she adjusted her slender black skirt and fixed her blouse so that it hung seductively over her shoulders. She wished in that moment she had not given him back his keys. It would have been more dramatic to come in on her own and surprise him. Shrugging and regaining a sense of her feminine power, she rang the doorbell and waited.

She was just about to hit the doorbell again when she saw a light switch on. She heard his footsteps and could feel him peering through the peephole at her. She felt his hesitation and grew disappointed. But at hearing the locks snap open, she put on her most seductive stance and lowered her eyes to give him a full upward glance. It was one of her favorite looks and she had practiced it long enough.

The door opened and Jaunice slowly looked up at him. He was wearing boxer shorts and a T-shirt. He was breathtakingly handsome and Jaunice regretted again allowing him to slip through her fingers.

David stared at Jaunice, leaning against the door in lazy disbelief. What did she want now? Hadn't they settled everything?

"Well? Aren't you going to at least say hello?" Jaunice asked in a subdued whisper.

"Hello, Jaunice," David said in a voice full of tired disregard.

Jaunice cleverly hid her disappointment both at his lack

of surprise of any sort and his bored demeanor. "Hello, David," she said in a husky murmur accompanied by a demure smile.

"What's going on now, Jaunice?" David demanded, having no patience with her.

Jaunice pouted, put her hands on her hip then swaggered up to him, saying, "Has it been that easy for you, David, to just let go?"

"Jaunice," David groaned, annoyed and wanting to just close the door on her. But he couldn't be rude to her the way he wanted to. He could only stand there and let her have her tantrum.

"Then it hasn't been easy, has it? Tell me that you haven't thought of me and that you truly don't want me anymore, David. Tell me that you're in love with Sionna Michaels and I'll cool my heels and be gone. But," she added hastily when he opened his mouth to speak. She put her hand on his shoulder, realizing as she did just how much she missed the feel of him. "But don't lie, because I won't accept a lie."

"Good, because the truth is Sionna Michaels is a wonderful woman whom I plan to spend a lot of time with. I like her, Jaunice. I don't want you playing games and trying to interfere with us again. Do you understand?" David was so abrupt that Jaunice nearly took a step back. It was like a stinging blow for him to so brazenly speak of his affection for another woman.

"And the question still is, has it been easy just letting me go?" Jaunice persisted. Her eyes were aflame with passion, from both her need to hear him admit he missed her to her need to rip Sionna from his thoughts.

"Jaunice," David sighed. He stared over her head down the dark street, wishing she would stop surprising him. She had no idea how relieved he was to be free of the puppet strings she had put on him. Yes, she was a beautiful woman, definitely a great lover. But it was over between them. He wanted to build a relationship with Sionna. He had learned years ago not to play games with a woman's heart.

"Jaunice, get in your car and go home. You're making a fool out of yourself," David said firmly.

"You bastard!" Jaunice yelled, so hurt she could have slapped him. David looked around at her unexpected outburst, expecting to see a ton of lights switch on at the sudden noise.

"Jaunice, cool it. I've got neighbors," David whispered anxiously.

"To hell with your neighbors!" Jaunice shouted, deliberately raising her voice as loud as she could. "They should know just what kind of lying—"

"Cut it!" David hissed, pulling her inside and slamming the door shut. "Have you lost your mind?" he demanded angrily. She had taken her game too far this time, he thought, furious with her.

Jaunice glared at him, bitter and full of resentment that he had so easily dismissed her from his life. "How dare you make me think . . . you made me think there was some chance for us?" Jaunice cried, real tears streaming down her cheek as she stood before him.

"Jaunice," David tried to interrupted.

"No!" Jaunice screamed. "Don't you dare try to shut me up. I came here because you made me think you just needed to think about our relationship. How could you fall for another woman without so much as a call to New York? I thought you loved me! I gave you everything I had, David Young. Everything!" she sobbed.

She was trembling and David moaned, feeling compassion for her obvious pain. He was frustrated. She had the incredible ability to make him feel guilty even when he hadn't done anything wrong. She hadn't even given half of what he had given.

"Jaunice," he murmured, pulling her to him. "Stop crying. You're going to make yourself sick." David wanted to find the right words to comfort her.

"I am sick. I'm sick with my love for you," Jaunice sobbed, relishing in his hold. She wrapped her arms about his neck and cuddled her face into his broad chest.

"Jaunice. You don't love me. You just hate to lose," David said, not moved by her words.

"You can call it what you want. I invested two years of my life in you and I can't just be expected to walk away from you."

"Jaunice, come on," David scoffed, holding her away from him so he could stare into her eyes. "I recall being the one told to get lost, taking a flying leap, leave you alone to put it bluntly. You needed to breathe, to think. You didn't want to get married or to move down here. And I couldn't move in with you because I would have invaded your space. You don't recall that?"

"Yes. But I wasn't sure yet. Now I am," Jaunice said so innocently that David laughed. He released her, realizing that yet again she had played him. Her tears were just a ploy to get him to give in.

"Now is too late," he responded as gently as he could.

Jaunice was stunned at his coldness. Her despair showed on her face and David felt chagrin that he had been too hard on her.

"I never knew how cold you could be. How cold in fact that you are," Jaunice murmured as she headed for the door.

"I'm sorry. I just . . . I never knew how to play games, Jaunice. It is what it is," David said, trying to make an appeal to her sense of fairness.

Jaunice turned dramatically at him in outrage by his statement. "No it isn't what it is. What it is, is David Young running into Sionna Michaels's arms. A widow, lonely, nothing more. A man spurned, by me I admit. She doesn't want you,

at least not after she gets over her husband's death!"
Jaunice added harshly.

"You have no idea what you're talking about," David
hissed, angry at her words. It was taking every ounce of
self-control he had not to stoop to Jaunice's level.

Jaunice, pleased to get a reaction from him, walked up
to him and said haughtily, "Oh, don't I? You were heart-
broken because I wasn't ready for your pretty, painted
world. And your girlfriend, she'll never, ever love you. Know
why, David? Because you are not Joey Michaels. Wasn't that
his name? You can't replace him, and that's the challenge
you'll have to face. And we both know how you are about
challenges, right David? You fail, at least with women, every
time," Jaunice added.

Her words bit into David, and with an angry hiss he
pulled her to him, swearing between clenched teeth.

"I want you to leave. I don't care where you go but don't
come back!" he spat out, then shoved her to the door.

"That's right, David. Act like a coward. That's why I never
wanted you to begin with. You're weak. Pathetic. A lousy
lover and a total loser," she spat out in return.

"If I'm such a loser, Jaunice, what the hell are you doing
here? What does that make you?" David growled, so angry
he was itching to slap her. She was deliberately provoking
him, he was sure of it. She wouldn't win. He opened the
door and waited for her to pass through it.

"I guess that makes me a loser too. At least, David, I'm
not pretending to be anything else," Jaunice added bitterly
before she stepped through the door. She barely had her
feet on the pavement before the door slammed behind her.
She paused, controlled her turbulent heart, and hastily
went to her car. It was over. She may not get him but she
was not going to give him up to Sionna Michaels. She had
Saturday's party and she was definitely going to teach David
a lesson he would never forget.

Twenty-eight

David was fuming. He was so riled up he couldn't stay still. Damn Jaunice. She was a bitter, evil woman and he couldn't believe he never knew it. What type of idiot had he been? What made him think she was the beautiful woman he had thought.

"Damn fool," he swore aloud. He was sweating with anger. Unable to rest, he switched on the television set, turned on ESPN and tried to get caught up in the game. But Jaunice's cruel words kept coming back to haunt him. Sionna was a widow and he knew she was still attached to Joey. But he wasn't trying to replace Joey. He just wanted to be a part of her life.

He was an idiot to allow Jaunice's words to affect him. She was so jealous and bitter she was capable of saying anything. At some point he had expected that he and Jaunice would be friends, but now he knew there was no way. She was too bitter and he thought she would never be trustworthy. Even if she didn't want him anymore, she definitely was too selfish to set him free.

Knowing he had a drama on his hands, he grew frustrated. What had Jaunice expected, that he would wait forever? He hadn't gone out searching for another woman to fall in love with. Sionna had found him. And he wasn't about to turn her away. She was far too perfect for him to ignore his feelings for her. He grinned to himself, realizing that he had fallen for Sionna almost the first night they went out. She had a real charm about her that Jaunice was lacking. Jaunice was made up from the floor up, David thought harshly.

Though Sionna wore makeup and definitely took care with her appearance, her soul was honest, her words were not rehearsed and her sincerity was a welcome respite from Jaunice.

Calming down at the thought of Sionna, he glanced at the clock and wondered if it was too late to call her. It was just past midnight. Impulsively, he grabbed the phone. Walking slowly about the house, he dialed Sionna's number.

"Hello," Sionna whispered, answering the phone on the first ring.

"Did I wake you?" David asked instantly, a smile coming across his face at the sound of her voice.

"No, I was just watching TV," Sionna murmured, sitting up in the bed and plopping her pillows behind her head.

"Oh, it's David by the way," David said hastily.

Sionna laughed and responded, "Did you think I didn't know that?"

"I'm glad to hear you did," David answered.

They fell silent and Sionna grinned, staring at her blanket. She was amazed at how girlish he made her feel, even just over the phone.

"Are you tired? I can call back tomorrow," David suggested, feeling foolish when the silence between them continued.

"I'm wide awake," Sionna answered truthfully. The moment she heard his voice she perked up and she couldn't sleep if she tried.

"Me too," David grinned, pleased that she wasn't irritated with his late-night call.

"I had a great time tonight," Sionna said truthfully. His presence was enough for her.

"So did I. I tell you, your sisters are something. I'm going to tread carefully with them," he added with a light laugh.

"They are very protective, like baby hens. But I love them," Sionna declared with a winsome smile.

"Are they still asleep?" David asked. Sionna giggled, tickled by his question.

"I don't see one reason for them to be awake," she responded.

"Okay, so it was a dumb question," David admitted. "I just wanted to know . . . if maybe you could come over."

Sionna's mouth fell open. She caught her lower lip between her teeth and considered his question. She wanted to say yes instantly but she worried about leaving the girls alone. And just who did he think he was making a booty call? she thought further, although she couldn't help grinning at the concept.

"I guess I'm asking for too much?" David suggested at her silence.

"You could be. Let me ask you this," Sionna added, feeling giddy with delight at his question. "Are you what my sisters call a good guy playboy? You know, the type of guy who does everything right but he's still playing the field?"

David laughed heartily. He had never been asked a question like that. He had to admit, though, that in college he had more than one girlfriend, often at the same time. But that game played itself out and even before he met and fell for Jaunice he knew he wanted to be a one-woman man. So, confident in his answer, he retorted, "If I was, would I admit it? But the answer is no."

"Uh-huh. Then my answer is yes," Sionna laughed, elated to be able to say yes without a qualm.

"Can I come by now to pick you up?" David asked, walking to his bedroom to start putting on his clothes.

"Pick me up? Why? Is it too late for me to drive, David?" Sionna asked.

"No, I just thought you might not feel like driving at this time of night," David answered.

"I think I can handle the drive. Give me your address and I'll be right over," Sionna suggested softly.

She was running her hand over the quilt when her eyes fell on the clock. She had to get the girls to the train station by seven A.M. She was taking a risk going out so late, knowing she had to run her errands early. But she had no wish to turn down David's offer. And though it would have been easier to have him come stay the night with her, she didn't want to subject the girls to her love life.

"Are you ready?" David asked, waiting to give her instructions. Sionna got out of bed, and as she looked through her closet for something sexy to wear, she answered, "Ready."

Twenty-nine

Sionna pulled up to David's house and whistled. She had thought Joey's house was beautiful when she first saw it, but David's was awesome. His was a full brick house at least three stories high. It was a huge lot with land for days behind the house. She drove up his driveway and felt as if she were invading his privacy with her harsh headlights.

She shut them off even before she parked the car. She had barely turned off the engine when he opened the door. He had been watching. She quickly glanced in the mirror and patted her ponytail. Another quick glance over her miniskirt and cardigan sweater and Sionna felt confident that she was attractive. Then, trying to quiet her wildly beating heart, she got out of the car and with a light walk met him at the front stairs.

"Hi," she greeted him, accepting his hand as he led her into the house. He was wearing slippers and a robe and Sionna was tickled. She wondered if he was nude beneath the robe. As he turned to lock the door she got a glimpse of his T-shirt and her answer to her question.

"Was it hard finding the place?" he asked, turning to her with a wolfish grin even as his gaze swept over her long legs clearly visible beneath her miniskirt. His expression warmed her all over, yet she somehow managed to answer him with a soft, "Not at all."

"Good. I still think I should have picked you up," David scolded. He escorted her into his cozy family room and offered her a seat on the love seat. Sionna sat down carefully, smoothing down her skirt as she did so.

"Would you like a glass of wine? A drink? Anything?" David asked, standing over her.

"I shouldn't," Sionna said hesitantly. "I have to get up early and get the girls to the train station."

"Okay." David dragged out. "Then how about a cup of tea or coffee? Believe it or not, I have both."

"Coffee," Sionna answered.

"Coming right up." David snapped his fingers and hastily went to the kitchen. Sionna sat quietly on the sofa, staring at the fire he had prepared. It was charming, even if it was still warm outside. She took a deep breath, then kicked off her shoes. As far as she was concerned, since they had made love once already, she could relax.

When he came back she had scooted comfortably on the sofa and had tucked the pillow under her head. He paused at the sight of her, pleased she had made herself comfortable.

"Here's your coffee," he murmured, setting it on the coffee table beside them as he sat on the love seat beside her, his eyes once again falling on her bare legs.

"Uhm, it smells great. What flavor?" Sionna gushed before taking a careful sip.

"French roast. It just smells good," David said.

"Oh," Sionna muttered. She set the coffee down and stared at him. "Your house is lovely. I would love to see the whole place."

"Yeah. All right, walk with me," David said, pleased at her interest.

Sionna stood up, then remembered she had taken off her shoes. She was about to put them back on when David stopped her. "Don't worry about it. You're at home. Let's walk," David insisted.

"Okay." Sionna complied. Accepting the hand he offered, she walked with him through the house. He took her to the basement, then up the stairs to the kitchen, and dining room then to the foyer. Finally they found their way to his upstairs and Sionna had to stop herself from gasping at the sight of his huge bedroom.

"Your place is incredible. You must have designed it yourself," Sionna gushed, walking over to the huge king-sized bed and sitting on the edge.

David considered her from the doorway, pleased by her comment. "I had some help, but I came up with the premise of the place," he admitted, crossing his arms over his chest.

Sionna eyeballed him with bold flirtation. He was virile and magnetic, and she didn't have much time. Giving him a mischievous grin, she stood up on the bed and stared down at him, murmuring, "I have only one concern about your house, David."

David grinned up at her, pleased by her bold stance and appreciating her playful mood. "And what's that?" he asked, indulging her.

"The heat in here," she stated. She pulled her sweater off and tossed it across the room before she continued. "Is it hot in here or is it just me?"

David laughed, shook his head and came to stand right in front of her before answering, "This place is on fire," he muttered. He cupped her buttocks and pulled her to him and began kissing her inner thighs, tasting her flesh as if it were the first time he had held her.

Sionna gasped, indulging in the sweet feel of his mouth against her tingling body. He released her buttocks and reached behind to unzip her skirt. She felt it flutter to the floor as he lifted her from the bed. Pulling her in front of him, he found her mouth and kissed her passionately. She returned his intense kiss, reveling in his hold, loving the crush of her breasts against his firm chest. She was indulged in the pleasure of making love to him, unashamed of her nudity as he dexterously removed her bra. Then he laid her upon the huge king-sized bed, and a moment later he was beside her. He fondled her flesh, pleasuring in the soft silkiness of her skin. His hands roamed up her flat stomach, finding their way to her breasts where he cupped them and fondled them until her nipples peaked with desire.

Sionna gasped, his kiss continuing to flame her loins, and finally she could take it no more. Before he could continue caressing her, she straddled him. Bending over him, she kissed his chin, his eye lids, and she found his earlobes where she gingerly nibbled and suckled them. He squirmed, tickled by her touch, turned on by the feel of her body pressing against his. Her hands danced along his chest where she gently raked her nails through the fine hairs she found. She pulled against his chest like a playful kitten, touching him and possessing him with her loving.

She rubbed her womanhood against his abdomen, fully aware that he was ready to enter her. But she made him wait, enjoying his hardness against her buttocks as she continued to tease his rising desire. David groaned, wanting her, his excitement compounded when she reached for him, slid the condom over his erect manhood and began to stroke him. He gasped as she moved faster and faster until he could no longer wait. With a sudden movement that caused her to gasp, he raised his hips, held onto hers and instantly entered her. Sionna tossed her head back, moving instinctively with him as he rose and fell, the gentle rhythm of his body penetrating to her very soul. His pace quickened. He grabbed her hands, holding them firmly against her thighs as he shot in and out of her without pause.

She moaned with pleasure, holding her own as she followed his rhythm. When he felt her shiver, his pace became even more demanding. Just as she climaxed his body tensed and his legs stiffened until a moment later, his body shuddered and he spasmed with a deep groan.

When they finished making love, Sionna lay content in

his arms. He held her to him, his heartbeat soothing to her. Sensing that he had fallen asleep, she peeped up at him. He was so peaceful and handsome. She felt good being in his arms. A content smile played across her mouth as she cuddled up closer to him. Her movement caused David to stir. Again, she peeked up at him. But he was still asleep. She was careful to lie still. She didn't want to wake him, not yet. She knew soon she would have to leave.

Sighing softly, she closed her eyes, wishing she could lie against his firm body forever. When next she opened her eyes she heard the birds singing and the first peek of daybreak. She yawned, then stretched before she panicked.

"Oh, no. The twins!" she blurted, jumping from the bed.

David woke up with a start at her outburst. "What? What?" he called, looking around groggily.

"I'm so sorry, David. I didn't mean to wake you like that," Sionna whispered, pulling on her clothes as she apologized.

"What's going on?" David asked, shoving off the sheets and sitting on the edge of the bed. At his movement, Sionna paused, drowning in his strong physique. David caught her gaze and grinned wolfishly.

"Are you trying to tell me something?" he asked, giving her a wink.

Sionna gave him a regretful smile. "Only that I have to go. I hate to go," she added hastily at his disappointed expression.

"I know, the twins, right?" he replied.

"Yes, I have to get them to the train station," Sionna answered, watching as he pulled on his T-shirt and shorts. "They're probably already awake."

"I understand," David said, walking to her and pulling her into his arms. "Just as long as I can see you again and again, I'm willing to let you leave now," he murmured huskily as he ran his mouth softly over her cheeks.

Sionna squirmed, thrilled by his touch. "Stop that or

I'll be forced to forget the twins are waiting for me," Sionna said.

"I wish you could," David groaned, his light nibbles quickly turning into passionate caresses.

Sionna closed her eyes, enjoying the feel of his mouth against her neck before he found her mouth. She was drowning in his passion, relishing in the electric shock he sent through her body. Caught up in his potent affection, she wrapped her arms about his neck and pulled him even closer, encouraging him to make love to her again. Sensing her arousal, David lifted her from her feet and laid her back onto the bed. Within moments she was stripped, and again they made love. When they were done, Sionna purred with pleasure. She could make love to him all day. She just wished the twins weren't expecting her. She sighed.

"Are you all right?" David asked, hearing her sigh.

"I'm fabulous. I just really have to go," she added, her voice heavy with disappointment.

"Then I promise not to detain you again. Just don't go teasing me again," he said, getting up from the bed and walking to the bathroom.

Sionna laughed, calling as he entered the bathroom, "I am not a tease." She reached for her clothes and paused. Staring at the disheveled sheets and pillows on the bed, a mischievous thought occurred to her. She glanced at the clock. It was already almost six A.M. and the twins were due at the train station by seven thirty. Grinning, she was sure she could make it. Impulsively she picked up the phone and dialed home. After two rings Tracy answered the phone, her voice still groggy with sleep.

"Terri or Tracy?" Sionna whispered, keeping her eye on David's bathroom door.

"Tracy. And where are you?" Tracy asked dryly.

"I'm with David. Listen, I know I have to get you down-town soon, so be ready. I just wanted to let you know I will be there," Sionna hissed, hearing the shower start.

"Who is that?" Sionna heard Terri ask.

"Sionna," Tracy answered.

"Hey, you two can talk after I hang up. I'll see you in a few minutes," Sionna muttered, then hastily hung up. The moment she hung up the phone, she tossed her clothes on the bed. Then, walking lightly, she went into the bathroom. She paused, staring at David with a cocky smirk.

David was washing his face, his eyes squeezed shut. Sionna boldly slid the shower door open. At the whiff of cool air, David's eyes popped open.

"Need help?" Sionna asked with a bold appraisal of his body.

"Absolutely," David agreed and pulled her into his arms.

Thirty

Sionna was singing to herself as she drove up to her house. She was elated, excited. David was everything she could ask for. And if what they say about moving too fast was true, she was willing to risk it. He was that great.

"Don't get out. We're going to miss our train," Tracy called, racing to the car before Sionna could turn it off. Terri and Tracy ran to the car, their bags in hand. They were angry with Sionna for being late. And to not even spend breakfast with them, Terri had complained, was downright rude. Tracy agreed. They were in no mood for further delays.

Sionna looked up at the girls as if they were strangers. They were like a douse of cold water, cooling the warm feeling that had coated her body since leaving David's house.

"You won't miss it. You have time," Sionna declared as Tracy tossed her bag into the backseat, then jumped in the front. Terri gave Sionna a loud huff as she buckled up in the back seat.

"It's after seven, Sionna. Our train leaves at eight o'clock. We have no time, thanks to you," Terri said testily.

"You two are so full of drama. Just buckle up . . ."

"We are," they chimed in together.

"And let's roll," Sionna finished, backing out of the driveway. She was about to drive down the street when she slammed on the brakes and asked, "Did you lock the doors?"

"Of course," Tracy answered with indignation.

"Unlike some people, we don't shirk our responsibilities on a whim," Terri said for good measure to annoy Sionna. But Sionna just laughed, tickled by their pouting.

"Some day, you two are going to fall in love with a man who is going to be . . . everything. He's going to make you sigh and laugh and cry and feel the ultimate joy. And then you will understand how I feel," Sionna commented, glancing at both of them.

"So David is everything?" Tracy asked, eyeballing Sionna as if daring Sionna to say yes.

"Almost. I want to take it slow, you know. With my emotions I have proven to be a little headstrong. This time I want to do it right. David and I will date and get to know each other and—"

"Make love even at the expense of people being late," Terri finished sarcastically.

"If you must know. Yes, we will make love. I'm a big girl, young ladies. I know what I'm doing," Sionna continued, not at all put off by Terri's statement.

"You should know you are not making a good impression on us. I wonder how Mom is going to feel about this?" Tracy asked, glancing in the backseat at Terri.

"She's going to be shocked," Terri answered in her dry way.

"Shocked? Please, she's going to be elated. Mom wants nothing less than to see me happy. With David, I'll have you two know, I am happy," Sionna declared with a haughty roll of her eyes.

"Don't let us spoil it, Sionna. I'm glad you're happy," Tracy declared, feeling a little guilty that she had allowed Terri's irritability to affect how she treated Sionna. Sionna was her idol. She wanted so much to be as independent and confident as Sionna was. The last thing Tracy wanted to do was make Sionna feel bad just because she was in love with David.

And just as Tracy was feeling bad for Sionna, Terri blurted, "I'm amazed that you can feel so strongly for this guy so soon after Joey's death." The statement was like a slap and both Sionna and Tracy stared straight ahead. It took Sionna a few moments to gather enough poise to respond.

"That was very unnecessary, Terri," Sionna began softly. Her eyes caught Terri's in the rearview mirror and Sionna silently applauded Terri for having the decency to at least humbly lower her eyes.

"I loved Joey. Certainly David can't change that fact. But I find David to be a wonderful distraction from the pain Joey left. Besides, whether I met David today or tomorrow or ten years from now, it wouldn't make a difference. Because if it's love, it's love. Who's to determine when the time is appropriate?" Sionna demanded, barely able to keep the choked pain from her voice.

"I'm sorry," Terri muttered.

"Yes, well, youth will do that to a person," Sionna snapped, no longer able to contain her irritation. "I wanted to spend this morning with you two. But things do come up, Terri, Tracy," she added with a glance at Tracy. "And it doesn't mean I love you two any less. I just needed . . . I wanted to spend time with David."

"I know. We understand. I'm really sorry," Terri added more sincerely.

"Well," Sionna sighed. "Let's just let it go. I'm going to come down and visit you and Mom in Georgia soon. I promise. And then we'll have a wonderful time together." Sionna made the decision impulsively, but she liked the idea of being with her family again and hoped when she visited them next she would have David at her side.

"Mom would love that. She misses you a lot," Tracy said.

"I miss all of you," Sionna said. Feeling a lot better and

with a reassuring smile, she added, "I'm sorry I wasn't here this morning."

"We know," they said in unison. They all laughed. Happy that the tension had eased between them.

"All right, you two," Sionna said as she pulled into the parking lot of the train station. "I want you to be careful. And when you get to New York, keep your eyes wide open and don't talk to strangers. Seriously. I mean it," Sionna insisted at their giggles.

"We'll be fine, Sionna," Terri confirmed. Sionna parked the car and helped the girls get their bags out the car. As they got on the escalator Sionna considered them with proud eyes.

"Do well in New York and make me and Mom proud," Sionna said softly. The look of motherly love set them aback. Terri swallowed hard, feeling as if she were going far away. Tracy had to hold back tears. They didn't say a word as they checked their tickets, then waited at Gate C. Finally the call for boarders came over the intercom and Tracy could no longer hold back. She turned to Sionna and with a burst of laughter and tears all at once, she hugged her sister.

"Don't let David go. He seems wonderful. Bring him to Georgia when you come. I don't mind him at all," Tracy added.

"I'm glad you welcome him," Sionna said, giving her baby sister a big hug.

"Sionna," Terri whispered, getting Sionna's attention.

"Yes, Terri," Sionna smiled, looking over Tracy's shoulder at Terri.

"I meant it earlier. I'm sorry. I can be such a sourpuss. And I liked David, too. Most importantly, I want you to be happy and to get over Joey and to move on. Okay."

She said it so innocently that Sionna could only laugh and nod, responding with a sardonic, "Okay. I'll get over Joey and move on. I promise."

Terri smiled, not catching the sarcasm in Sionna's statement. But when she said, "I love you, Sionna," Sionna's sarcasm faded and she pulled her sister to her bosom and whispered back a heartfelt, "I love you too."

The last call for boarding rung out over the intercom. Feeling a sense of family bond returning, Tracy and Terri raced for the train, waving good-bye to Sionna. Sionna waited until they were boarded before she turned away and slowly went back to her car. She was going to miss them, and she made a mental note to go home soon.

Thirty-one

David checked the back door to his house, then left the house whistling and tossing his keys in the air and catching them. He felt good. He couldn't remember when he had felt so good about a woman. Certainly Sionna was a dream come true. He got in his car and paused, feeling rather than seeing eyes watching him. He glanced around, certain he was going to spot Jaunice. But no one was there. After a moment, he shrugged, started his car and backed out of the driveway.

Sionna's name ran through his mind like a song. She was definitely the one, he was confident about that. And when the time was right, he was going to make his feelings known. But if there was one thing Jaunice had taught him, it was to slow down. He wanted to give Sionna a chance to breathe, to want him. And the only way to do that was to show her everything he had to offer without making a demand for her hand, at least not yet.

Pleased that he had figured out the situation, he grinned to himself, not noticing the curious glances his way as he headed for the office, prepared to finalize the designs. He had no clue how wired he appeared, and even Karen gaped at him. He was definitely a man in love, she decided as he entered his office and closed his door.

Jaunice's eyes narrowed the moment she saw David leave his house. He was a snake, a cad, a selfish bastard, she thought bitterly. She couldn't believe her eyes when Sionna came bobbing out of his house. Then, less than an hour later, David left, whistling like a schoolboy!

She was furious.

Angry with his ease at moving on without her, Jaunice waited impatiently for his car to disappear down the road before she quickly went inside. She had no idea how she was going to get inside until she realized she had not given David his key back, even though he had repeatedly asked for it.

Upon entering, Jaunice paused and glanced around her. The house was still, and as usual it was immaculate. She should be waking up in this house, she thought regretfully, always appreciative of the spacious design of David's home. Glancing over her shoulder as if she thought David would return at any moment, she hesitated before she gingerly began walking through the house. She paused in his bedroom doorway, staring into the room with narrowed eyes.

He had neatly made up the bed but she could imagine how ruffled it had been after he had made love to Sionna. The idea frustrated her immensely. To think she had thought he cared! She had poured her heart out to that man and still he had turned away from her.

Taking a deep breath, she continued to walk around the house, not certain what she was searching for, closure perhaps, she thought blandly. She just needed to be inside his house, to see what she was missing, if anything. She went back to the main floor, then hesitated, looking inside his private library.

The door was slightly ajar, and as always blueprints and sketches were all over the room. She pushed the door fully open and stepped inside the room. She glanced over the blueprints, the sketches, some memos. Then she froze.

Joey Michaels.

Who was Joey Michaels? She frowned. Why did his name sound so familiar? Of course, she grinned devilishly.

"Sionna Michaels," she murmured aloud. Curious, she leaned over the table and scanned the memo. Her eyes widened more and more as she read the degrading details of Joey Michaels's behavior at the company. What had David said? Ah, yes, he had died somehow. Miss Michaels was a widow. "That would be Mrs. Michaels," Jaunice corrected herself, feeling a hint of pleasure she hadn't felt in days.

Picking up the memo, she glanced around and found David's small copy machine. Hastily she made a copy of the memo, suddenly concerned that David would return and discover her rummaging through his things. That would never do.

When the copy was complete, she grabbed the memo and left the house. She had found more than she could have dreamed of. The question was, what did she want to do with the memo? How best could she teach Mrs. Sionna Michaels not to mess with her again? Shrugging, she got into her car deciding she had plenty of time to figure out how best the memo could serve her.

Sionna considered every stitch of clothing she owned, but was disappointed with the results. She couldn't believe she had nothing to wear. She had a dozen black dresses, yet none of them were right. She wanted to walk into the Buerhler party looking gorgeous. She still couldn't believe she was going to the Buerhler company party. Of course, now that she was rational and no longer looking for someone to blame, she knew they had not forced Joey to commit suicide.

Her teeth gritted with a power of their own as she thought of how humiliated and broken down Joey had been in those final days. It was going to take all her composure and dignity if she felt they were watching her in pity. But what they thought didn't matter. She knew the truth of Joey's suicide, and it was not a reflection on her, she silently declared.

Besides, she was there for David. She just wanted him to appreciate her all dressed up and sophisticated. Groaning, she looked again at her formal dresses and hated every one. Time was racing by. She only had one day to make up her mind. Finally giving up on her outdated and well-worn wardrobe, she got her purse and left the house. She was going shopping. If it took her right up to the minute of the party, she would find the dress that would knock David's socks off.

Saturday came with a rush of activity. David had gotten sidetracked by work, having promised the clean designs to Charles by Monday. When he looked up from his review of the designs, it was well past three o'clock. He jumped up, got his jacket off the back of his office door and left. He was close enough to completion to be confident he could finish the project on Sunday. He was exiting the building when he saw the rush of caterers and other personnel preparing for tonight's party, and Sionna instantly came to mind. Hurrying home, he quickly dressed before calling Sionna to see if she was ready. Of course, she was, and with a feeling of excitement at seeing Sionna again, he made his way to her house.

David was awed at the sight of Sionna. He would not have thought it possible if he had not seen her for himself, but she was even more beautiful. Her hair was pinned atop her head, with a few strategic ringlet curls dangling about her face. Her long, almond eyes were wide and enhanced by a light dusting of eye shadow. She wore a red lipstick that enhanced her sensuous mouth, a mouth his eyes fell on and couldn't look away from.

Sionna released a soft sigh, pleased by his stunned expression. It was an excellent accent to two long days of shopping for just the right clothes, sitting for hours to get the perfect hairstyle. She had taken great care with her makeup too. She had walked the mall for hours, searching nearly every store that had a dress displayed before she finally found the one. It was a sparkling silver-blue, spaghetti-strapped, ankle-length dress. It was formfitting with a low V-neck front. She had to have it. By the time the clock struck six, she was ready. His broad smile said it all. He liked her dress.

When he rang the doorbell, she didn't hesitate to open it. She had missed him. She hadn't called him Friday, and she supposed he was too busy to call her. First thing Saturday morning, he called to remind her about the party, as if she had forgotten.

"Wow," David whistled, a little at a loss for words at how breathtaking she was. "You look incredible," he said, his expression so full of awe that Sionna flushed.

"Thank you," Sionna responded humbly. "You look great, too," she added, stepping outside the house. They stared at each other again. Feeling a little uncomfortable beneath his ardent gaze, she breathed a sigh. "If you don't stop staring at me like that, I'm going to lose my concentration. So stop that," Sionna insisted, fumbling with the lock on the front door.

David grinned, appreciating her sudden bout of shyness. "Do I know you? Could this be the bold and beautiful Sionna suddenly shy and demure? Hmm," he said, teasing her. "I think I may like this new you a lot."

"Oh, please. I am hardly shy and demure. My mom has been trying to get me to at least pretend that I was for years," Sionna commented. Even as she made the statement, she couldn't deny that she did feel a little bashful beneath his admiring gaze. And even Joey had never made her feel so . . . desirable.

"I got to tell you, I was worried you would cancel on me," David admitted as they drove away.

"Why would I cancel?" Sionna asked.

David glanced at her, then answered, "I thought you may

be a bit uncomfortable about mingling with the men who . . . how should I say this?" David murmured, more to himself than to Sionna.

Sionna looked thoughtful. Realizing where he was going with his concern, she finished his sentence. "You were worried that I couldn't handle being around Buerhler, knowing that their firing Joey caused him to commit suicide."

"Yeah," David agreed, wishing he hadn't mentioned it at all. It was an idiotic thing to do just before arriving at the party.

"David, I'm not a fragile person. Besides, I knew they would be there when you invited me. I'm fine with it," Sionna answered, giving him a wide smile.

"I should not have brought it up," David apologized, giving her a doleful glance.

Sionna considered him with a tender smile. He looked like a reprimanded boy, except she hadn't reprimanded him. She hadn't complained at all. Turning in her seat to give him a intense gaze, Sionna soothed him by saying, "Don't worry about me, David. I'm a big girl. I know where I'm going and who's going to be there. Joey didn't do anything wrong, Buerhler did, so I have no reason to hide in shame. He was a broken man, yes, but he loved me and he loved his job. I have that and so I'm fine," Sionna finished with a proud smile.

David again glanced at her but didn't respond. The memo from Edgar McHughly about Joey's stolen designs instantly came to mind. Again, he regretted not telling Sionna immediately. And now was definitely not the time. The least he could do was let her keep her head up. One thing was for sure, he wasn't going to stay but a few minutes, long enough to show his face. The moment he was able to escape the party he was going to tell Sionna everything and clear the air. He was compelled to tell her under the circumstances.

Sionna relaxed back in her seat, content with being by

his side. Joey's memory was something she was proud of, and even though suicide was a taboo, she had known Joey like no one could. He was an honest, hard-working man, if a little moody. She had nothing to be ashamed of and Buerhler couldn't take that from her.

Still, when they arrived at the party, Sionna's pulse quickened and her heart beat wildly. It was a reaction she had definitely not expected. She attributed it to apprehension about walking in on David's arm, a very visible arm it was, she thought with an appreciative smile as he gently tucked her arm into his then escorted her into the building.

The party was held at the corporate offices of Buerhler. The same location where she and David had first met. When they entered the building, a few couples were mingling in the lobby. As they headed for the elevator one of the couples called David.

Sionna sensed his hesitancy, but he turned to them with a big smile.

"Hey man, you made it," the man greeted David, his arm possessively wrapped around the waist of the woman by his side. Sionna took the couple in, swiftly noting that they weren't the typical couple. The guy was a short, graying white guy with the attitude of a scruffy country boy. His mate was a tall, leggy blonde with deep blue eyes. She had a thin body with thin features and a pinched mouth painted a fiery red. She looked to be in her late forties and Sionna was sure she would look better if she had some weight on her. They were an odd couple, Sionna thought, although she was careful not to stare.

"Charles. Anne, how are you?" David asked, shaking Charles's free hand.

"I've been better," Anne answered, giving Charles a narrowed glance that told David she was referring to Charles.

David laughed, nodding his head. "I can understand that, with a husband like Charles."

"I'm not so bad," Charles retorted as his eyes fell on

Sionna with curiosity. "And who is this beautiful woman foolish enough to date you?" Charles added with a roguish laugh.

"Sionna, meet Charles and his wife Anne. Charles, Anne, this is my new sweetheart, Sionna," David answered, giving Sionna an intimate squeeze as he introduced her. Sionna grinned, saying, "It's nice to meet you." She felt a warm flush come over her as David introduced her as his girl. It was so sweet, she thought, giving him a sidelong glance.

David's eyes caught Sionna's glance and gave her a rueful smile. So they hadn't discussed how to introduce each other. Unless she complained, he was going to introduce her as his woman and that was that, he thought boldly.

"It's nice to meet you too, dear," Anne said, giving Sionna a smile that didn't reach her eyes. Sionna quickly noted that Anne seemed far less friendly than her husband did.

"So how did you two meet?" Charles asked, giving Sionna another curious glance.

"I'd love to tell you all about it, but right now, Charles, Sionna and I just want to get a bite to eat. I'll catch you later," David said, giving Charles a hefty pat on the back before escorting Sionna to the elevators.

"That's fine, later then," Charles said. He walked off with his wife, although they both continued to stare at David and Sionna in curiosity.

"I thought he was with the girl upstairs." Anne whispered as soon as the elevator door closed.

"Yeah, me, too," Charles said.

"Think we should have warned him?" Anne asked.

"Nope. We're going to just mind our business," Charles said. He turned his back to the elevators, refusing to indulge his wife's curiosity.

Thirty-two

Jaunice was extremely impatient. She thought David would have arrived by now. She had been at the party an hour and still there was no sign of him. She was tired of small talk and chitchat with his coworkers, particularly his assistant Karen, who felt obligated to be by her side.

"I cannot believe he could let you go like that. You're so gorgeous," Karen was saying. Jaunice gave Karen a tight smile that clearly showed her annoyance, but Karen didn't seem to notice. Karen had impulsively showed up at the party, curious about Jaunice and David. She also wanted to ensure that Jaunice didn't tell David how she got into the party, since it could cost her her job. Uncomfortable because of her relationship with Jaunice, Karen downed a few drinks too many, causing Jaunice to want the woman simply to get lost. She was definitely cramping Jaunice's style. Agitated by David's delay and starting to wonder if he was even going to show, Jaunice's eyes kept darting back to the elevators.

She was sipping her Cosmopolitan when the light over the elevator door lit up and Jaunice's world paused. She stared, Karen's voice fading into the crowd as she waited for the elevator door to open. The sight of them together was painful. They looked beautiful together, and she could have thrown her drink at them. Sionna stood beside David, regal and elegant in her long formal dress that accented her curves perfectly. David was handsome, too, standing tall and sophisticated in his black double-breasted suit. They were a beautiful couple and Jaunice felt suddenly nauseated. She watched in disgust as David and Sionna got off the elevator. Like a couple that had been together for years, they entered the room and were immediately swept up by the crowd.

David introduced Sionna around the room, keeping his hand on her waist as they mingled with the party. Neither of them felt the eyes on them that were constant and filled with resentment. Neither of them sensed her approach either. Sionna didn't even look back when a feminine hand gave David a light tap on his shoulder.

David was laughing at a story a different couple was telling them. When he felt the light tap on his shoulder he glanced back, and his laughter instantly stopped. Sionna was smiling at the couple when she sensed David's tension. She looked behind him at the woman who had caused him to suddenly stiffen, and she knew instinctively who the woman was.

Jaunice looked from David's stormy expression to Sionna's curious gaze and grinned wickedly. Her eyes held a devilish glare as she considered them. "Well, if it isn't the lovebirds," Jaunice hissed, her voice thin with dislike for Sionna.

"You must be Jaunice," Sionna suggested, keeping her poise as she turned her full attention on Jaunice. If she had learned one thing from childhood, it was to never keep your back to an enemy. And Jaunice was definitely the enemy.

"That's right. And you're David's latest fling. Nice to meet you," Jaunice said with such a nasty twist of her mouth that Sionna thought she must be in pain.

"Fling?" Sionna questioned, glancing at David. David was still staring at Jaunice, wondering what could have come over Jaunice to encourage her to crash his company's party. He knew without a doubt in that instant that he really didn't know who the hell Jaunice Sumner really was. This woman was a fanatic pest and he could not take it anymore.

"What's going on, Jaunice?" David whispered harshly, stepping so close to Jaunice that Sionna would have expected Jaunice to fall or at least step back. Jaunice held her ground, glaring up at David with pure malice.

"The truth," Jaunice whispered back. She flicked out the memo she had found in David's house. She had considered and debated what to do with the memo, certain that Sionna knew nothing about it. Her only problem was just what Sionna knew about Joey's situation at Buerhler. If she knew, Jaunice would claim that Sionna was a fraud herself. But if she didn't know, Jaunice would expose the secret and shame Sionna before the entire crowd. Either way, Jaunice felt she would win and David would lose Sionna.

David frowned, not understanding Jaunice's action.

"The truth is you shouldn't be here. I can't believe you pulled this crap," David murmured, glancing around to see if anyone was watching. No one seemed to notice the friction between them and he wanted to keep it that way, more so for Sionna than for Jaunice.

"Pulled what? You invited me, remember?" Jaunice smirked, waving the memo in front of her face as if it were a fan.

"I remember we broke up, too. Look," David added, losing patience and growing irritated with the constant movement of the paper. "What do you want?' he demanded.

"Nothing, just to wish you and her good luck." She pointed her head toward Sionna, who was watching them with quiet dignity.

"Sure, right, so now if you'll excuse us," David huffed, pulling Sionna even closer as he started to walk away.

Jaunice moved again to block him from leaving, saying hastily, "Just a second. I have something I would like to share with Sionna, although I am sure she already knows, right, David?" Jaunice asked, shoving the paper in Sionna's hand. "After all, I found this in your house."

Sionna frowned, glancing down at the paper, then up at David. For a brief moment she feared the paper was a marriage license or some other damaging piece of information on David that could put a whole new spin on their relationship. Taking a deep breath and giving Jaunice an exasperated glance, she opened the folded paper and with widening eyes read the memo.

David watched Sionna, having no idea what it was Jaunice had given her, but sure it was a lie, whatever it was. Confident he had nothing to hide from Sionna about his relationship with Jaunice, he glared at Jaunice, vowing to get a restraining order against her. She was simply out of control.

As Sionna read the memo, Jaunice grinned like the cat that swallowed the canary. Her grin widened even more when Sionna finally looked up, swallowed and stared with tear-brimmed eyes at David.

"Sorry, honey. But I knew David was too nice a guy to tell you the truth," Jaunice whispered, patting Sionna on the arm as if she were sympathetic.

Sionna yanked her arm away and took a step back, glaring at both of them. She watched David and with a voice that was suddenly choked with emotion, she asked, "You knew about this?" She crammed the memo in David's hand.

Frowning, he glanced at the memo and instantly recognized it. He looked sharply at Jaunice, his eyes fierce. "How did you get this?" he demanded. But before Jaunice could speak, Sionna gasped, ashamed to be with David as she realized by his question that he had indeed known. He had probably known from the very beginning, she thought miserably.

"You knew all along," she murmured, her eyes filled with tears.

"Sionna . . ." David began gently, trying to take her hand.

"No!" Sionna snapped loudly. A slew of heads turned their attention to them at her outburst. Feeling self-conscious beneath their curious gazes and the sudden realization that her husband had been fired for fraud, Sionna moved the bouncing strands of hair from her face and tucked it behind her ear, wishing she could shrink from everyone's view.

"I can't believe you allowed me to come here, knowing this. Why didn't you tell me, David?" she whispered in a stricken voice.

"I wanted to," David groaned. If ever there was a moment he wanted to take back, it was this one. How Jaunice had gotten hold of the letter, he had no idea. One thing was for sure, she had taken her jealousy too far!

"I can't do this," Sionna cried. Without another word she rushed to the elevator, the crowd of people a blur as she repeatedly pushed the button for the lobby. David moved to follow her when Jaunice paused him with a hand on his arm.

"David," she started. He halted and glared at her. Jaunice nearly gasped from the expression of sheer loathing that filled each crease of his frown and darkened his eyes.

"Don't touch me, woman! Don't you ever touch me!" he hissed so fiercely he could have been spitting. Jaunice removed her hand and watched wide-eyed as he hurried to Sionna's side.

She watched him beg Sionna to hear him out. Confident she had put a permanent dent in his plans to win over Sionna, Jaunice's mouth held a hint of a malicious smile. Her eyes caught those of a few people standing a few feet away. Suddenly she became a little unnerved at being left standing alone. It was as if their eyes were accusing her of something horrible. She had done nothing wrong. She had simply told the poor girl the truth about her husband. Still, she glanced around for a familiar, friendly face. She spotted Karen. Putting on a pretentious smile again, she headed for Karen. Any company was better than to be left conspicuously alone, especially after David's harsh outburst.

Thirty-three

"Sionna, you have got to listen to me, at least for a second," David begged, following her from the building. He had been trying from the moment they got on the elevator to explain why he didn't tell her, but she wouldn't listen. She kept turning her back to him, crossing her arms across her chest and staring at the ground. When finally the lobby door opened, she practically ran from the building, incensed that David was right on her heels.

"Go away, David," she bit out, raising her hand to hail a cab.

David grabbed her arm, holding it to her side to keep her from getting a cab. "Listen to me for just a moment. All right. I just didn't want you to be uncomfortable," David explained. "I thought it was something you didn't need to know," he groaned, hurting at how easily Jaunice had come between them. Somehow, she had found a way.

"Oh, so now you know me so well that you think you should decide what I need to know!" Sionna blurted, frustrated and hurt. How dare he determine what she could handle? She yanked herself free and again raised her hand for a cab.

"Would it have changed things? Would it make the pain of Joey's death any less to know the truth? And you tell me if the truth was something you really wanted, Sionna. You tell me that!" David insisted, his eyes catching sight of the cab just as it came around the corner.

"Yes. Yes. Yes. I wanted to know the truth. Can't you see, I needed to know. To understand, to understand why . . . how he could do such a thing," Sionna stormed, near tears. "Knowing the truth is so much easier than guessing. Now I understand him, David. Now I know who and what he was," she added just as the cab stopped. She opened the door, and before she got in the back seat she looked at David and said in a sad whisper, "The only problem is I don't know who you are. I guess I never did. Good-bye, David." She got in the cab and closed the door, leaving David standing in a heap of defeat, exhausted with the guilt that she had just lain on him.

Hurt, he turned and stared at the building. His pained expression quickly turned to fury as he recalled that Jaunice was still upstairs. Determined once and for all to let her know she had no part in his life or in his future, he stormed back into the building, brushing past everyone as he searched for Jaunice.

Jaunice brought her glass to her lips but she never took a sip. David got off the elevator, his breathing so heavily he could have been imitating a bull. She cringed, never having seen him so fierce. She saw the rage in his eyes, the intense frustration in his walk, the cold purpose in his frenzied search of the room. Her movement drew his attention. Involuntarily, Jaunice took a precautionary step back. Yet, even in her concern for her well-being, she noted with satisfaction Sionna's absence.

"You jealous bitch!" David called, not caring who heard him as he approached Jaunice. Several people paused at his words, gaping at him as he stopped short in front of Jaunice.

Jaunice scoffed with indignation, looking around in embarrassment, although she kept her composure.

"I don't have to take this," Jaunice said coolly. She sat her drink on the stand next to her and turned to walk away.

Furious, David swung her back around to face him. "You started this, now I'm going to finish it," David said between clenched teeth. By now a few people were openly staring. But David didn't care. Jaunice had gone too far and there was no way he was going to allow her to get off that easily. "How did you get the memo?" he demanded, his hold on her arm firm.

Jaunice considered him with steadily growing rage. He was forcing her to stand there and respond to his questions like a criminal. "I've been in your house many times, remember?" she mocked.

"Something I seriously regret," David snapped back. "I can't believe I ever loved you! You're a mean, nasty, conniving tramp. You don't deserve to walk on the same ground with Sionna. The last thing she deserved was your cruelty." David was so angry he had no idea his voice had risen to such a height that a hush fell over the room. Now all eyes were on them, but he didn't notice.

Jaunice noticed. Her face was hot with embarrassment. He was calling her out, making a spectacle of both of them.

"Let me go, David!" she hissed, keeping her gaze directly on him. It wasn't supposed to turn out this way. Sionna was the one who was to be shamed, not her.

"I'm going to let you go, don't you worry. But let me tell you this, I do not want you," he bit the words out so callously, that a slight murmur raced throughout the room. "You mean nothing to me anymore, Jaunice. How I can express that to you, I don't know. But you had better keep the hell away from me from now on. We are through. That's all I have to say. Now be gone!" he ended and released her with a slight shove that caused her to stumble.

Barely keeping her balance, Jaunice caught hold of the counter and cringed again. Shamed in front of all eyes, her first instinct was to slap David. But before she could move her arm to slap his face, he was halfway across the room. Before she could take a step to follow him, he was on the elevator. His harsh words and blatant rejection left her marked with humiliation as the doors slowly closed.

Jaunice could no longer control her sobs of humiliation. The room was still quiet as all eyes fell on her, watched her, waiting, expecting. Her embarrassment complete, she all but crawled to the elevator tearfully and waited an eternity to escape their knowing eyes. The moment she was out of the building, she headed straight for her hotel room. She was leaving Virginia. As far as she was concerned, David Young and Sionna Michaels could have each other. She never wanted to come back. Never.

Thirty-four

Sionna kicked off her heels and pulled off her dress the moment she walked into her house. With a tear-streaked face from crying all the way to the house, she ran up the stairs and jumped in the shower. It was the only thing she could do to wash away her tension, to ease her humiliation. She still couldn't believe David had known all along what Joey had done. She couldn't believe that a man so warm and sincere and passionate could lie so well. How foolish a woman she was. And all along, that woman Jaunice had planned to bring shame on her.

Sionna jumped into the shower, trying to cool her enraged soul. She washed the carefully decorated curls from her hair. She cleaned her skin of the makeup that she so rarely wore and completely washed away the new perfume she had bought. She wanted to be bare, alone, free. Free of the pain and of the truth.

Crying anew as she finished her shower, she had barely dried off before she pulled on a pair of cotton short pajamas. She wrapped the towel around her head and plopped onto the bed, a box of tissues in her hands. Wiping her nose, she tried to contain her sobs. But the thought that Joey was a fraud, a liar, a complete and utter loser, kept racing through her mind. And David knew all along. He knew!

Sniffling, she pulled on a pair of white ankle socks and went downstairs. The house was dark and she planned to keep it that way. She turned on a small lamp in the living room and started the fireplace. Taking a pillow from the love seat, she sat cross-legged on the floor right in front of the fire and stared into the flames.

How could she have been so naive? She had twice, back to back, misjudged men. She had prided herself for years on being a good judge of character. She had trusted her judgment so much she had not hesitated to marry Joey, believing him with his promises of the future, his passion of building designs and outbidding everyone. She had trusted him with her love and he had proven her to be a blind fool. And then came David. The same type of liar, only in a different disguise.

Yes, he had lied, Sionna insisted. She had told him about Joey. Explained her reason for coming to his office in the first place. They had talked, discussed Joey on more than one occasion. At no time did it occur to him that she needed closure, reassurance that she had not somehow inadvertently failed Joey. Holding back a sob, she closed her eyes and rocked back and forth with the pillow tucked securely between her arms.

She lay on her side and tucked the pillow under her head. She just wanted to crawl into a ball and disappear. It hurt too much to think that David had so cruelly betrayed her trust, if not her love. Still rocking back and forth, a last tear slipped from her eyes as she drifted off to sleep.

David drove like a madman through the city. He could not believe how in one heart-wrenching moment Jaunice had come between him and Sionna. He wasn't sure what hurt worse, that Sionna thought he was a liar or that she was willing to say good-bye to what they had without hearing him out. The last thing he was going to let happen was a big misunderstanding to keep him away from the woman he loved. And he did love her, he thought.

He loved her without a doubt, he realized, speeding even more. He glanced in his rearview mirror, then at the road, and raced on. He had to get to Sionna tonight, clear the air tonight, before she closed the door on them forever.

One thing was for certain, Jaunice was not going to ruin this one true love he had found. And he was no fool. Jaunice was no more in love with him than he was with her. She only wanted him for the challenge the situation had presented. If he had never met Sionna, he was sure Jaunice would still be in New York, singing her tune of needing space and not able to commit to him. And he, like a dense idiot, would have accepted her line, even though he knew she just didn't want him.

Sionna, he groaned inwardly, blindly driving through the night. Sionna was sincere, loving, kind. She had no games, no tricks to hand him. She was a genuine woman in every sense of the word, and he needed her. It was a revelation for him because he had not really thought it through, but being with Sionna made sense. All he wanted in a woman he had found in her. All that any man could need, she had to give. He loved her and she had to accept it.

He grinned, realizing even as he raced to Sionna's house to explain his role in withholding the memo from her that she had to love him as well. There was no way he could have such a powerful emotion for her without a mutual connection.

Calmed by his belief that she had to love him, he released a sigh and completely missed the stop sign. He only had a brief moment to see the tractor-trailer coming right at him before it smashed into his car and sent his Acura spinning. It only took a few seconds before his car was practically wrapped around another parked car and he was thrown from the vehicle.

Thirty-five

It was just past dawn when Sionna, cramped and uncomfortable, woke up. She blinked and sat up, realizing she had slept in the living room. Coming to her feet, she picked up the pillow and tossed it back on the love seat. She looked at the fireplace to be sure no small flickering fires remained before she headed straight for the kitchen. Without thinking about it, she reviewed her caller ID on the telephone. She felt an intense sense of regret when neither David's home number or cellular phone number came up on the line. He hadn't even bothered to call.

She released a deep sigh, realizing that she had given him no reason to think he should or could. Feeling a slight headache coming on, she went upstairs and looked in the medicine cabinet for her Advil. She opened the bottle and took two with a glass of water. Then, feeling sad and weighted down with depression, she went to her room and lay on the bed. She lay on her back and stared at the ceiling, once again overcome with anger that David had so blatantly lied to her. She couldn't, no she wouldn't, let him hurt her, she decided. She would stop thinking about him. Maybe she could just go to Georgia, stay with her mom awhile, maybe even move back to Georgia. After all, her experience in Virginia had been as negative as it could get.

Groaning in frustration, she switched on the television set and sat back on the edge of the bed with her remote control. She switched through all the local all-news channels and stared at the set, barely listening to the news. She should go back to work, she thought, watching the weatherman's prediction of sunny days ahead.

But that was not an option right now, not until Mr. Eikton was comfortable she could handle the job. She sighed, dropped the remote control on the bed and got up to leave the room. She needed a cup of coffee. Then she could think about what she was going to do.

She made her way back downstairs, stopping to glance out the window into the street before she headed for the kitchen. A small part of her wanted David to appear, to beg her forgiveness to make it all better. But she was being irrational.

She didn't really know the man. She had made a mistake and that was that. Setting her chin firmly and proudly in the air, she went into the kitchen and prepared a pot of coffee. After she filled the coffee machine with water, she watched the water drip into the pot with a hypnotic rhythm. When she realized she was allowing herself to mope over David, she switched on the radio. She need to hear music, watch television, do anything to help her get past her initial stage of grief.

The coffee was ready and she was reaching for a coffee mug when the news brief caught her attention.

". . . last night on Maple Avenue. The drivers of both the Acura and the tractor-trailer are listed in critical condition. This WTOP news segment is brought to you by Safeway . . ."

Sionna set the mug on the counter, frowned, then shrugged. Her concern was completely unwarranted. Her frown increasing, she made her coffee, trying to remain calm as she went into her family room and switched on the television set. All the while she prayed it wasn't David's Acura, that she was being irrational because of her traumatic experience before with Joey.

She turned to the news, and with hands that trembled

with a will of their own, she stood, listened and waited. It was excruciating, the wait. No accident was mentioned through an entire segment. Feeling as though she would lose her mind when the commercials came on, she sat on the sofa and tucked her feet under the pillow, watching the television set anxiously.

The news came back on and she sat up, staring at the television as if she were half blind. Again the reporters went through political news, the weather, sports, more news and then nothing. She could have screamed.

She took a sip of her coffee, glancing away for only a moment. It was in that moment that the picture of the car accident appeared on the corner of the screen and the reporter, live on the scene where the accident occurred said, "Melissa, it was just last night that this was the site of a critical accident. A blue Acura with one passenger and a Food Chain tractor-trailer collided here last night. Both drivers were taken to Howard University Hospital where they were immediately listed as critical. The accident held up Maple Avenue traffic for hours."

"Melissa?" the news host asked, looking intense. "Any word on how the collision occurred?"

"Yes. The driver of the car apparently ran the stop sign and the tractor-trailer hit him. As you can see by the bent sign behind me, Kevin, the Acura was totally destroyed. It's a miracle that the driver of either vehicle survived."

The reporter had barely finished her commentary when Sionna jumped from the sofa, spilling her coffee on the coffee table as she did so, and ran to the phone. First she called David's house, praying he would answer. After four rings she panicked. When he didn't answer, she hung up and dialed again. She dialed his home several times before she called his cellular phone holding back a sob. Again, no answer. Full of panic, she called his office even though it was Sunday. Once again, as she expected, she received no answer.

She set the phone down and grabbed hold of the counter. Closing her eyes she prayed that David was all right. She couldn't go through a traumatic loss again. She couldn't handle that type of pain again. Afraid of getting bad news, but needing to know, Sionna picked up the phone and called information for the number of Howard University Hospital. As soon as she had the number she hung up and dialed, anxiously waiting for an answer. To complete her frustration she received an answering service. She tried to be attentive and listen carefully, but she was relieved when she finally got a live voice.

"Howard University registration, this is Ms. Adams," the female voice answered.

"Yes, I'm trying to find out about an accident victim," Sionna said, her voice edged with nervousness.

"And the patient's name, please?" Ms. Adams asked.

"David Young. He would have come in last night," Sionna added.

"Just a moment," Ms. Adams said, then put Sionna on hold. She waited anxiously, hoping that he wasn't the victim, although her gut instinct told her that he was.

"Ma'am?" Ms. Adams said.

"Yes," Sionna answered quickly.

"There was a Mr. David Young who came in last night. Are you a family member?" she asked.

"No. No," Sionna again responded quickly. "I just would like to see him."

"Visiting hours are over at six o'clock on Sundays," Ms. Adams explained.

"Thank you," Sionna whispered, then asked, "Is he Okay?"

"I wouldn't know, ma'am. I only know that he is in recovery, on the fourth floor."

"Thank you," Sionna said again, then hung up the phone. For a moment she was dazed. It was David. Her gut instinct was right. Looking around in a flurry of worry, she turned off the coffeepot, switched off the radio and television, and raced upstairs to dress. Right or wrong, she had to see him. She had to make sure he was all right.

Thirty-six

Sionna found David with ease. The nurses were kind and kept telling her how lucky he was. He was all right. She was utterly relieved. Arriving in his room, she half expected to see him sitting up and ready to leave. But it was a shock to see the tubes running into his arms and nose. He was sleeping peacefully. Walking softly, she came to stand at his bedside. He didn't move. If the nurses had not made everything sound so positive, she would have thought he was dead, he was laying so still.

"David," she leaned over and whispered in his ear.

He groaned, opened his eyes and stared into her face. "Am I dreaming?" he asked in a voice barely audible.

Sionna smiled, holding back tears so he wouldn't worry. "No. But I wish I were. I wish you weren't hurt and in here," she murmured. She sat carefully on the edge of the bed and gently took his hand.

"I'm sorry, baby," he murmured.

"Don't try to talk, okay. We have time to talk later," Sionna insisted. "I just . . . I'm just glad you're all right!" she breathed in relief.

"I took a bad hit. Wrecked the car, they tell me," David said.

Sionna put her hand to his mouth and whispered, "Hush. You need to rest."

"I need to talk to you. I . . ." David tried to say.

"No. I will leave. I mean it. You have to get better, then

we can talk. No," she said firmly when he opened his mouth to speak. "Please wait, David. I don't want you to lose what little strength you have. We have time, I promise," Sionna reassured him with a big smile.

David sighed, closed his eyes and opened them again. "I am a little tired," he admitted. As easily as he had awakened, he slipped back to unconsciousness.

Sionna stared at him, admitting to herself with a great lump in her throat that she was definitely in love with him. It wasn't like anything she had ever experienced. Loving Joey and losing Joey had been painful, yes, but she never felt the instantaneous love for him that she had felt for David. She loved him, she thought in agony.

"I won't lose you, David Young. I won't," she murmured, kissing him softly across his forehead.

For several days David stayed in the hospital. Whenever he awoke it seemed that Sionna was there.

She was there when the police came and took their report. She was there when they informed him that the other driver was doing well also.

She was there when the news reporter closed his story on the accident. She was there when he was fined but not charged, thankfully.

She was there when the doctors said he was getting better. And she was there when they finally released him, insisting that he stay home at least another week to ensure that he was all right.

He had miraculously escaped the accident and come out practically unscathed. After three days in the hospital they were confident he was strong enough to go home, as long as he took it easy.

The ride from the hospital was noncommittal. Sionna was so relieved to have him coming home with her that she was too choked up to speak. David was contemplating how finally to explain the memo about Joey to her. It was time, he thought, but he had to be patient. One thing was for sure, Sionna had comforted him and given him hope that through it all, maybe she could forgive him.

His house was cool when they entered it. David turned the air down, then turned to Sionna. She had not moved from her spot just inside the doorway.

"Sionna, have a seat, please," David said, sitting on the sofa and considering her with pleading eyes. Sionna complied. She sat beside him and he immediately took her hand.

"I guess you'll need to go car shopping now," Sionna said with a laugh, feeling a nervousness she couldn't explain.

David stared at her, loving every feature of her face. He reached up and with a loving hand caressed the smoothness of her cheek. Their eyes caught and he leaned forward and kissed her. It was a warm kiss, not the passion-filled kiss of a lover, but the moving, longing kiss of love.

"Will you let me explain now?" David asked, pulling away from her. He knew she had forgiven him, although they hadn't discussed it. But he wanted her to know the truth, not the drama that Jaunice had prepared for them.

"Yes," Sionna answered, looking at him as if to say it was all right. She understood. Those days he spent in the hospital gave her a chance to analyze the whys and hows of his behavior. And she had come to her own conclusion: that he had wanted to spare her the pain of knowing just what kind of weak man Joey really was. And for that she could not blame him, she had decided. She could only love him more for trying to protect her.

"I never meant to hurt you," David began, holding Sionna's hands against his chest.

"I know that, David," Sionna said as she smiled, giving him a consoling gaze.

"I kept that memo from you because . . . because I

thought it would hurt you more to know than if I kept it from you. I found it a few days before I asked you to the party. Then I worried that even though you didn't know what went down, others would. I don't know what I was thinking, Sionna, by letting it go so far."

"You didn't let it go so far, David. Jaunice did that for you. I forgive you, don't you know that?" Sionna asked, staring intensely at him.

"I know and I'm happy. I just wanted to keep from hurting you more. To let Joey rest in peace. And I tell you Sionna, to be honest, I didn't want to give him any more power over you than he already has," David blurted, his insecurity about Joey spilling forth.

"Joey doesn't have any power over me, David. I loved him. I trusted him. And I lost him, before he committed suicide," she added firmly. "You never had any fear of his coming between us."

"Yes, I did. You're a passionate woman. Your love for him was clear. You sought me out because of him, remember? You loved him in a way that I can only hope you will someday love me," David admitted. Sionna laughed, unable to contain herself at his statement. David looked a little uncertain, baffled by her hysterical laughter.

"Is that such a ridiculous concept?" he demanded, hurt by her laugh.

"Oh, no, please," Sionna answered, trying to contain her laughter. "Don't misunderstand. I'm not laughing at the idea that I could love you the way I loved Joey. I'm laughing because I love you in a way that I could never have loved Joey."

"I'm confused," David said slowly, trying to grasp what she was saying.

"I love you silly," Sionna blurted, her laughter gone as she gazed deeply into his eyes. "I love you completely. Can you understand that? I was so worried, so unbelievably afraid when I went to the hospital to see you. Do you realize that when I heard about the accident, even before they said what type of car it was, I instinctively knew it was you? I lived with Joey for three months and had no clue what he was going through or in fact what kind of a man he truly was. Yet with you in just a few short weeks, I feel as if there is nothing I don't know. And all of the surprises that are in store for our future, I look forward to them," Sionna said with such sincerity that it was David's turn to laugh.

"What?" she demanded. It was her turn to be confused.

He pulled her to him, holding her like a child in his arms. Then he said in a husky voice, "Do you know how adorable you are?"

"Yes," she laughed, completely unabashed as she considered him.

"You see," he said. "You have everything, and I do mean everything, that I need. You have just made me a very, very, let me repeat, very happy man," David said. With a playful growl, he nibbled at her neck, causing her to squeal and squirm away from him.

David's teasing nibble quickly became a passionate flutter of kisses that soon found her mouth. Beneath his sweet kiss, she stopped squirming and wrapped her arms around him, returning his passion with all her love. Aware that he was still healing, she gently pulled him closer to her and delicately removed his shirt. Within moments he had done the same to her and they lay together, making love in a gentle motion, their mutual love for each other bonding them in sweet ecstasy.

Thirty-seven

It was late and David was exhausted. He pulled his new Acura into his driveway and carefully turned off the engine. The lights were on in the house and he knew instinctively that Sionna was still awake. Over the past few weeks she had been unable to sleep until he got home. He smiled, his exhaustion forgotten as he thought of his beautiful Sionna. He got out of the car and on feet that felt much lighter just because he was home, he opened the front door.

As usual, Sionna greeted him with a bright smile. Her cheeks were flushed and a little fuller, but David loved it. She was standing at the foot of the stairs, one hand holding the rail, the other resting on her round, full belly.

"I thought you would never get here," she scolded.

"I will climb mountains and swim the deep sea. No matter what it takes, Sionna Young, I will get here," David said warmly, walking up to her and kissing her forehead.

Sionna grinned, loving his expression of love. "Oh, you missed it. He kicked," Sionna gasped, quickly grabbing his hand to touch her belly.

"He did it again," David said in excitement.

"Oh!" Sionna gasped, but this time her expression was filled with discomfort.

"What? Is it time?" David asked, instantly nervous.

"No. No, it's been happening like that all day," Sionna said calmly, although if she had to guess, she would guess it would happen soon. But she didn't want to worry David. He was tired enough. When the time came, she would know and she would not hesitate to tell him.

"All day?" David helped her to the sofa. "Why didn't you call me?" he demanded, standing over her after helping her raise her feet and sit back comfortably.

"David, if every time I had a slight pang of pain and called you, you would go crazy. Trust me, love. I'm fine," Sionna insisted. Then the labor pains began. "I take that back," Sionna gasped, squeezing the arm of the sofa as she lifted her body to rise up with the pain.

"I knew it. Okay, I'll call the doctor. The bags are ready," David babbled on, running through the house in a panic.

When labor pain subsided, Sionna called to David. "David, perhaps you should just take me to the hospital. We can call the doctor on the way." The moment she was finished speaking another set of labor pains hit her, and she tensed.

"Breathe, baby. Breathe. Remember. I got your bags," David called, seeing her tense. Sionna breathed hurriedly, recalling her instructor's examples. But it didn't work. The pain was still there and didn't leave until the contraction had subsided.

"David!" she called, anxious when he disappeared for a few moments. He came out of the garage, her coat in his hand, and helped her to the car.

"You know I wasn't gone far. Let's go."

"Drive carefully," Sionna said sternly, giving him a narrowed glare. Over the past year, it was her traditional statement to him each time he drove anywhere. After his near-fatal accident, she couldn't let him go anywhere without reminding him that it was better to be safe than sorry. She had gotten into the habit of telling him to drive safely and David, rather than becoming annoyed with the reminder, loved her all the more for it.

"Absolutely."

* * *

David Young Jr. was born at 3:36 A.M. and weighed seven-and-one-half pounds. He was beautiful and the spitting image of his father. David had stayed at her side throughout the entire ordeal of her labor, but with his love and a whole lot of determination, she had suffered it out and won the greatest prize of all, a healthy son.

David gently moved her hair from her face, smiling proudly at his wife. He had barely slept when the nurse came into the room with their son, cleaned and wrapped tightly in a blanket. She handed David Jr. to Sionna, then with a smile, she left the room.

"Ooh, he's beautiful," Sionna cooed, staring into his sleeping face with a joy that David appreciated. He looked from his wife to his son and felt a burst of pride. He still was amazed that he had won Sionna, that she loved him enough to marry him. It had happened so fast he was still spinning. She had sold Joey's house and moved in with him, and a week later they were married. It was the best thing that had ever happened to him.

"He takes after his mom," David grinned, sitting beside her and looking over his family with pride.

"I beg to differ. I see David Young Sr. all over him," Sionna declared.

David considered his son. He was a handsome kid, he thought in agreement with Sionna. "Whoever he looks like, I love him. Just like I love his mother. Congratulations, Mrs. Young, you have just become a mother," David said as if he were making an announcement to the world. Staring into each other's eyes, they both knew everything was going to be all right. And with David Young Jr. to guide them, Sionna knew the future was going to be very, very bright indeed.